The Change

The Chase Runner Series

Book 1: The Chase
Book 2: The Choice
Book 3: The Change

The Change

The Chase Runner Series

By
Bradley Caffee

MOUNTAIN**BROOK**FIRE

The Change
Published by Mountain Brook Ink
White Salmon, WA U.S.A.

The website addresses shown in this book are not intended in any way to be or imply an endorsement on the part of Mountain Brook Ink, nor do we vouch for their content.

This story is a work of fiction. All characters and events are the product of the author's imagination. Any resemblance to any person, living or dead, is coincidental.

Scripture quotations are taken from the King James Version of the Bible. Public domain.
ISBN 978-1953957-09-2

The Team: Miralee Ferrell, Alyssa Roat, Kristen Johnson, Cindy Jackson
Cover Design: Lynnette Bonner

Mountain Brook Ink is an inspirational publisher offering fiction you can believe in.
Printed in the United States of America

To Lauren, my friend,
who has encouraged me every step of the way and
is a "Sheila Kemp" in her own right.

"There is no fear in love; but perfect love casteth out fear."
—1 John 4:18a

Acknowledgments

All glory to God and his Son Jesus Christ from whom all good things come. There is no other way to say it. Writing this series has been God's grace to me in dark years. Thank you, Father, for bringing light to my darkness and showing the reality that there is no fear in love. I pray you are pleased with how your work in my life has been poured onto these pages.

Thanks also to: My wife and my love, Tirzah. There have been moments when I doubted that I could do this, and you have been the keeper of my dream. You haven't let me doubt myself. Thank you for always reminding me to celebrate the wins and helping me pursue joy in this world of writing. You are the best! I love you.

Samantha and Hunter, you have grown up with Dad chasing this crazy writing goal. I hope in some small way, the birthing of this series has shown you that dreams are possible. When God gives you a task, pursue it with your whole heart. I love you both.

Miralee Ferrell, it has been humbling to have you celebrate my work and to notice my progress as a writer. I have never felt adequate to the task, but your encouragement and love for these characters has meant the world to me. Thank you for taking a chance on me.

The team at Mountain Brook Fire continue to be my patient support behind the scenes as I take too long to respond to their emails as I'm often crushed under the weight of my small business. Most of us have never met face-to-face, and yet I feel like I have a group of friends cheering me on. You guys rock!

Sarah Freese, my agent, for connecting me to my publishing family and celebrating each step of the way.

Lauren, my first reader, who this book is dedicated to. Your unquestioned friendship and help when you had every reason to not have the capacity to read and assist my writing has made this series possible. I am so thankful for our nearly twenty years of friendship.

My beta team—Greg, Nikayla, Lauren, Kyla, and Becca—thank you for celebrating with me from the day this manuscript was first finished.

To the fellow writers at Realm Makers and the Blue Ridge Spec Fiction Writers, I love being part of a village that truly cheers when others win. You gave me a place to belong when I was without community. May the force be with you!

To all my readers, new and old, what a journey it has been. I pray Willis, Perryn, and the gang have blessed your life as much as they've blessed mine. May you find this chapter a satisfying close to their story. More books to come!

Chapter One

My name is Willis Thomson, and I am free from the Law.

"Patient 842, are you still with us?" The voice blared in the smothering darkness. Willis stared into the blackness without responding. "Patient, we aren't asking much of you. Is it really worth all this?"

My name is Willis Thomson, and I am free from the Law.

"Patient 842, your rehabilitation will be much smoother if you accept your position here. We simply need a token response from you of your openness to the process. Just four words." Silence fell over the chamber as the voice waited for his response. Willis's breath came in gasps as he managed his panic. Sweat beaded upon his forehead and rolled down his face, joining with the involuntary tears that quietly seeped from the corners of his eyes. "The law is good. That's all. Four words. You can do it—and this can end."

My name is Willis Thomson, and I am free from the Law. He repeated the phrase over and over in his mind. It was the one thing keeping him sane. His wide eyes scanned the darkness for the millionth time in the days and weeks he'd been kept here. *Or has it been months?*

"Patient 842—"

I won't do it. I can't.

"Four simple words."

No. No. No.

"Don't make us do this to you."

I won't.

"We can help you. Give us a chance."

Liars!

"Patient, this ends one of two ways. Don't make this harder on yourself."

I can't.

"You can accept this or resist, but eventually you'll give in. Why drag it out?"

Please don't.

An audible sigh could be heard as if the voice forgot to mute itself.

"Last chance."

"The—" Willis began.

"There you go."

"The Law—" Willis paused for a long breath.

"Come on. You've got this!"

"The Law is—GONE!" Willis shouted into the dark void.

Pain. The electrical impulse coursed through his body, white flashes filling his vision despite the darkness of the room. His back arched involuntarily off the table. His wrists pulled at the restraints, reopening the raw wounds on his skin that hadn't been able to heal properly. He screamed to the point his voice broke.

The shock ended, and his body slammed back onto the table. Sobs welled up inside him, and he clenched his eyelids shut.

"You disappoint us, Patient 842. It doesn't have to be this way."

Willis's lips trembled as he sucked in a breath. He searched the suffocating blackness as if looking for an explanation he could give to the voice.

"Why—why don't you recode me and get it over with?" Willis's voice was hoarse and barely audible.

"All in good time, 842. For the time being, we suggest you work with us."

Willis breathed deeply and set his jaw. He gazed upward at the supposed ceiling and willed his tears to end. *I can't let them break me. I can't. I can't.*

Another audible sigh could be heard. "Okay, Patient 842. Let's begin again." The voice paused. "Four words."

My name is Willis Thomson, and I am free from the Law.

Chapter Two

Perryn roamed the halls of the new Underground headquarters. The empty hallway of the abandoned school echoed her breathing, and she strode toward the training center, keeping her footfalls light. Most were still asleep, and she envied them. Rest had been hard to come by since their arrival at the converted school.

A quiet conversation up the hall drew her attention. Approaching slowly, she listened outside the door.

"Chief, it's been four months since the raid. We need to get started again." Lydia's voice was strained.

"I know. It was arrogant of me to think we could move so fast," Kane replied. "It cost us so much—so many."

"But why can't we—"

"Because I don't know what we're supposed to do. Everything was clear before. Stop the Coalition. Help the Liberated. Even the rescue mission to save Brenda was clear to us until—" Kane stopped.

"She changed everything. Didn't she?"

Perryn winced at the mention of Jez. She'd changed everything. All that was clear had become muddied from the moment they discovered her on that operating table in Solution Systems. Whether it was agreeing on what to do with her to responding to her violent means of passing the trials, she created confusion for everyone.

"She did," Kane growled giving away his still raging anger over Jez's betrayal.

"Kane, I haven't given up on you. None of us have."

Perryn's eyebrows rose at Lydia's use of Kane's name. *I don't think I've ever heard her say that.* She searched her memory, confirming her thoughts. A long moment of quiet passed, and Perryn realized she was listening to far too personal a conversation. She moved on past the doorway window, but not before noticing that Lydia had reached across the desk to take Kane's hand. Neither saw her as she walked by.

Lydia and Kane? Together?

The training center used to be the gymnasium of the school, which was bracketed by other classrooms used to teach shop or automotive skills. The Underground had converted all of these to help everyone stay in shape and train new recruits.

A door to one of the side rooms outside the gym opened, and three older teenage members of the Underground burst into the hallway laughing.

"There's no way that's true!" the young girl shouted, oblivious to sleeping people elsewhere in the building.

"Uh-huh! I'll show you later," one of the boys replied.

"He's just jealous," the other laughed.

"Jealous? Why would I be—"

The three stopped dead where they stood when they noticed Perryn. She breathed to gather her patience and smiled at them.

"Good morning, guys!" she said.

"Uh—good morning, Perryn," the girl responded.

"What's so funny?"

"Oh—it's nothing. Really." The girl smiled pleadingly at the boys.

"Yeah, nothing. Uh—sorry, we've got to go," the first boy added.

"Yeah. Okay." Perryn watched them as they walked while trying not to appear like they were hurrying. *This is getting old.* She was done with having conversations cut off when she entered rooms.

Since the disappearance of Willis, several members of her Underground family had tried to help her see that her thoughts about him were simply a recoding manipulation. She'd resisted their attempts, and they'd ceased trying to persuade her long ago.

It was a kindness, she realized, but it made her feel like an outcast among her own people. At first, it was a relief. Now it was maddening. It cut her to the heart anytime she saw Brenda put on a brave smile in front of her, and the guilt of seeing Kane lose his confidence in leadership was more than she could bear.

Enough is enough. If they won't bring it up, I will. Her shoes slapped the floor as she stomped into the training center in hopes of locating a friend. Opening the door to the room, she wasn't disappointed.

Sheila stood on the other side of the gym, her shirt soaked with sweat. She stared at the bar above her, her brow pinched in exasperation.

"It doesn't get any lower," Perryn said, smirking as she approached. "That's why it's called a 'pull up.' You have to pull yourself up."

Sheila started at her voice but smiled when she noticed Perryn. She sighed and placed her hands on her hips. "That's easy for you to say. I've been doing these a couple of weeks. You grew up a Chase runner. You've been doing these since you were what—eight? Nine?"

"Seven actually."

"Seven? For real?"

"Yeah. My parents were killed in a car wreck that year. My aunt tried to take care of me for a while, but she turned me over to the Alliance for Chase training when she couldn't make ends meet. I've trained ever since."

"I'm sorry."

Perryn shrugged. This wasn't where she wished the conversation to go. "Try gripping the bar this way." Leaping for the bar, she demonstrated the hold, trying to shift the subject away from her childhood. She lifted herself five times before jumping down and turning to Sheila.

"Show off. You're not even out of breath," Sheila joked.

"Whatever. Now you."

Sheila shook her head and reluctantly stepped under the bar. Leaping, she grabbed the bar and managed three pull ups. On the fourth, her arms shook under the strain and gave way.

"Not bad," Perryn said, and she meant it. "For having started recently, you're doing well. Most people can't even do one."

"Whatever."

"I mean it." Perryn grabbed Sheila's arm and traced the muscles in her shoulder and arms with her free hand. "See, that definition wasn't there before."

"Yeah, well, I've got a long way to catch up to you. That's why I get up so early to work out. It's a bit embarrassing to work out in front of everyone else."

"Why are you doing this, anyway?" Perryn pointed to the bar.

"As the Watcher, I had a purpose." She turned to Perryn. "I had a place to help you all. Since the raid, I'm an extra body taking up space. I figured I'd better get into shape to help everyone once we begin running missions again."

Perryn nodded, seeing her opening. "Things have changed."

"You can say that again."

"Speaking of change, I feel like everything is different."

"That's understandable. The Underground was raided, and we relocated here. People join us every week, but we've spent these months having to rethink everything we were doing. We can't suffer another invasion like that."

"That's not what I mean." Perryn sat, turning away.

"Explain."

"I mean that it feels different between us. You, Kane, Brenda, and the group—why don't any of you ask me about Willis anymore? It used to be the constant topic of conversation. I hated that I couldn't go a day without one of you talking about him. But this—this is worse."

Sheila circled her, her gaze softening. "How so?"

"It's obvious everyone wants to know where he went, but no one wants to talk about it in front of me. I can't help but think everyone is mad at me for causing him to leave. Are you, Sheila?"

Sheila raised her eyebrows at the question. She grabbed a towel. Rubbing her face with it, she sat down on a bench. She bowed her head and took a couple of deep breaths. It was something Perryn loved about Sheila; she took her time with words. She wouldn't speak until she was sure of what she intended to say. Perryn waited, giving her space to think.

"Sit down for a second." Sheila said finally, patting the bench beside her. Perryn joined her. "Perryn, you're family to all of us. We love you. We love Willis. We know what things were like before the raid, but your heart is your own. It's not our place to try to force you to believe something you can't. Whatever you decide about Willis, we'll love you either way. It's why we don't bring it up. We respect your space."

The words made sense to Perryn, and it frustrated her that she couldn't argue with them. She wanted to be offended that they weren't trying harder to convince her, but she couldn't decide why that was.

"I guess I expected you all to keep hounding me about him, especially after he left." She paused. "That was my fault, wasn't it?"

"Perryn"—Sheila placed her hand on Perryn's—"where is this going?"

"I—" she hesitated. "I used to dream about the future he and I had together. We would finally have a quiet life that we've both imagined. Then, the invasion—Jez—what she said to me—I have every reason to doubt his feelings for me were ever real, but I also am equally sure how I felt about him. At least, that was before—" Her voice trailed off without completing her thought. "Anyway, I don't want everyone tiptoeing around me over this anymore. Whatever my feelings, I need to sort them out myself."

"Yes, you do," Sheila agreed.

"But I can't with him gone. And I can't help feeling like everyone is forced to miss him because of me. And Brenda—it's not fair to her."

"What are you saying, Perryn?" Sheila gave her a hopeful look.

"We need to find him. Wherever he went, we need to find him

and bring him back. Not for me—but for everyone, especially Brenda."

Sheila smiled and glanced down. She squeezed Perryn's hand gently. "Would you believe there's already a plan in the works?"

Perryn smirked. "Yeah. That would be Kane's style. I suppose everyone was waiting for me to come around?"

"Something like that. It was Jaden's idea. Wouldn't let anyone do anything until he was certain you were okay. Somehow he understood you would be."

"I guess I need to go tell him, huh?"

"Might be good start. Want my help finding him?" She pointed toward the doors.

"No. I've an idea where he'll be later today."

"Okay. Seriously, though, you need to keep it a secret."

"Talking to Jaden?"

"No, about the fact I can't do more than three pull-ups." She squeezed Perryn's hand again, and the two laughed quietly, the sound softly echoing into the silent training room.

Chapter Three

Jaden was sitting on the stairs at the front entrance. It was the same place he sat the day Father Anthony had led the newly arrived group to him after the invasion. Everyone had thought him dead when the space station exploded after the Chairman launched a missile on live television. The stairs were a spot he retreated to on a regular basis, and she'd expected she could find him there today.

"Hey, stranger," she said quietly as she approached.

"Hey, Perryn," he said flatly. He didn't look up.

"Mind some company?"

He smiled shyly. "No, not at all. In fact, I think I probably need some."

"Today is the day, isn't it?"

"Yeah. It's been six months."

Perryn sat down next to him and leaned against his shoulder. She sighed. When they'd been first reunited with Jaden, the group had been so shocked that they peppered him with questions for hours. They asked where he'd been and how he found the Underground. Of primary interest had been how he'd avoided the Chairman's missile strike. His story of stowing away on a supply ship, locating his mother, and returning had impressed even Lydia. The two of them had taken refuge in a large crate, which required they sit quietly for three days as they were loaded as cargo on the next transport.

Perryn remembered crying as he told them he learned the living conditions on the station for slaves had caused an infection to spread among the population. The slaves had never rioted on the station as the Chairman suggested, they simply grew desperate for help and broke into the medical wing. After they'd returned to

Earth and gone into hiding, his mother revealed that she'd contracted the deadly virus. Two months after her rescue, Jaden had been forced to say goodbye to her as she succumbed to the illness. That'd been six months ago to the day.

"She would have liked it here," Perryn suggested.

"Definitely. Though she would have had a thing or two to say to the kitchen crew. No way last night's dinner would have passed her inspection." They laughed gently together at the thought.

"You okay?"

"Yeah. I'll be fine. I miss her, that's all." He sighed. "And I wish she could have experienced more of this life."

"At least she got to experience it—freedom, I mean. For a time, she was free."

"Yeah—at least there's that."

"You know, when my parents died, I felt like I had to think about them every day. I believed I'd be a bad daughter if I ever forgot about them. At first it was easy, but as time passed, I would have a day here or there that they wouldn't come to mind. I felt horrible at first, but I eventually decided they wouldn't want me to spend too much of my life dwelling on their passing." She took a deep breath, remembering her parents. "So, I picked a spot at my aunt's house under a tree where I would spend time with them in my mind each month. I called it my 'family tree.' It helped me to know I would 'see' them each month at the tree. And that helped me live the other days well."

"I like that." Patting the stair, he said, "It's not a tree, but I guess this is my spot for the moment. Thanks for joining me at my 'family tree,' Perryn."

The two of them sat silently for a long moment. They stared out the high windows in the hall, the ones not boarded up. The sunlight poured in, and they could see the clouds passing on the pale blue of the sky. When Jaden took a deep breath, Perryn realized he was ready. She nudged him with her shoulder.

"Hey, I hear there's a plan in development to get Willis."

"What? Where did you—?" He appeared startled, and she laughed.

"Don't worry. I brought it up first. No one spilled the news until I was ready."

Relief flushed his cheeks. "I told them not to say anything until you were okay to hear it. We don't want to pressure you, Perryn."

"I think we need to find him, Jaden, but I want you to know my feelings haven't changed. This isn't my rescue mission; it's ours. He's a friend to all of us, and I don't want our history to cause everyone pain. Brenda needs her son back. Kane needs to stop beating himself up. And I—" Her voice trailed off as it had with Sheila.

"And you?" Jaden waved a hand in a circle, encouraging her to complete the thought.

"Well, let's say I owe him. He shared his family with me after the Chase. I can share this one with him."

"That's all?"

"Hey, don't make me regret this decision. That's all." She elbowed him to let him know she wasn't angry.

"Okay, then," Jaden said, holding his hands up in mock surrender. He took another deep, slow breath. "For what it's worth, that's good news. Really good news. And I needed some today." He stood up and turned to her smiling. Holding his hand out, he offered it to her. "Should we go find Kane?"

"I'm guessing Sheila's already on it, but yeah." She took his hand, and he helped her up. They walked toward the corridor that led to the offices.

"You know what?" Jaden smiled.

"What's that?"

"What my mother would have liked most about this place is everyone takes care of each other because it's the right thing to do. It's all she ever dreamed about—living free among people who took care of each other the way people should." He smiled broadly, and she was glad to see it. "Let's get going. We could use some fresh ideas for the plan. It's not ready yet."

Chapter Four

Click.

The sound of the door latch roused Willis. Even before he opened his eyes, he could tell something was different. A brightness shone through his eyelids, and he was aware the light in the room was on. Someone was moving next to the table, and he struggled to awaken. He couldn't be sure if it was from sleep or drugged unconsciousness. He sensed the person near him, and he strained to open his eyes.

It was the sting of the antiseptic on his skin that yanked him to alertness. His eyes shot open, and he instinctively tried to sit up. The restraints restricted his movement to his neck causing his head to whip backward to the table. Frantically, he searched around to see who was in the room. Jez sat next to the table. She'd loosened one of the restraints and was blotting the wounds on his wrist with a cloth.

"Jez? What are you—?"

"Shut up, Willis." Jez curled her lips at him. She kept her eyes glued to her task.

"But what—?"

"I said shut up."

She poured more antiseptic onto the cloth and jammed it on the underside of his wrist. The solution lit the raw skin on fire. He sucked in a breath to manage the pain. He could see her smirk as she watched him try not to react to the sting. Trying to wrench his arm free, he found himself too weak. He stared at her with questioning eyes.

Noticing him, she rolled her eyes. "Don't get any ideas. They're moving you on to phase two of what they do here."

"But I never—"

"Broke? Don't be too impressed with yourself. Neither did I. Yet, here I am, cleaning you up because they told me to."

"Phase two? What does that—"

She mashed his hand back down on the table, silencing him, and worked the buckle of the leather strap with the other hand. "Don't ask. I can't tell you anyway. Will, it's better to go with it. The process is so much harder if you resist, but they'll win in the end either way." She tightened the restraint and moved around the table to his other wrist.

The pain as she sterilized the wounds on his other wrist caused him to seethe with anger. The fog in his mind cleared, and he glared at her.

"You shot Perryn." The words hung heavily in the air between them.

"Mmm-hmm." Her answer sounded apathetic, but she still wouldn't meet his eyes.

"You told her I didn't love her."

To that, she simply nodded.

"She believes you."

Jez stopped and placed the cloth on the edge of the table. She finally glanced at him and took a breath. "You told me to interpret what they put in my head."

"So, you shot Perryn!?!" He was shouting.

"It was either that or shoot you."

"I'd rather be dead."

"Well, you're not. I know you hate me, but I can live with that. I have to. I'm nothing here. I went from their chief asset to their slave."

"Whatever. I don't care." He turned his head away from her.

"As far as they're concerned, I'm a failed experiment. They sent me to kill you, and instead I did what I did. That's why I'm in here bandaging your wounds instead of out there. I can think of a million things I'd rather be doing."

He didn't respond.

13

"Will, listen." He bristled at the name. She was the only one who called him Will, and he hated how she used it to get his attention. "Hate me all you want, but you need to know they've learned their lesson. They'll recode you, but not before they change you. That's why they want you healed. They don't want you distracted by—"

A sharp rap at the door cut her off. Willis could see from the corner of his eye the air of fear she wore as she stared at the door. She turned back to him, and she lowered her brow.

"Fine. Whatever. Have fun as they mess with your head." She grabbed the restraint and tightened it violently, crushing his wrist inside. He grit his teeth, refusing to let her see his pain. Picking up the cloth and antiseptic, she threw the door open and stormed out. A man with wire-rimmed glasses, the same he'd seen his first day here, stood outside the door. He shot an angry glare at Jez as she left. Returning his gaze to Willis, he closed the door, leaving him alone in the room. The man shuttered the window on the door. The lock latched into place and the lights went out.

They'll recode you, but not before they change you.

"Patient 842?"

Willis jolted to consciousness at the voice in the dark. How long had he lay there in the darkness? Frantically, he scanned around to see the source of the voice, but blackness was all that greeted him.

"Good day to you, Patient 842." The voice sounded different than prior days. No longer mechanical, but more human. He turned to his left and realized the source was in the room with him. "Yes, I'm here with you, 842. My name is Dr. Campbell." A single light turned on to a dim glow. In the near darkness, he could see a man sitting near him. Though his face was in shadow, Willis could make out the wire-rimmed glasses on his face. This was the mysterious man who had watched him through a window since the first day at Solution Systems.

"You're wanting to watch more closely as you torture me? I won't say what you want me to say." He wasn't sure if antagonizing his captor was a good idea, but it made him feel strong for the moment.

"Yes, we've become quite familiar with your strength. It's quite impressive. Most of our patients reform far more quickly. Your resilience requires us to graduate you to a new and more radical approach to our work here."

"Phase 2," he whispered, remembering Jez's words.

"Regrettably, Patient 1 informed you of this before you could hear proper explanation," Campbell shook his head. "No doubt you've prejudged the process you're about to undertake. I'm sorry to say that it will make harder on you. Hopefully, we can recover much of that ground in this conversation."

"Patient 1?"

"Yes. She carries that designation because it was in her that we made most of our discoveries."

"You mean, the hundredth recoding?"

"Yes, and no. While our original mandate was to unlock the secret to recoding well into the hundreds, our greatest discovery was the process that made passing that barrier possible rather than the recoding itself. When we searched beyond the physical recoding, we realized why so many of our experiments failed following Patient 1. We discovered something that made her—" He paused and stared at Willis over the frames of his glasses. "—well—unique."

Where was he going with this? Deciding that more information could help him figure out what they were up to, he kept the conversation going. "Something made Jez unique? What was it?"

"In short, Patient 842—you."

Willis stared at him quizzically. *How in the world do I make Jez unique?*

As if Dr. Campbell could hear his thoughts, he continued, "Yes, you. She was quite fond of you during your training, you know." Willis's stomach lurched as he heard what he'd suspected about Jez stated out loud. He nodded. "She was a fearful, young girl who spent each day attempting to avoid her presumed death upon recoding. For much of her time on the station, that meant aligning herself with you. That alignment transformed into romantic feelings that rooted so deeply that her very survival was essentially connected to being with you."

"So?"

"842, how does a young woman go from hopelessly in love with a young man to wanting him dead?"

Willis could only stare. His eyes adjusting to the dim light, he could see Dr. Campbell's disappointment.

The man let out a frustrated sigh as if he couldn't understand how Willis wasn't getting his meaning. "She changed. Fundamentally, she changed. Survival is one of the most basic human instincts, and hers transformed from being connected to you to requiring your removal. To put it in non-scientific terms, she changed into a new person."

"Because of—me?"

"Yes. Your actions forced her to reinvent her entire psychological profile. The hundredth recoding was impossible because so much of the persona was lost by then that the brain couldn't handle the strain of recognizing the cloned DNA in the replacement body. This psychological rebirth, as we like to call it, essentially reboots the brain's awareness of self and sets a fresh starting point from which recoding can take place!" His words were almost giddy as he explained the science. "While we don't yet fully understand why the brain is able to do this, the connection is undeniable."

Willis's mind hurt trying to grasp it all. He closed his eyes and shook his head. "So, that's why you were able to turn her into a super-soldier?"

Dr. Campbell's eyes darkened at Willis's words. "That was the short-sighted goal of the previous Deputy Chairman of the Western Alliance. He believed a different breed of army could quell the unrest by force. It wasn't until our Deputy Chairwoman took office with the full support of the Chairman that Project Rebirth could truly be realized."

Willis remembered the name 'Project Rebirth.' Sheila had passed that information to the Underground along with his mother's whereabouts while still operating as the Watcher. Realizing he was about to get information the Underground had merely guessed at prior to the invasion, he probed one more time. "And what was that?"

Dr. Campbell smiled, his crooked teeth making the grin appear sinister. "We've developed a near perfect process of transforming the human mind's sense of self. We can tell people, not simply what to think, but also how to think of themselves. It's the ultimate tool to bring the world back into alignment with the Law. No policing will be required. No coercion. No force. The world will *want* to follow the Law." Campbell's eyes widened as if in awe of his own work.

Willis shuddered. *Could it be possible? Could they change people that much? Could they change the world?*

"Why don't you recode me? Couldn't you tell me what to think?"

"All in good time, 842. You will be recoded. But—Patient 1 showed us our own failure. Unless we change the way you think first, you're free to interpret a suggestion in your recoding as you wish." Campbell's eyes returned to Willis. "Patient 1 is an imperfect prototype no longer useful to our cause. You, Patient 842, will be the first in a new generation of citizens completely loyal to the World Coalition!"

"Don't bet on it," Willis said, shaking his head.

Dr. Campbell smirked. "You think I've shared too much with you. That's the beauty of our process. It doesn't matter what I reveal to you. Nothing we do or say to you will involve anything less than the truth. The truth, Patient 842—that is what will change you."

Willis's eyes grew wide.

"Let's begin. Shall we?" Dr. Campbell smiled.

Chapter Five

Willis squinted at the bright lights of the hallway. He searched around in his confusion, trying to make sense of his surroundings. The hallway appeared like the one they'd raided to rescue his mother, but he couldn't be sure it was the same. His eyes adjusted to the sterile fluorescence.

He was bound to a wheelchair around his arms and ankles. Wires had been taped to his scalp, which they'd shaved for that purpose. Several nicks still stung from the rushed haircut, the adhesive of the tape pulling at several barely healed wounds. Similar wires were attached to his chest.

Dr. Campbell walked alongside the chair, staring down at his notes. He couldn't see who was pushing the chair.

"What—why—?" Willis stammered, unable to finish his thoughts. He realized his mouth was impossibly dry.

"Stay calm, Patient 842. You're dehydrated, and I can imagine it's difficult to talk." Dr. Campbell nodded without even glancing up.

"Awake—?"

"You want to know why we haven't sedated you." Campbell spoke as if he'd been waiting for this question. "It's an understandable inquiry. You simply need to know that we can't risk allowing drugs to interfere with your readings. We're breaking incredible ground through you."

Nearing the end of the hallway, a door opened to the left. Jez emerged carrying a tray of instruments. She stopped abruptly at the sight of Willis and Dr. Campbell, surprised to see them in the hallway.

"Ah, Patient 1," Dr. Campbell began.

"I told you not to call me that." Jez spoke through gritted teeth.

"Watch your tone, *Patient 1*." He didn't try to hide his smile as he emphasized the name. Jez breathed deeply in anger. "I want you to be ready to process Patient 842. Clean him up and get him fluids. We can't have him passing out on us."

"I thought you said I wouldn't have to—"

"You will do what you're told."

Jez's eyes squeezed shut. Her face flushed with anger as she appeared to try to contain her response to Campbell.

"Have I made myself clear, Patient 1?"

The tray flew from her hands, landing in a metallic crash on the floor to Willis's right. Her eyes opened with wild fury, and her hands balled into fists. She lunged for Dr. Campbell. A baton jutted out from behind Willis wielded by the guard that'd been pushing him. He recognized it as a much larger version of the shock sticks the Underground had used for their trials.

The baton met Jez's ribs before she could reach Dr. Campbell, and Willis saw her body crumple mid-air. She fell to the floor with a grunt. Immediately she tried to stand, but the baton found its mark a second time. This time, the guard held it there for several seconds. When he stepped away, Jez lay on the floor weeping, her arms wrapped around her middle. Dr. Campbell sighed heavily. Producing a syringe from his lab coat, he knelt beside the incapacitated Jez.

"Like I told you, Patient 842, this one is a failed experiment." He injected the serum into her neck, which made her wince. "Once a valuable asset to us, her failure to follow orders upon your capture has led to a cascade effect in her brain allowing her to question all suggestions we've given her through recoding. This neuro-booster—a genius invention of my own—allows our work to take greater hold, but you've seen what happens when it begins to wear off." He held up the empty syringe with pride.

Willis stared at him with questioning horror.

"You wonder why we keep her, don't you? Remember, 842, she's the beginning of our research. One doesn't simply throw away your original specimen because a greater one has been found. Too much has been invested. Besides, you can see the effect of the serum already doing its work, though the duration of that effectiveness is lessening. Pretty soon, she'll need to be on a constant drip of it to stay in line."

Willis examined Jez. Her eyes had dulled, no longer full of fire. Her body relaxed on the floor, and her features grew flat. She stared into the distance as if none of them were there with her.

"There we go. Much better," Campbell began. "Patient 1, you'll complete the task I've given you to process Patient 842?"

"Yes, Dr. Campbell." Jez responded without glancing at him. Her voice sounded void of emotion.

The guard wheeled Willis toward the last room of the hall. Dr. Campbell followed, leaving Jez laying on the floor. The door opened. Willis's breath caught when he saw beyond into the room. The table he'd been strapped to earlier was vertical, each restraint ready to receive him.

Willis stood strapped tightly to the vertical table, bound in several places on his limbs as well as his waist and head. A clean hospital-style gown had been placed on him. What he guessed was hours later, the door opened revealing Jez. She again carried a metal tray, except this one held various cloths from which wisps of steam arose.

She gazed at him, expressionless. "Let's get this over with," she remarked.

He watched her through half-drowsy eyes as she placed the tray on the counter in the corner. Picking up one of the cloths, she approached him and reached toward his face. He sucked in a quick breath as he tried in vain to pull away.

"Relax, Will," she said, pausing. "This cloth is hot, but not enough to burn." She wiped his forehead and temples with the flat of her hand. Readjusting the cloth around one finger, she traced the lines of his face. The steaming cloth gave off an antiseptic odor that awoke his senses. He watched her eyes as she worked, studying her.

"I—I—don't understand what they're—" he whispered still struggling to speak. He was surprised to find he wasn't angry at her. After the scene in the hallway, a tiny swell of compassion for her had formed in his gut.

"Let me guess. Lots of bright lights and random pictures for hours—that's what they did to you."

He couldn't nod, but his eyes must have communicated she was right.

She moved on to scrubbing his arms. "Yeah, I've seen them doing that to people. Practicing to get ready for you, I guess."

His eyebrows scrunched in question. Seeing him, she smirked and let out a chuckle.

"They're measuring your reactions to stimuli," she said mimicking the voice of Campbell as she quoted him. "First they show you a bunch of pictures and flashing lights. They measure everything. Your heartrate, your hormone levels, brain waves—everything."

"Why?" he whispered, trying to glance over at her.

"It tells them everything they need to know for what they'll do next."

"Which is?"

"Nice try. Been ordered not to say any more. And as you saw, I can't resist."

She placed the used cloth on the tray. Picking up a tourniquet and needle, she banded his upper arm to find a vein. Sterilizing the area, she inserted the needle and hooked up intravenous fluids. A moment later she was done, and he raised his eyebrows to let her know he was impressed.

"Done it a million times since they made me the grunt around here." She started the fluids dripping into the line. "There. You'll start feeling better soon." She stepped back to meet his eyes.

"Thanks," he whispered again. He meant it.

She studied his face for a moment. "I don't hate you, Will. I know you might hate me. I hate me. I hate what my life has become, but I don't hate you." She approached, her face directly in front of his. Tears welled up in her eyes, and her lips trembled. "I wanted us to be more. Then, I didn't anymore when I thought your choices would kill me. But—when I was with the Underground, and everything was different—I hoped—"

She leaned forward and kissed him lightly on the cheek.

Willis stared, unmoving.

Stepping back, she wiped her eyes with her finger. She wrapped her arms around her middle as if to keep herself from bursting. "I know it can never be. Not after betraying you twice. I never desired to hurt you or Perryn or anyone, and I'll never get to make it right. On the station, I was scared to die. Here, I had to do what they told me. I hate my life, Will. I hate what they've made me to be."

Her eyes met him. The hardness in them was gone, worn down by months of cruelty at the hands of her captors. Pretense was stripped away. All her bravado and manipulation he'd known from her was missing.

"And for what it's worth—" she swallowed hard, "I'm sorry."

Willis felt no anger or revulsion. He pitied her for what they'd done to her. *They destroyed her life in the name of sick science, and now she's their slave. Here she is, reduced to nothing. Could this be the real Jez?*

"Jez, I—" he started.

"No, don't," she interrupted. She held a hand up to stop him talking. "I don't want you to say anything." With that, she turned to grab the tray and threw the door open.

He could hear her sniffling as she ran down the hallway.

Chapter Six

"That's it! Hand over hand!" Lydia cupped her hands on either side of her mouth. Afternoon training had started, and numerous members of the Underground stood drenched in sweat. Perryn walked with Jaden, and she could see the focus on Lydia's face as she watched the two rookies struggle with the obstacle course.

"Captain?" Perryn began.

"How's it going, Perryn?" Lydia never took her eyes off the course. She walked away, following the movements of the trainees. Perryn followed.

"We were searching for—"

"The Chief. I know."

"Do you know where we could—"

"No! No! No!" Lydia was shouting again, and Perryn needed a moment to realize it wasn't at her. Both trainees had fallen on the mats below, and Lydia's frustration was obvious. "You're stronger than you realize. Don't give up the first moment it's hard!" She was standing over the two fallen trainees, gazing down on them. "Get up, back of the line."

"Captain, please. I'm sorry to interrupt, but—"

"Not now, Perryn."

"But—"

"I said, 'not now!'" Lydia snapped. She glanced at Perryn for the first time and immediately deflated, seeing her hurt. Her shoulders slumped as she let out a long sigh. "I'm sorry, Perryn. I didn't mean that."

"Is everything okay?" She could see Lydia drift away for a moment in thought.

"Yes. I mean—no. I mean—" She sighed again. "I've got a lot

on my mind. The Chief will be here in a few minutes if you want to wait for him."

"Sure thing. Can we—help in any way?" Perryn raised her eyebrows with the question, not sure there was anything she could do.

"Unless you know a way to motivate this group, then no. This is the new group of Liberated that arrived last week through Father Anthony's work, and they're not used to this kind of training."

"Hey, Perr," Jaden said, catching up to her. He'd been chatting with the tired trainees in the line. "Pretty defeated group back there."

"We were talking about that," Perryn responded.

"I got an idea." He smiled broadly. "Let's show them how it's done—it'll give them a breather, and maybe inspire them a little bit."

"Are you always this positive?" Lydia shook her head in mock disgust.

"No." Perryn smiled. "Sometimes it's worse."

Jaden snorted a laugh as he turned to run back to the start of the line. Perryn smiled and rolled her eyes. Lydia let out a single laugh and shrugged.

"I'll try anything with this group," Lydia suggested.

Jaden and Perryn stood next to each other. The trainees had gathered, their line becoming a half-circle with each trying to get a view of the spectacle. Jaden jogged lightly in place, loosening up. "You ready for this?" He nudged her playfully with one hand.

"You mean to smoke you on this course? For sure," she retorted, unable to hide her grin. "Remember, I've been training with the Underground longer than you have."

"Yeah, but I've got a secret weapon." He lifted one leg to stretch his right quadricep.

"Sure, you do." She bent sideways to stretch.

"No seriously."

"And what would that be?"

"I'm not telling." He switched legs. "That's what makes it a secret."

Perryn tisked with amused annoyance. "That's because you're full of it."

"Not kidding," Jaden said in singsong.

"Oh yeah, prove it." Perryn turned to Jaden and crossed her arms.

Jaden sighed and turned to Perryn. She matched his stare. He chuckled and readied himself to run. His mouth stretched into a smile. "I told Lydia to blow the whistle when I had you distracted." At that moment, the whistle sounded, and Jaden took off. Startled, Perryn froze for a moment before leaping forward to start running.

"No fair!" she cried out. Picking their favorites, the trainees shouted, urging them on.

She ran up the ramp to the balance beam on the other side. Throwing her arms to her sides to steady herself, she crossed the beam with three skips to find Jaden halfway up the rope on the other side. He was laughing out loud, and it was slowing him down.

"You're seriously going to pay for that."

"Gotta catch me first!"

She pulled at the rope, hand over hand, until she reached the top. Ahead lay a bar above her head littered with holes on both sides. Scrambling across the platform, she bent to pick up two wooden pegs. In one motion, she inserted the peg in her right hand into the side of the post and swung her body to reach with her left. The left peg found its mark, and she yanked at the right side to free her handle to move it forward. Glancing to her right, she could see Jaden missed on his release and had to stop his swing to pull the peg free.

Here's my chance. Methodically, she moved forward, marveling to herself as each peg pulled free flawlessly. Together, she and Jaden leaped and landed with a simultaneous *thump* on the far platform.

"Struggling, are we?" she joked breathlessly as she ran forward.

"Not at all." Jaden laughed as he matched her pace.

Both slid down a pole to the floor level, which placed them at the foot of a vertical climbing wall. Perryn smiled, knowing this is where she would make her move. Grabbing the first handhold, she hauled her body upward, her foot finding its mark on a block jutting out from the wall a few feet off the floor. Both climbed like four-limbed spiders to the point where the wall sloped back toward them slightly for several feet. Jaden began his slow, partially upside-down ascent with calculated ease. Perryn, however, stopped.

She took a deep breath and squatted as low as her arms would allow. Summoning all her strength, she sprang upward and outward letting go of the wall completely. She reached for the corner where the wall turned vertical again and smiled inside as both hands found their grip above the edge. Curling her body, she brought her legs upward to allow her feet to find their hold on the slope below her. She clenched her jaw as she pulled with her arms, resuming her vertical climb.

"Where did you learn how do that?" Jaden laughed from below her.

"Let's—call it—my—secret weapon." She spoke between gasps of air, partially from her exertion and partially from the laughter bubbling up inside her. Finally, her hands found the top of the wall, and she hoisted herself over the edge. She allowed herself two deep breaths.

She stood as Jaden's fingers found the edge. Turning, she grasped a bar that was attached to the zipline. She jumped and smiled as the rush of air blew in her face during her descent. The line caught at the bottom throwing her forward. She landed catlike and took off running back toward the crowd of onlookers whose cheers bounced off the walls of the gym. She could hear Jaden's feet land behind her.

Throwing herself to the floor, she slid a couple feet and army-crawled underneath the wires. Back and forth, she swiped at the floor with her forearms and feet. A tug on her right foot caused her to lose her rhythm for a moment. She peeked back to see Jaden's hand wrapped around her toes. He pulled her backward a few feet. "Whatever, cheater!" She laughed, resuming her crawl. Emerging from the other side, they scrambled to their feet and ran side by side. The finish line nearing, Perryn reached out a hand to Jaden's shoulder and shoved.

He stumbled, his feet pounding the floor as he caught himself. Perryn leaned across the finish line and collapsed on the mat. A second later, Jaden collapsed next to her. Their chests heaved up and down as they tried to catch their breath. Perryn turned to Jaden, who was already watching her. The corners of her mouth pulled inward as she tried to contain her amusement, but it was to no avail. Together, they burst out in a laughter that echoed throughout the gym. Their laughter was so hard that the crowd joined in their delight.

Lydia approached and stood over them, a smirk on her face. "I don't know what that was, but at least you got them all to smile." She reached out a hand to Perryn, pulling her to her feet. The two of them both grabbed the hands of a still snickering Jaden, yanking him upward. "See, everyone," Lydia shouted to the group, "it's possible. Who's next up?"

Perryn punched Jaden in the shoulder. "Look at you, cheater."

"Cheater? Who was pushing who there at the end?"

This brought another fit of laughter that ended in a long sigh. They stretched lightly to ease complaining muscles. A loud *bang* reverberated off the walls, bringing the entire room to silence. Turning in the direction of the sound, Perryn saw Kane storm into the gym, Sheila by his side.

His eyes appeared like saucers, and his stride told everyone this wasn't a casual drop-in. As they approached, the tears welling in Sheila's eyes became visible, and Perryn sucked in a shallow breath. Perryn's smile disappeared. Turning to Lydia, she could see her face wore grave concern.

"Something's happened," she whispered to Jaden.

He didn't answer.

Chapter Seven

"What do you mean raids?" Lydia pounded the desk in desperation.

The group huddled in Kane's office. Lydia had immediately dismissed the trainees, and the five of them had retreated behind closed doors to talk. A knock moments later brought in Maria and Chris. Perryn reached out to hug Maria, a common greeting for them. Maria had been her rock during these months, always loyal and quick to defend her. The seven together were Kane's senior staff, his most trusted people. They were often privy to information that wasn't shared with others.

"For weeks, we've been intercepting transmissions between high ranking officials in the Coalition, thanks to Chris," Kane said. "We learned that Law-keepers were massing in Central City, but they were careful not to give specifics in their communication. Everything hinted that something was coming, but nothing could be deciphered."

"How'd you know about the raids, then?" Maria smacked nervously at her ever-present gum.

"Because of this," said Chris. He picked up a remote and turned on the monitor hanging from the wall. The screen faded into color, and a news broadcast could be heard mid-sentence.

"…would only comment that the dissidents were connected to the terrorist organization known as the Underground. In a bold move to establish peace in the Western Alliance, the Deputy Chairwoman authorized the neutralization of several installations known to be sympathetic to the terrorist cause."

Penny, the Deputy Chairwoman of the Western Alliance, appeared on screen. She stood outside one of the Alliance buildings. She was dressed in Alliance yellow from head to toe, and her bracelets jingled incessantly with each hand motion. A breeze blew the few strands of hair that she hadn't managed to perfectly paste into place.

"We cannot permit the presence of those who would threaten to undo the great prosperity we enjoy here in the Western Alliance," Penny began, her voice sick with sweetness. "We have given every opportunity for these confused rebels to see the grace we have extended, but our patience has limits. As Deputy Chairwoman, I will lead us to be an Alliance that honors the glory of the Law and respects our Chairman, no matter the cost."

The screen cut away to the image of an armored vehicle equipped with a steel battering ram crashing into the front a building. Stone dust filled the air around the vehicle, and debris fell as it backed up for another blow to the building.

"That's the Central City Mission!" Sheila gasped.

"Is Father Anthony—" Perryn started to ask.

"No," Kane interrupted. "His current safehouse remains unknown to the best of our knowledge. He has relocated as many as possible there. But—the mission was destroyed."

Turning back to the broadcast, the Chairman appeared. His wire-rimmed glasses glinted in the studio lights that'd been set up in his office. He sat on an ornate sofa, legs crossed, his hands folded on his black robes as he gazed at someone off camera.

"The Law is to be trusted. That is the grave problem going on in our world today. Former law-abiding members of our great Coalition have taken it upon themselves to depart from the Law. It is a breaking of faith. They have broken trust with the Law, and thus have broken trust with those who follow the Law. We have made great strides to restore peace to our Coalition around the globe, but there yet remain a few holdout rebels who wish to continue to promote their false doctrines."

"And what will be done about those rebels, as you call them?" a voice from off screen asked.

"I wish to address my children across the globe, those citizens who have remained faithful. We will with certainty quench the angry fire of these rebels. They breed fear through terror. But be warned, my loyal citizens—like a wounded animal, they are more dangerous than ever. These so-called Liberated will not hesitate to harm you or your loved ones, and they will do so without remorse. Compassion is not in their nature. Apart from the Law, they know not what it means to serve another. Please stay clear of them and report anything suspicious to your local Law-keeping office. My children, in the meantime, know you are in my heart."

The screen cut away to more images of uniformed Law-keepers raiding buildings and bringing out crowds of people in handcuffs. The reporter wrapped up the report, and Chris flipped off the television.

"I can't believe it," Lydia whispered.

"Those people. They were no threat. They were normal people!" Perryn jabbed a finger at the blank screen.

"This is bad." Maria nodded.

"Chief, what are we going to do about—" Jaden started.

Kane held up a hand to silence the group.

"I'm afraid there's little we can do. Intelligence says the raids took place simultaneously and appeared to be over before we found out."

"But Father Anthony, he's not safe!"

The group murmured in agreement.

"No, he's not. Plans are being made to abandon the safehouses within the week. It takes time to relocate new Liberated here without being detected. Father Anthony has told me in no uncertain terms that he intends to see the process through prior to coming here himself."

The group stood in heavy silence. It was Jaden who finally broke it.

"Kane, we need to advance our plans to find Willis." His voice sounded loud in the quiet room. "Perryn has, well, agreed to the idea."

Perryn tensed as the people in the room turned slowly toward her.

Kane lowered his voice. "Is that true?"

Perryn cleared her throat, giving her a moment to choose her words. "Yes. Yes, I did. Not for me, but—it's not fair to everyone else that he remains out there. It's not fair to Brenda."

Nods could be seen around the room. Maria stepped in closer to her and grabbed her arm in reassurance. Kane rubbed his face with his hands and let out a long sigh. Perryn could see the weariness in his eyes. He gazed at her a long time and glanced toward Lydia, their eyes communicating.

"We—are going to have to postpone any plans of finding Willis," Lydia stated carefully.

"What!?" Jaden burst.

Kane held up a hand to calm Jaden who fidgeted, seemingly ready to storm the city by himself. With his other hand, he stroked the thin beard growing in on his chin. Taking a long breath, he scanned the room. "For a long time, finding Willis was a top priority. Our numbers are regrouping, but we've not been positioned to challenge the Coalition for a long time. But—these raids—they change everything. People need our help, and it's up to us to try." The words filled the air like a cloud of smoke that might choke anyone who tried to enter. Lydia moved a step closer to Kane as if to protect him from the accusing glares around the room. Perryn understood his reasoning, but the tension in the room buzzed like an angry hornet's nest. One wrong move could unleash panic.

"Chief has gone over the options," Lydia broke in. "In fact, we've gone over it many times. Willis was one of us—"

"Is," Sheila interrupted. "*Is* one of us. I imagine none of us wants to talk about him like he's dead."

Perryn sucked in at the words. *Dead?* She hadn't considered that being an option. They all assumed that he was alive, but she hadn't considered that something may have happened to him. *He's one of the most recognizable faces in the world.* The idea turned her stomach sour.

"I didn't mean to imply that," Lydia corrected. "There's no

reason to assume he's in danger. He left under his own terms and may very well be living quietly somewhere."

"Listen," Kane said. "The sooner we get all the people from the safehouses around the city relocated—" He paused to glance at Perryn. "—the sooner we can start searching for Willis."

"Kane, you can't seriously—" Jaden began. Perryn stopped him with a hand on his shoulder. He was defending her as he'd done for so long.

"I know," Perryn said, "that I'm the reason no one has searched for him."

Jaden turned and gazed at her, his eyes softening with sadness.

A single tear collected at the inside corner of her eye and threatened to fall down her cheek. She glanced down to hide it. "I know if I had said something, he might be here helping us plan to evacuate the Liberated out of the city." The tear escaped, catching on her upper lip before falling to the floor.

"Perryn, you don't have to—" Sheila started.

"No, I do. I do because it's true. Willis is out there. Maybe he's fine. Maybe he's not. All of you have had to live with that burden because I couldn't get over myself." Perryn sniffed. Breathing deeply, she collected herself to go on. "We have a crisis in the city. People like us are in danger, and we need to do something. That's why we're here. When we do find Willis—"

"And we'll find him," Kane added. Everyone nodded, including Perryn.

"We will," Perryn continued, "and I'll have to live with whatever state we find him in. But—we are the Underground. We're the hope of the Liberated everywhere. If we don't stand up to the Coalition in the middle of this, people might think we're gone for good. People might give in to their fear and lose hope. Willis wouldn't want that."

Jaden straightened at her words, his face growing serious. Perryn turned to him. "And if the world loses hope—" she started.

"Then we've lost already," Jaden finished.

Perryn nodded with a deep breath. She turned to the room around her. Their agreement was obvious.

"Very well," Lydia said. "We proceed with evacuations. Chris and Sheila, I want you to examine all the intelligence and see if you can decipher which of the remaining safehouses are most vulnerable."

"On it." Chris nodded.

"Maria and Perryn, I want you to prepare quarters for all of the evacuees. Set up in the auxiliary gym until we can sort out how many we need to work into the barracks."

"Maid duty for us, Captain." Maria smirked, squeezing Perryn's arm.

"Jaden, you'll take over training the recruits for a while. I think you won their respect in the gym. Can you handle it?"

"Sure thing," he smiled.

"Chief and I will try to contact Father Anthony on a secure channel to get word on his progress. We'll know more once we get his update. Everyone clear on their responsibilities?"

Everyone nodded again. The atmosphere had lifted, and Perryn could sense that everyone was glad to have something to do.

Lydia ended the meeting. "Okay, dismissed."

"Okay, girl. Are you for real about this?" Maria questioned. "I mean, are you *for real* about finding Willie-boy?" Maria hadn't wasted thirty seconds as they walked the hallway to the auxiliary gym before her questions burst from her lips.

"Yes, I am." Perryn kept her tone calm.

"Because you know I've got your back if you don't want to."

"It's the right thing, Maria."

"Did new-guy-Jaden put you up to this?"

"Not at all." She smiled. Maria was a loyal friend, but she could be overly passionate sometimes. "I mean it, Maria. It's time to find him as soon as we get the people out. It's not fair for everyone to have to sit around wondering, especially Brenda."

"Yeah, I guess so. Not fair what he did to you either."

"Can we not get into that?"

"Okay, but I'm not going to let them forget it." She pointed backward to Kane's office. "They may not believe it, but you know I'm with you. How did you not end up with Jaden anyway? He's pretty protective of you."

Perryn rolled her eyes. "It's not like that. It was never like that. We're friends. That's all."

"Friends, huh? Well, I think your *friend* is pretty hot. You think he—" Maria raised her eyebrows.

"Be my guest, but I don't think you're his type."

"Oh yeah, what type is that?"

Perryn laughed. "I honestly have no idea. Do whatever you want." Their laughter echoed off the stone corridor.

They rounded a corner and descended a short flight of stairs. The auxiliary gym was a smaller gymnasium, barely large enough to fit a basketball court, but it would make a perfect temporary shelter for evacuees to be placed once they got the cots set up. Pushing open the double doors, the smell of wood floors and dust greeted them. High windows on the left allowed sunlight to pour into the gym, which appeared as two rectangular beams of light. Dust particles floated in the beams, disturbed by their entrance.

Maria coughed. "Where are the cots?"

"In the storage room in that corner." Perryn pointed to a metal door and frowned. A large padlock could be seen above the door handle. "—which happens to be locked."

"Got the key?"

"No." Perryn sighed in annoyance. "I bet Kane has it."

"I'll get the blankets from the laundry and meet you back here." Maria rolled her eyes as she walked away.

Perryn retraced her steps back to Kane's office. The door was closed and the blinds pulled, but she could tell the light was on. Muffled voices could be heard. She stood by the door listening silently. She could hear Lydia and Kane speaking, and she dared to peer through a crack in the blinds where they hadn't quite closed.

Her eyes grew wide.

Kane was standing in front of Lydia, his eyes drenched with tears. Lydia was gazing into his eyes with her hands placed affectionately on either side of his face. Her thumb slowly stroked his beard.

"I—I don't know what to do anymore," Kane said through tears. His deep voice betrayed a slight rasp.

"Kane, you can't be so hard on yourself. You aren't responsible for what happened." Lydia pled with him. "You built something great here. Something that gave people hope, and it will again!"

Kane dropped his gaze in defeat. "I should have acted sooner. I should have done something these last four months. I should have—"

"Rested. You needed to rest. We all did."

"But the dead. The ones who got arrested."

"Were taken by the Coalition, not you. I've said it and will say it again and again until you believe it. The invasion wasn't your fault."

Perryn could sense that this was a conversation they had many times. She turned right and left to check the hallway, grateful no one had entered to see her watching through the door. She blushed as she intruded on their moment, but she had to know if her instincts from earlier were correct. She peered back in the window.

Lydia wiped a tear from his cheek. She leaned forward and kissed Kane tenderly. Kane's huge form leaned forward and wrapped Lydia in both arms, burying his face in her neck. She returned the embrace. They held each other for a long moment until Kane let out a deep breath, his body relaxing. He pulled away slowly, smiled, and kissed her on the forehead. Lydia grinned from ear to ear.

"Perryn?" a voice whispered from behind her.

Perryn jumped at the sound, nearly gasping and giving away her position to Kane and Lydia. She whirled around and found Brenda's smiling face. "Brenda! I—" she whispered back.

"I'd scold you for spying," Brenda kept her voice hushed, "but I'd have to scold myself as it's how I found out."

"You knew?"

"Kane and Lydia are incredible leaders and soldiers. They can control their emotions and reactions in any crisis. Yet when it comes to love—their body language betrays it every time if you know what to look for." Brenda laughed softly.

"I wasn't meaning to—I mean—I—" Perryn stammered.

"Relax, Perryn. It's nice not to have to carry the secret alone anymore. In fact, I'm sure they'll be relieved, too." To Perryn's horror, Brenda knocked on the door to Kane's office.

"Enter," came Kane's hurried voice.

Brenda opened the door. Kane and Lydia had moved several feet apart. Lydia stared at some papers trying to appear occupied. Kane was sitting at his desk, but his posture was unnatural.

"Okay, you two. I told you the secret would get out if you weren't more careful," Brenda warned.

"What do you mean?" Lydia protested.

Brenda stepped to the side revealing Perryn. Perryn longed to crawl in a hole and die of embarrassment. "I—I—needed the key to the cot storage." It was all she could say.

"You guys might want to do a better job of closing the blinds on the door." Brenda snickered.

Lydia's face flushed bright red. Kane wouldn't take his eyes off his desk but appeared to be trying to contain a smile. Brenda glanced at Lydia and then to Kane and back again. She burst out laughing. Lydia let out an embarrassed chuckle, and so did Perryn, who was sure her face matched Lydia's. Kane's smile spread fully across his face.

"You two are so pathetic," Brenda joked, entering the room. She motioned for Perryn to enter and closed the door. "You can't keep this a secret forever."

"Yeah, well, we didn't know how to tell everyone. Besides, we didn't want it to be awkward for—" Her voice trailed off, and she wouldn't meet Perryn's gaze.

"Oh come on," Perryn said, realizing Lydia's meaning. "Everyone has got to stop tiptoeing around me. I'm fine." She let out an exasperated sound.

"Sorry," Lydia said.

"It's okay. Just no more." Perryn shook her head at the two of them. "So—can I get that key by chance?"

The group laughed again, and Kane reached in his desk. Handing her a key, he smiled. "You might want to wait to tell Maria what you know," he said.

"Uh, no. I tell her, and the whole place knows." Perryn held out her hands as if to push the idea away. "I love that girl, but she can't keep her mouth shut about something like this. Trust me, I'm telling no one. This is yours to tell whenever you think you need to."

"Well, thanks for that." Kane turned to Brenda. "You may want to go with her. I think she has some news you'll want to hear."

Brenda glanced quizzically at Perryn. "Come on," Perryn said. "I'll tell you on the way, and then you can help us set out some cots."

Chapter Eight

Sweat beaded on Willis's forehead. Strapped to a table, he'd been left under the lights for what felt like days. Four blinding lights that shone bright enough to even light up under his eyelids when he closed them. He hadn't slept in forever, both from the light and the shock the table would give him anytime his exhaustion allowed him to nod off. His clothes were drenched in sweat from the heat of the lamps, and his body ached down to his bones. A clear bag fed something he couldn't identify into his vein.

The lights went out, their glow extinguishing leaving the faint outline of the still-red-hot filaments in each bulb. Willis tried to look around, but even his head was restricted.

"Patient 842," came Dr. Campbell's voice over the speaker, "congratulations. I believe we're ready for the next part in this."

"What do you hope to achieve by this?" Willis's voice croaked, and his mouth chafed like sandpaper.

"Try not to talk, 842. You must be quite thirsty at this stage."

Willis didn't want to respond, but the mere mention of thirst made him suck inward. He stared around into the blackness of the room, four spots still lingering in his vision.

"Let's start with exhibit one, shall we?" Campbell said.

A screen illuminated in front of him. His eyes required a moment to adjust. The picture was of several young boys in uniform. He recognized the logo from the Lake Placid Training Center. He found himself in the photo, barely a teenager. His body was lean and athletic, but his face still held onto some of its boyish roundness.

"Can you identify this photo?" Campbell waited for him to answer.

"Yes," he whispered.

"The name of the young man on the right?"

Willis studied the photo for a moment. "Mark-something."

"You were friends. Were you not?"

"Yes. We trained together in Lake Placid."

"Very good. Can you tell me what happened on February the year this was taken?"

Willis furrowed his brow. "He left the center."

"Not left, dismissed. Am I correct?"

"Yes." Willis wasn't sure where he was going with this information.

"Dismissals happen under recommendation from a trainer or squad leader. Tell me, who recommended young Mark's dismissal?"

"I did. I was squad leader."

"You did. And why?"

"He'd peaked in his ability. Our squad was losing ground in the point system, so I needed to recruit a faster runner to take his place." Willis spoke slowly, his mind unable to connect what Dr. Campbell was implying.

"You wished to replace him?"

"Yes. Well, no. He was a nice guy, but we needed someone better."

"You wished to replace him?" Campbell repeated.

"I didn't want to, but we'd fall in the standings. I had to."

"So, you sent him home?"

"Yes."

"Would it surprise you to know that young Mark is dead?"

Willis's eyes shot open in surprise. *Dead? How could he be dead?* "He's dead?"

"Young Mark went home to a family that needed his government subsidy to put food on their table. His return home sent his family into starvation. He got work at the port in his city unloading cargo ships. Safety standards aren't what they once were at the ports, especially for those who would hire such a young worker. I'm afraid a harness broke free, and he was crushed under several cargo crates."

Willis's breaths quickened at the news. "I—I—how could I?"

"Did you ever ask him about his family?"

"No. We mostly focused on training. We—"

"So, Patient 842, could it be said that your failure to get to know the story of your teammate ultimately caused his death."

"What? No! Well, I guess—"

"Perhaps it was an early leadership mistake. How about this one?"

The picture changed. This time, Willis was older and wearing his red uniform from the space station. His arm was around a young black male, who smiled brightly for the camera and wore the same uniform. It was an earlier member of the Red team, one whose spot he ultimately recruited Jez to fill.

"And this one's name?"

"Jenkins."

"Ryan Jenkins to be exact."

"Yes. But we called him Jenkins."

"And what happened to him?"

Willis paused, not wanting to answer. "He died in recoding."

"Another teammate dead? Is that so?"

Willis's anger burned. "That wasn't my fault!" he shouted, and it stung like blades in his throat. He took a couple of breaths to recover. "It was his one-hundredth recoding. He didn't survive."

"Did you know he was so close to his one-hundredth?"

"Yes. He told me, but we were winning. It's why he desired to be on our team so badly. We won every month, and he avoided recoding."

"So—what happened?"

"That—that was an accident." Willis felt panicked at this point. He could barely catch his breath. His mind swung like a pendulum between anger and fear.

"An accident during a training exercise. Am I right?" Campbell didn't wait for a response. "Fell off a ledge and broke two vertebrae on impact. Taken immediately to recoding, correct?"

"Yes—but—"

"And why was he on that ledge?"

"Because I told him to climb up there. We believed we could shave a few seconds off our run. But—it was an accident! I didn't mean to get him hurt. It just happened."

"But you were aware of his ninety-nine recodings?"

"Yes, but—"

"And you sent him up there anyway?"

"Yes, I did—"

"Would you not say that was careless of you as a leader?"

Willis stared at the picture, panting wildly. His eyes watered, and he blinked hard to keep from crying. Each time he opened his eyes, Jenkins stared at him.

"Tell me, 842," Campbell continued, "what did he say to you as they took him away?"

"He said," Willis whispered, "'Please don't make me go. Please.'" Willis's lip trembled at the memory.

"On to the next picture," Campbell said flatly, and the screen changed.

Hours passed. Campbell mercilessly made Willis relive memories from all parts of his life. They rehearsed the young girl in Lake Placid Willis had turned in for stealing. They discussed the time he'd angrily hit a boy in the training center lunchroom with his tray and sent him to his first recoding, mocking him as he cried when they took him away. Pictures of former teammates, one after another, flashed in front of him. They even made him watch the replay of Jez being hauled away to her hundredth recoding on the station.

Jez's screams still echoed in the room as Willis lay there. His chest heaved as the sobs threatened to surface at any moment. He searched the darkness in vain for sympathy.

"Please stop," he whispered to no one in particular. "Please stop."

"Patient 842, I believe we're nearly there. Tell me. Where was this picture taken?"

The screen changed. There before him, suspended above him in the darkness, the image of his family at the lake cabin after the Chase shone. His father was smiling, his years creasing the corners of his eyes as he smiled. His mother's gentle expression showed pure happiness. Her hand rested upon Perryn's shoulder, whose smile betrayed her feelings as she held Willis's hand.

"Where did you get this?"

"Tell me, 842," Campbell continued ignoring him, "what happened to your mother?"

"She—she was captured."

"And?"

"And brought here."

"You can imagine what it was like for her here. 842, why was she arrested?"

His lips shook as he tried to speak. "She—was protecting—us. Hiding—me."

"Very good. How about the young woman? She appears happy in this photo."

"She was."

"Was?"

He swallowed hard, his tongue catching in his parched mouth. "She—she—no longer trusts me." The words stabbed at his heart as he said them. His body trembled with heartache.

"And your father?"

Willis didn't answer. He stared at the image of his father. He remembered the angry words he'd spoken, the last he would ever say to his father. The smile in the picture seared into his mind. His father loved him. He was so proud of him. He hadn't deserved what came to him.

"842, your father?"

"He—he—died."

"Keep going."

"He was shot by Law-keepers."

"And why?"

"For protecting me."

"Could you not stop it?"

"I—I—" The image of his father's execution burst in his mind. His indecision while hiding in the trees. The flash of the muzzle. The report a split second later of the pistol. His father's limp body falling hard to the ground. His mother's wails over his body.

"You, the great leader of Red Team. The one whose life saw so many others cast aside for your benefit. The one who never doubted that *he* would run in the Chase. The one who never lost a race, no matter the cost. The strong, confident leader who wouldn't fail—could...you...have...stopped...them!?" Campbell shouted.

Willis could barely breathe. He was sucking in so quickly, he nearly passed out.

"842! Answer! Could you have stopped them?"

"Yeeeeeeessssss!" Willis shrieked into the dark room. His voice broke, and he coughed, tasting blood. The sobs came with abandon. He moaned with sorrow. His cries bounced off the walls and echoed into the hallway beyond.

Willis's insides split, as if his soul were attempting to claw its way from his body, and he could sense darkness infecting his entire spirit. His heart pounded to the point he worried it would burst. Doubt and regret and fear ate at him like carrion birds over a carcass. His crying stopped, and he stared blankly into the darkness, his breath in shallow gasps through his gaping mouth.

Right there, strapped to a table, Willis broke.

Chapter Nine

The gray wall stared back at Willis. Through his half-open eyelids, crusted with salty residue from tears long since run out, he could make out a crack in the stone. It ran from the floor upwards at an angle, meeting the corner near the ceiling where it disappeared from view. He gazed at the crack blankly. His soul froze as cold as the stone wall, and it too was cracked in every direction.

His body lay limply on the table where they'd left him. Hours had passed, and he could barely keep conscious. His swollen tongue stuck to the roof of his mouth. Not that there was anyone to speak with him. Campbell had raised the lights abruptly. He congratulated him, calling what happened a 'breakthrough.'

"Welcome to the new you, Patient 842," he'd said.

With that, Willis was left alone. Without food and minimal water, his muscles ached, feeling both small and heavy. He was still strapped to the table, but they could have left him free. He couldn't move.

I've failed. I've failed everyone I've ever known. The idea repeated over and over in his mind. The confidence he'd always carried oozed out of him like fluid from a septic wound. *I've failed—everyone.*

His thoughts returned to the image of his father. *I could have stopped them. They were searching for me, not him. I could have left the trees and let them have me. He'd be alive. He'd be with Mom. We never would have found Jez, and she would never have hurt Perryn. Everyone would have been better off, and I would have been brought here anyway.* The idea grew in his heart, its roots wrapping around his entire being.

It's all my fault. Everyone is hurting because of me.

His eyes glazed over, and he resumed staring at the wall. Would they come in again or let him waste away in this room? They could do what they wished. He no longer cared.

Thump.

The noise at the door broke the silence of the room. The handle jiggled, followed by the muffled sound of someone cursing. A moment later, the door burst open. Jez entered dragging the body of an unconscious guard. Reaching to take the guard's key card still stuck in the door, she closed the door with a soft click.

Had he not been curious about the guard, he would have told her to leave him alone, to leave him to sink deeper in his thoughts. Instead, he stared flatly at her unable to do much more. She rushed to the table, her fingers shaking as she fumbled with the restraints. She was breathing quickly. He glanced at the guard on the floor and then at her. Their eyes met.

"Shut up," she whispered.

He stared at her without answering or reacting.

"I said shut up," she repeated. "We don't have time to argue about it." She'd freed his head and worked on his arm.

"I don't—understand," he said, a barely audible whisper.

"Orderly showed up an hour early to give me my neuro-booster," she started, working on his leg. "Dr. Freak-show's way to stay ahead of my 'relapses' as he calls them. It won't be long, and he'll have me on a constant line feeding it into me like they do you." She stopped to hold up the IV line and stared at him. "I can't let that happen." Ripping the line out of his arm, she rounded the table and started on his other leg.

"Orderly—what? Where?" His head was in a fog, and he couldn't put a full sentence together.

"Knocked him out. Shoved him in a closet. I'd say we have about ten minutes before he's discovered." She moved to his other arm.

"But—what are you—"

She ripped the last restraint off his arm and grabbed his shoulders. His body spasmed as she pulled him upright. The room spun, and he might have vomited if he had anything inside him. Grabbing his face in her hands, she made him gaze up at her.

"Will, there's no time to fully explain. I'm done being their failure. I hate them, and the best way I can hurt them is to take you with me. Got it?" Her eyes were wild as if lit on fire, and she waited for his response.

"You're—helping me?" he whispered.

"Don't let it go to your head." She rolled her eyes. "I expect you to help me once we're out of here. I've no place to go, but I think you might."

He stared blankly, unable to consider how to answer.

"Well, you didn't say 'no' at least." Putting his arm around her shoulder, she hoisted him to a standing position. This time he did vomit—bile burning his throat. She sniffed in disgust as she glanced at her shoe. "Guess I've deserved that in some way." Hobbling to the door, she quietly opened it and peered out.

Willis could see her eyes taking in every bit of information they could in a single pass. Her body tensed as if ready to spring, and then it relaxed. Seeing an empty hallway, they stepped out. They walked, or rather she dragged him down the hallway to the stairwell. Producing the guard's keycard, she scanned it.

Nothing.

She scanned it again cursing. This time, the door clicked, and they burst into the stairs. He swayed like he was going to tumble down the flight, but her grip was firm. The air was cold, and his body shivered in the thin gown he wore. On the landing, she shoved him against the wall, the stone feeling cold on his bald head. She put a finger to his lips to silence him. Down the stairs stood two guards, talking about the upcoming Chase and who might win.

"I don't think the Western Alliance has it this year," one guard said. "Word has it that a runner out of Federation of Island States is going to win it all."

"You didn't hear?" The other guard huffed. "The Chairman was no fool when he blew up the space station. I heard all the runners were evacuated secretly after the riots broke out. That all-girl Gold Team is supposed to be in this year's Chase."

"Phew. I hope so. Otherwise, it'll be years before we can win—"

"Hey!" Jez startled both of them as she walked down the flight. Willis stood on the landing out of sight, his arms shaking as he gripped the railing to hold his body up. He peered through the rails, thankful the guards were fixated on Jez. "Dr. Campbell sent me down with a delivery for the captain."

Both guards glanced at each other. The first spoke. "You don't have clearance for this floor. Law-keeping personnel only. No botched experiments allowed." Both guards laughed.

"Fine." She shrugged her shoulders. Willis saw her turn to leave. "I hope you have a good answer for Dr. Campbell when I tell him you slowed his work."

"Hold it right there!" the second guard barked. He held out his hand. "Give it to us, and we'll deliver it to Captain." He snapped his fingers twice to let her know he meant business.

Jez let out a long sigh. Turning back, she held out her hand as if to give him something. As he extended his arm to grab it, Jez grabbed his index finger, violently bending it backwards. Even up the flight, Willis could hear the bone crack. In one motion, Jez shoved the broken hand backward, forcing the yelping guard into the wall. At the same time, her right foot shot into the air, the instep connecting with the soft tissue beneath the first guard's chin. He flew backward into the corner, gasping for air.

Retracting his broken hand, the guard on her left reached for his weapon with his good hand. Jez's palm shot upwards striking his chin. His head snapped back and to the side. He fell in a heap, no longer conscious. She took the guard's pistol from its holster and turned to the first guard who was still trying to suck in a full breath. She raised the pistol and struck him across the face. He, too, crumpled to the floor.

"Botched experiment, am I?" She spat on one of the unconscious guards. Shoving the pistol in her waistband, she returned to Willis who was ready to collapse. "You'd think they forgot what they did to me around here."

Grabbing his arm, they resumed their descent. In what seemed like hours of effort, they finally reached the first floor. The door beeped as she unlocked it with the keycard, and they slipped through. Darting to a dark corner on the left, Willis's legs wobbled, and he fell to the floor.

"Stay quiet," she whispered as she turned to peer around a parked truck. How she believed he had the strength to make any sound was a wonder to him. She returned a moment later. "Three guards in the parking bay. Stay right here." She pulled the pistol from her waistband.

Creeping around the backside of the truck, she tiptoed along the wall. Willis could see under the truck to the three guards in the distance from his floor view. Two were conversing, while the other was walking the perimeter of a patrol truck with a digital screen in his hand. Occasionally, he would check off something and resume his examination of the vehicle.

"You want to finish that inspection already, Cooper?" one called to the man with the screen.

"I swear you guys must go off-roading every time you drive this thing," he laughed in response. "You guys are keeping me busy, that's for sure."

"Tell you what," the third said, "you keep that thing running smoothly without the higher ups knowing, and we'll take you out sometime. Wally here knows all the best spots, right outside the city."

"Mmm-hmm, whatever."

Out of nowhere, Jez leapt on the two chuckling guards. She kicked one in the gut, and he doubled over with a grunt. The second received the barrel of the pistol to his head, and he fell to the ground. A kick to the face of the first guard sent him sprawling. Before the man with the screen could respond, he was facing the barrel of Jez's pistol pointed right at him.

"Who? What are you—" he stammered.

"Quiet," she demanded. She approached and unholstered his weapon. She threw it under a nearby truck without ever taking her eyes off him. He slowly raised his hands in surrender, the screen still in one of them. "Do you have a family?"

"A family? What? Why?"

"A family—do you have one?" she shouted, emphasizing her words by extending the pistol further.

"Y-yes, I have a family."

"Do you want to see them again?"

"Of-of course."

"Then do as I say. In the corner over there, start walking." The two slowly moved in Willis's direction. The man turned the corner of the truck and stopped when he saw Willis on the floor. "Pick him up and load him in the patrol truck," Jez snapped, jabbing his back with the end of the gun.

"Okay-okay. Don't hurt me." Up close, Willis was surprised by the man's youth. His hands shook as he reached down to grab Willis's weakened body. "Please, I have a wife and a child. I won't do anything, I promise."

"Get him in the truck."

The man grunted under Willis weight, but he managed to carry him across the garage. Jez opened the back of the truck, and he placed Willis roughly in the back seat. Motioning with the pistol, she beckoned the guard to get in the driver's seat. He complied. She climbed in the rear cab with Willis and slammed the door behind her.

"Get us out of here. Say whatever you have to, but remember I've got this gun pointed right at you the whole time. Got it?"

"Y-yes." He fired up the engine of the patrol truck and moved slowly toward the entrance. "I-I don't normally drive the vehicles at this time of day. They'll know something is up."

"Better make up a good lie, then."

The garage door opened, and the truck pulled into the sunlight. Willis squinted at the brightness. Jez grabbed a tarp she found in the back and covered the two of them. He could feel the truck slow to a halt at the guard station.

"Bit early for you to be taking one of these out for a test drive," the guard said to their driver.

He laughed nervously. "Wally and Ryan did a number on this thing today. I don't even know what's wrong with it, so I thought I'd drive it around a bit to get a feel for what it's doing."

A moment of silence passed.

"That doesn't fit with procedures. I'm going to have to call for clearance."

"No!" the driver blurted. Willis tensed, sure the man would silently tell the guard to check the back. "I mean, come on, I'll never get home in time if I don't get on this. I'm behind as it is, and Sarah has a special meal planned for tonight. I—I'd hate to miss it."

Another moment of silence passed. Willis saw Jez tighten her grip on the pistol, ready to move into action. That's when the alarm blared.

Bwwwahhh. Bwwwahhh. Bwwwahhh.

"Floor it!" Jez yelled. Without hesitating, the driver hit the accelerator. The lowered gate cracked. Bullets ripped through the air, shattering two of the windows.

"The—the barrier is coming up. We aren't going to make it," he shouted.

Throwing off the tarp, Jez rose to peer out the window to see the two pillars rising from the ground. "Faster," she cried. Willis could hear the engine roar as he hit the accelerator to the floor. A moment later, the truck lurched and a loud crunch came from behind Willis. He was left to guess, but it felt like the rising steel barrier had managed to catch their rear bumper as they'd barely cleared it.

"Turn here, and head south," Jez told the driver. Without a word, he followed her directions. "Okay, Will. It's your turn. I got you out. Tell us where we can go."

He bit his lip. "Central City Mission," he croaked.

"Did you hear that?" She tapped the driver with the barrel of the pistol. "Know where that is?"

The man winced. "Y-yeah, but we can't go there."

"Yes, we can, and you'll take us there."

"No, you don't understand. You can't go there. It's—it's not there."

"What do you mean?" Jez pointed the pistol at him where he could see it.

"I—I mean they burned it down. The Coalition. They—they've been arresting the remaining terrorists." Willis winced at the word *terrorist*.

Jez turned back to Willis. "Got another place you can get us into?"

He searched his mind, trying to remember the location of the other safehouses the Underground used. If the driver was right, they'd be clearing out from the city. His brain felt like mud, and he clenched his eyes trying to remember something. The image of Sheila coming to the Underground and describing her flight from Penny entered his mind. The safehouse she'd gone to was one of the most hidden in the Underground network. He hoped they'd hadn't already abandoned it.

"Yeah," he whispered. "There's an alley behind the old arena. Go there."

"You sure?" She gave him a worried frown.

"Yeah."

"Good," she said. She flopped to a seated position next to him. "I hope it's not far."

Willis spotted the sweat gathering on her face, and he would have asked what was wrong if it wouldn't have alerted the driver. The hand holding her pistol was trembling, and fear crept into her eyes. He noticed she was clutching her side with her free hand.

Willis could see the blood soaking into her shirt around her fingers.

Chapter Ten

"No one is answering," the driver said a second time.

"Knock again." Jez pounded a fist on the truck window. She glanced at Willis. "You sure this is the place?"

"I—I think so," he guessed. He was certain this was the place Sheila had used when she escaped from Alliance headquarters, but there was no way to know if it was still in use after all this time.

Thud.

Jez and Willis snapped their heads in the direction of the noise. The driver lay in in heap on the ground, a telltale dart in his shoulder. Further down the alley, a hooded figure could be seen standing in the shadows created by a small camouflaged door that sat open. Dart pistol still raised, the figure approached the patrol truck.

Willis saw Jez's hand tighten on the pistol grip. He reached out and grabbed her wrist gently.

"No, whoever that is, they're Underground," he said.

She winced in pain as she adjusted her position. "Yeah, that's the problem. If you remember, I'm not exactly popular with the Underground."

In his weakened state, his mind was still not moving quickly, and it was a moment before he put together what was about to happen. If Jez was the first person the figure encountered in the vehicle, things might not go well. Trembling, he uncovered himself and turned to his side. Placing his hand in front of him, he pushed. His body, emaciated and dirty, complained as though hundreds of pounds rested on his arms. He strained against his weight, lifting his body high enough to be seen through the windshield.

The figure stopped. Willis couldn't see the face, but he was sure the hooded person was staring right at him.

"Willis, my son, is that you?" The voice sounded so familiar, but it was not until the figure threw his hood back that the kind eyes of Father Anthony confirmed Willis's hope.

The world was spinning, and Willis's vision blurred. Breath wouldn't come to allow him to say anything. He stared, willing his silent plea to be heard by Father Anthony. The dart pistol lowered, and Father Anthony approached with caution.

"Willis, is it really you?" His eyes were wide with amazement. Willis slumped back down, his strength failing him. "Sister Josephine, come quickly."

"On my way," her voice responded over a radio.

Father Anthony rushed to the back of the truck and threw open the door. Willis squinted in the light, and he saw Father Anthony jump backward at the sight of Jez. He raised his dart gun. She sat slumped against the side of the vehicle, shaking and trying to contain the blood seeping from her side. Her right hand still gripped the pistol, but it lay flat next to her as if too heavy to hold.

Willis held up a trembling hand to signal that Jez was no threat. He forced air to expel from his lungs.

"She...rescued...me." It was all he could get out, but it was enough. Father Anthony angled the pistol downward.

The main door flew open, and a rush of footsteps could be heard. A moment later, a young woman dressed as a nurse appeared next to Father Anthony. She, too, stepped backward at the sight of Jez in the vehicle.

"It's okay, Sister," Father Anthony assured. He grabbed her arm gently. "Willis, here, has vouched for her."

In a flurry, Sister Josephine rushed back to the door and emerged with two assistants pushing stretchers. The first moved Willis with surprising ease onto one. The second stopped short when he noticed Jez's pistol.

"Relax," she said. "You'd be dead already if I planned to use this." The orderly reached out his hand, and Jez let out a cry as he helped her move to the back of the vehicle. Sister Josephine examined the wound and sent a knowing glance at Father Anthony.

"She'll make it," he assured. "Do what you can to stop the blood flow, but we'll have to operate once we arrive at headquarters." Willis gave him a questioning glance. "Yes, my son, we're taking you somewhere else. We're in the middle of our final evacuations. In an hour, we'll have you reunited with your friends and family." He smiled warmly, and Willis's lip trembled with hope.

Beep.

The group stopped and listened.

Beep.

The sound came again.

Beep.

One of the orderlies stepped closer to the driver's window. Slowly he opened the door and peered inside. "Father?" he said slowly.

Beep.

"What is it, my son?" Father Anthony inquired.

Beep.

"I'm not certain, but I think it's a tracking device. This truck is sending a signal."

Beep.

"Quickly," Father Anthony began with great concern, "it won't be long before the signal locks and the Coalition knows where—"

Beeeeeeeeeeeeeep.

No more time was wasted on words. Father Anthony grabbed Willis's stretcher and shoved it toward the door. Jez cried out again as the other assistant pushed hers. Entering the hallway beyond the door, Sister Josephine opened a cabinet and produced a large handbell, which she rang furiously.

"Evacuate. Everyone, evacuate. This is *not* a drill," Sister Josephine shouted as she ran down the hallway with the bell.

Seconds later, doors opened, and people emerged. Cries of

panic filled the hallway with a cacophony of noise. Families picked up crying children, while others gripped a few meager possessions. All appeared as though they were packed and prepared to leave.

"Leave your bags!" Father Anthony shouted. "The Coalition is on its way! Make your way to the vans immediately."

Bang!

A flash and puff of smoke set off screams as people fled down a side hallway. At the far end, sunlight poured through the smog where a door once stood. A second later, uniformed Law-keepers emerged with rifles raised. Shouts of "get down" were barked. Several people complied, lying flat on the floor in front of the soldiers.

Willis's stretcher twisted to the side, and Father Anthony yanked him down another side hallway. Jez's stretcher followed.

"Don't worry, my son." He smiled warmly as he nearly ran with the stretcher. "Our vans are ready, and our escape route is below ground. They've no doubt surrounded the building, but we'll get outside their circle."

A set of double doors banged open as the stretcher struck them, and the group emerged into a large warehouse. Families were quickly loading into vans, which were already running and filling the room with exhaust. In the distance, a shot was heard, causing the room to fill with more screams.

The front van slammed its doors and drove off down a ramp that sank into the floor. It disappeared into the tunnel beyond. Father Anthony pulled the stretcher to a halt next to the last van and motioned to the orderly to load Willis. Jez cursed as they folded her into her seat.

"Mommy!" The cry came from a little girl lying on the ground clutching a skinned knee. Father Anthony rushed to her side and picked her up. Whispering a word in her ear, he ran her to the second van and into the extended arms of her mother. The van screeched away as Willis landed in his seat, the orderly jumping in after him. Father Anthony turned to rush to their van, the last to leave.

Bang!

Another explosion jolted the hastily barred door to the garage, and a Law-keeper emerged through the haze. Turning to the van, the muzzle of his rifle flashed.

Father Anthony stopped running. His eyes shot open wide, and he fell to his knees. Blood began to spread across his chest where the bullet had ripped through his body. His face relaxed into what Willis would later swear appeared like a state of peace.

The tires squealed, and the van lurched. Shots rang out, and everyone in the van ducked. The door still open, Willis dared a glance as they sped toward the ramp. Father Anthony still knelt, his head down and hands gently laid on his knees as if in prayer.

He was gone.

Chapter Eleven

Sheila sat on the roof top staring out at the skyline of Central City in the distance. She held her tea in both hands to warm them as the air was uncomfortably cool. Still, it was the one place that she and Lydia could talk without being heard or disturbed. Typically, no one was allowed out here, but Kane had authorized it for Lydia's sake.

"So, how many know?" Sheila smiled.

Lydia sighed, her breath visible in the cold air. "Well, since Perryn found out a few days ago, we're up to three. But—Brenda and Perryn don't know that you know."

"Let's—keep it that way for the moment." Sheila chuckled, pointing to the space between their chairs. "I'm getting all the girl-talk I can handle right here." The two laughed.

Lydia had changed since arriving at the new headquarters. She'd dedicated herself to the training of the recruits, but the raid had softened her. Sheila guessed that was why she finally entertained the idea of a relationship with Kane. "There are no guarantees," Sheila had told her shortly after arriving at the converted school. "If you don't tell him, you may not get the chance later." Little did she know that it meant she would become Lydia's confidant as she and Kane awkwardly worked out their growing relationship.

"So, when are you guys going public?" Sheila raised an eyebrow.

"I don't know. He's still so unsure of himself. I don't want him to appear even more vulnerable."

"You know that everyone would approve, don't you?"

"That's what you keep saying."

"Then what is it?" Sheila turned to her.

Lydia stared down at her coffee cup and bit her lip. She ran her finger around the rim of the cup several times before looking back up. Taking a deep breath, she said, "It will make it real."

"And that's bad because—?"

"Sheila, you know how I feel about him, but what I haven't told you is that I can't stop thinking about the future—our future. I mean, what are we going to do—leave the Underground, get married, have children, and let someone else pick up the fight? That wouldn't be right. So, where does that leave us?"

"Hopelessly in love and with every reason to anticipate the future," Sheila suggested. She smiled at Lydia but regretted her comment when Lydia turned away.

Lydia shook her head. "No, love has no place in this fight. It's a distraction. Despite my efforts, I'm not helping him. He's so broken over the invasion. He still believes that everyone that was lost is on him. I—I'm not helping. I'm giving him something else to be afraid of losing."

Sheila straightened and set her cup on the ground. Reaching for Lydia's hands, she cupped them in hers like her sister used to do. "You know how I became a journalist?"

"No, you never told me."

"My sister, Audrey—she made me follow my dream. She believed in me more than I believed in myself. Even when she was sick and near death, she always had a word to help me not to give up on my future." Sheila took a deep breath to settle her heart, which always fluttered with sadness when she talked about Audrey. "I remember prior to my first live broadcast, I called her terrified. I was so worried I would forget everything and mess up my chances of becoming the inter-alliance journalist I aspired to be. She said to me, 'Kemp, we tell people the truth because it's one of the greatest ways to show them love exists.' I've never forgotten that."

"I don't understand." Lydia wore confusion all over her face.

"You said that love is a distraction in this fight, but I think this fight is all about love. The world is free from the Law, and they need to be told that it's okay to live that way. We tell people the truth, and in doing so, love them. So, our fight is one to show that love exists. I think—love has everything to do with what we do."

"But that doesn't mean—" Lydia glanced away again.

"Yes, it does, Lydia. What you and Kane have is special and rare, and the world could use more of it. Thinking about the future would be good for all of us."

Lydia closed her eyes as she spoke. "I want to believe you're right. Kane told me he's not felt like this since he lost his family. He's given so much in this fight, and I think he deserves to be happy."

"Then I think you've answered your own questions." Sheila let out a chuckle, sitting back in her chair. She enjoyed talking like this with Lydia. More than anyone, she connected woman-to-woman with Lydia in a way that reminded her of Audrey. This time, she played the part of older sister.

"Did you know he had a child?" Lydia opened her eyes. "Kane, his wife was expecting when he was taken from them."

"A child?" Sheila whispered. "I heard he had a wife and that she died after he went to prison, but a child—who knew?"

"It's not a secret, but he doesn't talk much about it."

"It's Kane we're talking about, right? I'm pretty sure he'll never be accused of over-sharing about anything." They laughed again.

"Yeah," Lydia chuckled, "I suppose you're right." She stared down again, her voice lowering. "He's lost so much. This world has taken more than its share from him, and he doesn't owe it anything. And yet, he leads the Underground anyway. I—" Her voice faltered, and tears rimmed her eyes.

Sheila straightened, taken by surprise at Lydia's rare show of vulnerability. "What is it?" She placed her hand on Lydia's.

"I hope he'll be happy with me. I—I don't know if I can ever live up to the ghosts of his wife and child."

She squeezed Lydia's hand in assurance. "You don't have to

be them. You don't have to replace them. You be you because that's who he's in love with."

"How do you know?"

"Because we both know that Kane doesn't do anything halfway. He's not in this as some kind of reminder of the past. He's in it with both feet for what it is."

Lydia nodded silently.

The two of them sat in silence for several minutes, Sheila never removing her hand from her friend's. She stared at the city skyline in the distance and breathed in the silence of their remote location. *Yes, what they have is special and so important.*

It was then that she noticed a quiet drone begin to grow. She squinted her eyes to see the source of the noise, but she saw nothing. She turned to see if Lydia had noticed. Her eyes were hawk-like as they scanned the horizon. She'd heard.

"What is that?" Sheila craned her neck for a better view.

"Engine. No, engines. More than one." Lydia said. Sheila could see the switch from vulnerable friend to soldier as Lydia's face hardened. Slowly, Lydia's hand reached for her radio. "Chris, come in."

"Here, Captain. What's up?"

"What time were we expecting the last of the safe house transports?"

"Not for a least another hour. Why?"

"Because I can hear multiple vehicles from the roof."

"Vehicles?"

"Yes, and they're approaching—fast."

Lights flashed throughout the building as silent alarms alerted everyone of the incoming danger. Sheila darted between people rushing in the opposite direction, making their way to the basement to hide. Families carrying whimpering children and new untrained members were unfamiliar with the defense protocols, and their concealment was considered priority. Sheila, though, had trained since their arrival and followed Lydia to the armory.

Watching Lydia, she could see her ability to lead people. With some, she was the Captain, giving firm orders that filled them with confidence to do their job. With others, she was the soft voice of assurance as she directed them to the basement. *Yes, Kane has chosen well whom to love.* She allowed the thought to take hold amid the near chaos.

Approaching the gym, a set of locked double doors had been opened. Maria and Chris were furiously handing out dart guns of various sizes to members of the Underground. When Sheila reached the front of the line, Maria handed her a pistol and motioned her on.

Doors had been barred, reinforced, and locked throughout the building leaving the front lobby as the one easy point of entry. The lobby glass had been boarded from the inside for safety, but it was the most obvious point of entry from the outside. Sheila rushed to her designated position behind a pillar that stretched from floor to ceiling. She crouched to one knee, checking to make sure the safety on her pistol was in the off position. To her right, Lydia assumed a similar defensive posture. Kane, Chris, and Maria were all there along with many of the longest standing members of the Underground. She couldn't see them, but she understood from drills that Jaden and Perryn were on the second floor overlooking the lobby area.

The silence in the room was heavy with the occasional scrape of a foot being repositioned sounding loud enough to send Sheila's skin into goosebumps. She had to remind herself to breathe.

This is your first action, Kemp. Don't blow it. She found herself assuming Audrey's tone in her head.

Gradually, the drone of the engines could be heard growing louder as the unknown vehicles approached. Everyone's shoulders tensed visibly as the speeding cars could be heard turning on the vacant street where the old school was located. Gravel crunched as tires pulled into the lot out front, and Sheila raised her pistol.

Van doors opened.

Footsteps crunched on gravel.

Muffled voices spoke, not trying to go unheard.

Sheila stood and stepped out from behind the pillar. *That doesn't sound like Law-keepers ready to invade.* Lydia was motioning furiously for her to get back to her position, but she walked forward. Slowly and softly, so she could still hear the sounds from outside, she moved toward the doors.

Bang! Bang! Bang!

The pounding on the door halted Sheila. *Who would knock?*

Bang! Bang! Bang!

"Help! Please help!" came a muffled shout. "Please open up! She's hurt!"

"Sheila? Kane? Anyone?" This new voice sounded strained and was barely audible through the door.

Sheila turned back to Lydia, who was emerging from her position. She pointed to her ear as if to ask, "Does that person sound familiar to you?" Lydia shrugged and shook her head. Turning back to the door, Sheila began walking.

Bang! Bang! Bang!

The pounding was louder and more desperate. She hurried forward. Grabbing the bar across the doors, she lifted it out and set it to the side. Almost at once, the door burst open. People streamed inside.

A mother emerged first, carrying a small girl whose cheeks were stained with tears. Three young teenagers came next, one pulling along what must have been a younger brother who couldn't have been more than five. An elderly couple entered, the man with his arm around his wife with one arm and holding her hand with the other in a protective posture.

"Sheila?" the definitely familiar voice asked.

Sheila whirled back toward the door to find herself staring face to face with Willis. His cheekbones protruded from obvious weight loss and his face was sallow in color. His shoulders slumped and his lips were heavily cracked. He was dressed in nothing more than a hospital style gown, and Sheila's mind flashed to her own reflection in the mirror when the Alliance had released her from prison.

"W-Willis?" she stammered. She stepped forward, noticing his gait. He was barely able to walk. She rushed to him and threw her arms around him. He stank of sweat and cottony breath, but she didn't let go. He trembled violently, and she had to hold him up to keep him from collapsing.

At this point others emerged from their hiding places. Running footsteps could be heard as Jaden pushed his way past those on the stairs. Kane slowly walked to them, letting out a sigh of relief. He shook hands with one of the van drivers. Lydia immediately issued orders for Underground members to holster their weapons and help with those in need.

Conversation exploded in the lobby as people inquired about what had happened. They were obviously shaken, and the multitude of answers kept Sheila from understanding any of them. She pulled away from Willis, keeping her hands on him to support him.

"Willis, what happened? How did you get here—with these people?" She stared into his eyes, desperate for answers.

"She—she saved me. She's hurt," Willis whispered, barely able to speak. It was then that a hush fell over the room like a smothering blanket.

Sheila peered past Willis to see what had caused the reaction. Two men were holding up a lean, muscular girl with short, black hair. Her hands clasped a piece of blood-soaked cloth over her side, and her eyes darted left and right as if searching for an escape.

"Don't everyone say 'hi' at once." Jez half-laughed while grimacing in pain. The men held her up and half-carried her to a nearby chair.

Instantly, Kane flew forward, throwing one of the men aside with his right hand. With his left, he grabbed Jez by the throat and lifted her effortlessly out of the chair and against the wall. The other man helping Jez backed away, an expression of fear on his face.

"Kane, no!" Lydia screamed, momentarily forgetting to use his title and running to his side. She grabbed his arm with her hand. His eyes, wide in their fury, flashed at her. His teeth were bared, and he appeared as if he might crush Jez.

"Two times, I've let her live. Two times, she's betrayed us," he growled. The room stood stunned by their Chief's loss of composure. "There won't be a third."

Lydia reached up and touched Kane's face tenderly. "Please, this isn't you," she pled. He hesitated for a moment, seemingly unsure, then his eyes softened, and he lowered Jez back to her chair. Jez gasped for breath as he let go of her, and she appeared as though she couldn't decide whether to hold her throat or her side. She pointed at Willis.

"Ask—"

Cough.

"—him."

Cough.

Jez's words rasped through her injured throat, and several moments were needed for them to register in everyone's mind. Faces turned to Sheila and Willis. Sheila stared back at Willis. "Jez, here? With you?" She had a thousand questions in her mind, but these were the two she could verbalize.

"Saved me. She—" Willis's eyes rolled backward, and he fell forward into her arms, unconscious, succumbing to his weakened state.

"Willis? Willis!" Sheila shouted as she lowered his body to the ground. "Someone, help me!"

Perryn stood at the top of the stairs rooted in place. Her dart gun hung limply at her side. Down in the lobby, Lydia was shouting to get Willis to the medical wing along with Jez. Guards were selected to follow Jez, and Kane ordered they shouldn't leave her side. Whispers could be heard spreading through the room as members of the Underground shared their theories as to what was happening. The refugees from the safehouse mostly stood dumbfounded by what they'd seen, not understanding what was going on. Somewhere, a refugee baby was crying followed by the gentle shushing sounds of her mother.

Kane's face turned grim when he received the news about Father Anthony.

Willis? Jez? The names rolled in her mind like earth giving way into an avalanche. Her senses were overloaded, and she couldn't make out what was going on.

When Willis entered, her heart had gone to war with itself. Part of her had longed to rush down the stairs with Jaden to greet him. The other part twisted her stomach into knots. Seeing him so weak and helpless, her gut soured with concern.

Jez had been another matter. She hated Jez for leading the Coalition to the Underground, costing the lives of so many. Yet, under the surface, she couldn't help but feel as though she owed Jez. She was the one who had removed the veil and helped her see Willis for who he was, a man who pitied rather than loved her. When Lydia persuaded Kane to let her go, she found herself surprised at her own relief.

I need to talk to her, was all she could think. Questions flooded her mind, particularly about why Jez and Willis had arrived together. It was a bizarre sight considering the last time she saw them together, but so was the idea that Jez may hold the answers she needed. She sat down on the steps, folding her arms across her knees. She rested her head on her arms and breathed deeply. *So many questions.*

"Girl, you okay?" Maria stood nearby. When Perryn didn't answer, she sat without another word.

Perryn glanced—much of the room had started to disperse. That was okay with her. She needed time to sort this out. Somewhere, she could hear Lydia barking orders to move the vans to a safer location and to let those hiding in the basement come out. Kane was sitting in a chair, his face in his hands. Jaden had apparently rushed off with the medical staff to see to Willis. She was thankful for that. He would try to cheer her up if he was here.

"I don't know." She sighed after a moment. She studied Maria, whose face wore both concern and determination.

"Everyone's seeing to everyone else." She elbowed Perryn playfully. "Thought someone ought to check on you. You know I still got your back, right?"

"I know." Perryn's voice was flat and emotionless. She didn't know how to feel.

"Willie-boy and crazy girl coming here together? What's up with that?"

Perryn sat silent.

"Yeah, you don't need to say it. I already agree. It's messed up." Maria leaned over and rested her head on Perryn's shoulder. They sat that way watching as dart pistols were collected to return to the armory. The tension of a possible invasion had morphed into the more familiar scramble to help the injured and frightened. With mechanical precision, refugees were handed blankets and shown to rooms. Perryn never ceased to marvel at how the Underground could help lost people feel at home. So quick was the work that soon Lydia returned and sat next to Kane, not hiding her hand in his.

"I need to talk to her," Perryn finally said.

"Her? To who?"

"Jez. I need to talk to her."

Chapter Twelve

Perryn approached the hospital wing. It was a series of administrative offices that'd been converted, but they sat nearby what used to be a nurse's station and contained the one semblance of medical storage in the building. Several people were being checked out, though most appeared simply shaken up by the experience. The elderly man sat as a medic listened to his heart through a stethoscope. His wife stood next to him, her brow creased with worry.

"His heart has never been very good. Are you sure he's okay, young man?" the wife said.

The medic removed the stethoscope from his ears and turned to her, smiling. "We'll have the doc check to be sure, but I don't hear anything abnormal. We're not fully equipped for all conditions here, but we do our best with what we have."

"See?" the elderly man said to his wife, thumping his chest with a hand. "Strong as an ox. The old ticker isn't giving up on me yet." He turned to the medic. "I told her she was making a fuss over nothing."

"I'm sure she is." The medic nodded. "All the same, let's have the doctor examine you once she's done with the more critical patients."

The man nodded and grabbed his wife's hand tenderly.

"Thank you, young man," she said.

Perryn smiled at the interchange as she passed. Kindness, which felt like a luxury in her previous life as a Chase runner, was commonplace here among the Underground. Making her way to the end of the hall, she saw several bandages being applied to scrapes from falls during the escape. Another was being treated for a twisted ankle. Yet another sat with her arm in a sling, a pained expression on her face as she waited for her pain medication to take effect.

It'd been a miraculous escape for those who made it to the vans. The news of Father Anthony had spread quickly throughout the Underground. It was a heavy blow to all of them. *I can't believe he's gone.* She remembered his gentle smile when they met in the recoding center after the invasion. On each subsequent visit to the school to deliver new refugees, he'd always made a point to check on her.

Continuing past the various families, she reached the end of the wing. Her smile disappeared when she spotted the two remaining doors. Behind one, she realized, lay Willis. Dehydrated and malnourished, the doctors had forbidden anyone besides Kane, Lydia, and Brenda from seeing him until he improved. She was thankful not to have the choice. *I'm not sure I'm ready to see him.* She was partially grateful for his return. It would at least put an end to the guilt over his absence, but the conflict inside her raged. She couldn't bring herself to speak with him—not yet.

The room across the hall was guarded. A man stood armed with a dart pistol, and she could tell that Kane was taking no chances with Jez. As she approached the guard, he held out his hand.

"Sorry, Perryn," he started. "No visitors. Chief's orders."

Getting closer, she recognized him as Bryan. He was the Alliance transportation official that'd smuggled her and Willis into Central City. She'd located him and helped his escape to the Underground two months earlier. It was one of the few missions Kane had authorized since the raid and only because she'd insisted. She hoped that favor would be worth something.

"Bryan, can't I see her for a moment? I need to talk to her," she pled, trying not to sound desperate.

"I'm sorry, but Chief said—"

"Chief would understand why," she interrupted. "Come on, a few minutes."

Bryan glanced around uncomfortably.

"Perryn, I shouldn't." He paused, again glancing around. "Okay, but you have three minutes—four tops."

She patted him on the arm as she approached the door. Reaching for the handle, she paused. *What am I going to say?* Taking a deep breath, she turned the handle and entered before she reconsidered.

Jez lay on the bed, partially inclined. She could see the extensive bandages poking out from underneath her shirt where the doctors had tended to her bullet wound. Both wrists were handcuffed to the bed as were her ankles. *Kane is definitely not taking chances,* she marveled.

She worried that Jez was asleep until her eyes snapped open. She glowered at Perryn. They'd never liked each other. Whether on the station or in the Underground hideout or even here, no love was lost between the two of them. And yet, they were linked. One moment in the tunnel during the raid changed everything when Jez had shot her and changed her mind forever. She considered leaving, but Jez spoke first.

"Enjoying the view?" She squinted at Perryn.

"I—I wasn't sure you'd be awake."

"With what they've got for pain medication around here? Doubtful. Sleep is going to be a little hard to come by." She jerked at the handcuffs. "Especially when you can't do anything but lay in the same position all day."

"Can you blame Kane? I mean, you—"

"Betrayed everyone? Shot you? Allowed the Coalition to kill or imprison many of you?"

Perryn stood dumbfounded. She didn't know how to respond.

"No, I don't blame him," she said, answering her own question. "I suppose being a prisoner of the Underground is preferable to being a prisoner of the Coalition."

Perryn felt her minutes ticking away. "Listen, I need to talk to you. I need something from you."

Jez studied her for a moment, and her mouth grew into a smile.

"Ah, I see. So, my words did their trick, did they? Let me guess, you can't even bring yourself to visit him."

"They won't allow visitors for him, yet," she said dodging the implication.

"I'm sure, and you want to know if somehow I can sort out the mess in your head. You're hoping I can undo what I did."

Perryn affirmed the thought with her silence.

"Sorry, no can do. Not because I wouldn't, but because I can't. I could tell you all day that I lied or didn't know what I was talking about or made the whole thing up. My words would have no effect. That idea is coded into you."

"I don't think you made it up," Perryn said, as Jez clamped her mouth shut in surprise. "It all rings true as I look back on our history. Did he pity me? Maybe. But I can't sort that out until I'm sure that I am thinking for myself." The two stared at each other for several long seconds.

"Well, I wish I could help." Jez's voice was softer, and Perryn supposed she might mean it.

"I see." Perryn couldn't hide the disappointment in her voice. "I guess I'll go then. I hope you heal soon." She turned to walk out of the room.

"Perryn?" Jez spoke suddenly. Perryn turned, startled that she couldn't remember Jez ever using her name. Jez's eyes appeared glassy as if she might cry, and she kept glancing away as if looking too long would keep her from holding the tears back. "You've every right to hate me. Everyone here does. But for what it's worth—you're not the one he pities. I am."

Perryn froze in shock. Never had Jez ever spoken like this around her. This was the Jez who wouldn't think twice about destroying another person if it meant bettering herself. Her countenance shrank to something small, her toned frame appearing to wither in front of Perryn.

She backed her way to the door, unable to take her eyes off this version of Jez. Turning to the door, she dared one more glance backward. Jez had laid her head down and stared out the window.

A single tear clung to her cheek, finally landing with a patter on the pillow.

She stepped through the door and closed it quietly behind her. She squeezed Bryan's elbow in thanks as she silently walked away.

I have to figure this out. Jez had essentially told Perryn the implanted thought was false, yet her mind rejected the notion. *Jez was right. Her words weren't enough.* She still doubted Willis had little more than pity for her.

She raced down the hallway to find Kane. She'd used her favor with Bryan. Kane was going to have to take her to see Willis.

Chapter Thirteen

Willis opened his eyes. The sterile fluorescence he'd grown used to at Solution Systems had been replaced with a softer light, and he had to remind himself where he was. He lay on a bed next to which sat a small end table and lamp, which was the single light illuminating the room. The shades were pulled, but he could tell it was evening. Fluids dripped from a clear bag hanging to his right and creeped down into his arm.

"Welcome back to the land of the living," Lydia said to his left. "Your mother will be right back. I insisted she go get something to eat. She's been here since you arrived."

Willis smacked his lips in a vain attempt to moisten his dry mouth. "What is this place?" His voice was barely a raspy whisper.

"This is the new home of the Underground. It's pretty amazing. Once you're stronger, I'll show you around."

Willis glanced at the window again. "It's above ground?"

"Yep. An old school building. Kind of makes the name 'Underground' a little ironic, doesn't it?" They both chuckled. "Chief will want you to brief him on where you've been and what you learned. Jez filled us in that you were at Solution Systems, so anything you can share with us would be helpful."

Willis nodded. He would share what he learned with them, but it would have to end there. *Too many people have been hurt on my account. No more missions for me.* His hands trembled, remembering the list of those who had come to harm. He tried to catalogue all the things he'd learned in his head to share them later. That's when it hit him.

"Kane! I have to talk to him!" He shot up in bed, and he cried out from the pain in his head.

"Whoa! Hold on!" Lydia said, reaching out to calm him. "Slow down. That's too much, too soon. Kane's away running for supplies to provide for the new families. He won't be back until tonight."

"But I have to talk to him, now!" he said through clenched teeth, trying to contain the pain.

"Why? What is it? The Coalition?"

He shook his head, which he regretted. "It's about Sandra."

Lydia's eyes grew wide at the name of Kane's wife. "What about her, Willis?"

He placed his hands on his temples and fell back to his pillow. "She's alive. And so is her child," he whispered.

"Alive?" Lydia whispered, more to the room than to Willis. Turning back to him, she leaned toward him. "Are you sure?"

"Yes, I met her living on the streets after I left. She's been searching for Kane since she saw him run the Chase. She believed he was dead. He needs to know. She's out there somewhere."

Lydia backed away from the bed. Her lip trembled, and her breath quickened. Suddenly, she lunged at the bed and grabbed Willis's shoulders. She stared at him face to face.

"Willis, you can't tell him," she said, an expression of desperation on her face.

"What? Why?" His eyes widened with astonishment.

"It—it will break him."

"But he has to know. It's his wife and child!"

"I know—and he will." She paused, searching for what to say next. "I—I need—I need to find her first." The words hung in the air, filling the room.

"I don't understand."

"I know. Kane isn't himself. Ever since the raid—well—this will destroy him. Knowing they were out there this whole time will be too much for him to bear. I need to find them first, so he knows they're okay."

"But—why you?"

"Because it has to be me."

Willis had no idea what she was talking about, and he stared at her.

"Willis, you have to promise me you'll keep this quiet."

He didn't answer.

"Promise me!" She shook him a little, which made his temples pulse even more. Her face filled with fear.

"I—I promise."

Lydia stood and slunk away from the bed. "Okay," she whispered. "Good." She was trembling as she reached for the door handle. "Thank you, Willis." Then, she disappeared out the doorway.

Chapter Fourteen

Sheila stepped out onto the rooftop. She couldn't see Lydia, but she could hear her shuddering gasps coming from behind an old air conditioning unit. She padded across the roof and around the metallic box. Lydia sat on the roof with her face buried in her hands. Her sobs came in great heaves that barely allowed her a breath before they resumed.

"Hey," Sheila said softly.

She sat down beside Lydia and placed her arm around her. Lydia shook with each breath. What could have upset her so much? Holding her friend, she waited for her body to calm before speaking again.

"Been searching around for you. What happened?" Sheila paused for an answer.

Lydia glanced up, but not directly at Sheila. She wiped her nose on the back of her hand, all efforts at being composed abandoned. "She's alive."

"She who?"

"Sandra. Kane's wife. Willis met her out there." She nodded to the skyline of Central City.

"His wife is alive?"

"She's searching for him. And—and there's a child." The tears resumed, and she pressed her fingers into her eyes.

It can't be. Sandra's alive? "Does Kane know?"

Lydia sniffed heavily. "No, and he can't. You can't tell him."

"Lydia, you can't keep this from him. It's not fair."

"I know!" Lydia bawled, striking the roof with her hands.

"Then, what do you intend—"

"I'm going to find her."

Sheila's heart shattered. She understood the full extent of Lydia's tears. *She loves him enough to return his wife and child to him, even at her own expense.* The thought tore through her like lightning splitting a stormy sky, and she sucked in a deep breath.

"Oh, Lydia," Sheila whimpered, her own tears falling. She rested her head on Lydia and held her friend.

The two sat in silence. Sheila imagined how Audrey must have felt comforting her after her mother died. Sheila had been away on assignment and had been inconsolable when she returned to learn the news. Audrey, despite her condition, had taken care of her for days. Most of all, she never left her side, and the two sisters grieved together.

"You're grieving, Lydia, and you should. But—are you sure you should be the one running off to find her?"

"Yes." Lydia didn't hesitate. "I love him, Sheila. I need to do this for him, so it won't break him."

Sheila thought of her sister again. "Then, you won't do it alone."

Lydia straightened and turned to her. "No, Sheila. I can't ask you to—"

"You didn't. I'm volunteering. If you refuse, Kane won't have one foot in the door of this building before I tell him. Deal?"

Lydia stared at her through red, swollen eyes. She nodded slightly and leaned into Sheila. "I don't know how we're going to do it," Lydia started. "We can't ask for help from the intelligence officers here without an explanation, and neither of us is familiar enough to hack Coalition systems. Anyone we ask for help will ask for Kane's authorization first. And—we can't run around the city blindly calling her name. We're out of options, and we haven't even started."

Sheila bit her lip for a moment. "That's not entirely true. What if there was someone who could help us?"

"Who?"

"It's a crazy idea, but there's someone who knows the Coalition better than anyone else here. The Coalition tracks everyone, and there's someone who has had access to their network."

"Sheila," Lydia's tone grew serious, "who?"

"People won't like it. Some may even think we've betrayed the Underground."

"You don't mean—?"

Sheila nodded. "Jez. We need to break her out and take her with us."

"Sheila, I don't think—"

"I know. But we either do this or tell Kane." Sheila paused and considered her words. "Willis trusted her enough to allow her to be brought here, and I can't ignore that. Lydia, she saved him from that awful place. Maybe it was to save her own hide, but she saved him anyway. And that gives me an idea on how to strike a deal with her that'll stick."

Chapter Fifteen

Night had fallen, and Perryn walked with Kane quietly through the hallways of the hideout. He'd been reluctant to give her permission to see Willis, but she promised it was necessary. She'd asked as a friend, not a member of the Underground. With a sigh, he said he would escort her.

The medical wing was a ghost town compared to earlier. Most of the minor injuries had been treated, and the newcomers were shown to their living quarters. Other than a few rooms housing sleeping patients, the hallway was empty. Their footsteps, though quiet, echoed in the darkness.

A new guard had replaced Bryan outside Jez's room, and he stepped forward at their approach. Kane raised a hand to let him know to stand at ease. He turned to Perryn.

"You sure you want to do this?"

"No, but I think I need to." She'd answered more honestly than she intended.

"Want me to come with you? Might make it easier to see him with someone else there."

"No thanks. If we're going to talk, we need to *really* talk. You sure he's awake?"

"He slept most of the day away. Nurses said he's refusing drugs to sleep. Can't blame him after what he went through. I expect you'll find him wide awake after so much rest."

"Okay." She turned to stare at the door behind which Willis lay. Kane walked away. "Kane?" She waited for him to turn back to her. "Thanks. I mean it." He nodded with a grin and continued walking.

She stared at the handle to the door and was aware that the

guard behind her was watching her. Most of the Underground had heard her story by now, and she felt the heat of his stare creep up the back of her neck. She took a deep breath and let it out. Grasping the handle, she turned it.

The room was dim, with a single lamp illuminating it. To the right, a table sat empty other than a clipboard with notes about Willis's condition. The carpet was worn and smelled slightly musty. To her surprise, the blinds were open to the lights of the city in the distance.

"I told them to keep them open." Willis's voice startled her. She turned to him. He wasn't watching her, but rather he gazed out the window. His cheeks were drawn, though they had more color in them than when he'd arrived. While she could still see evidence that he'd once been a Chase runner, he was skinnier than she'd ever seen him. His hands appeared skeletal, and his lower ribs were visibly protruding. "Where the Coalition kept me had no windows. I got so sick of seeing the same four walls. No change. No variation. I told the nurse that if I was going to be up all night, I at least want to have a view."

She stared out the window with him. City lights blinked in the distance. Some areas were well lit, indicating the presence of Alliance structures. Other sections were nearly dark, as power usage was strictly monitored for regular citizens. She heard him move on the bed and realized he was gazing at her. She hesitated to turn to him.

I have no idea what I planned to say. Deep in her gut, a knot formed choking her thoughts. Had she made the right choice coming here?

"I'm sorry," Willis said, breaking the stalemate.

The words broke her attention, and she turned without thinking. His eyes were mournful, and he appeared like he had an incredible weight upon his shoulders. Their eyes locked for a moment.

"I really am sorry," he said again.

"I—I don't know what you mean." She was at a loss for words. *What could he possibly be sorry for?*

He took a deep breath as if trying to control his emotion. "You got hurt. Not getting shot, and that's enough. No, you got hurt in every way. Your body. Your mind. Your—heart. And it's my fault."

Her brows furrowed. "Willis, I don't think—"

"I do. My life has been an endless line of people who have been damaged in the wake of what I believed were good decisions."

"That's not true." She couldn't believe his candor nor understand why he would be saying these things.

"Yes, it is." His tone was more forceful, and his voice rasped. He breathed heavily and dropped his gaze. "I never meant for anyone to get hurt. I never meant for *you* to get hurt. If I had known, I never—" His voice trailed, and his head dropped. "Everyone around me---everyone I love, gets hurt in the end, and I can't let it happen again. I'm so sorry."

She gaped at him in silence. The confident, sure-handed Willis was gone. From the day she first met him on the station, he'd been the most driven and single-minded person she'd ever known. He had an answer for everything. He understood his purpose. Even after his father had been killed, it simply took the idea of his mother's rescue to refocus him. Replacing that man was a trembling shell, crippled by self-doubt. He was broken.

Her insides twisted until some part of her came close to snapping, and she worried she might begin to cry. She heaved a sudden breath to contain the tears and took a step toward him. A battle between her mind and heart raged.

"Willis, I don't know what happened to you or what the Coalition did to you, but I do know you can't take the blame for what they did to people around you." It came out more intense than she'd intended. He straightened at her tone.

"Yes, I can!" His chest heaved with shaky breaths as he nearly yelled the words. A vein pulsed on his bald head. "No one is safe around me! I'm so sorry you got hurt, Perr. I never wanted you to—" He was crying. "When I left after your recoding, it was to let you be happier. Now, I know I can't be around you because you'll be safer without me. Maybe what Jez did was for the best."

"Willis, you can't—"

He lifted a trembling hand to stop her. "Perryn, thank you for coming to see me, but you're better off without me." He laid on the bed and turned away from her, signaling the end of the conversation.

She stared for a moment, wondering if she should speak to him again but then thought the better of it. Quietly, she opened the door and stepped out. She walked quickly down the hall until she rounded a corner out of the guard's sight. That's when she broke into a run. Tears streamed from her eyes.

Her brain told her it was better this way. If he'd never truly loved her, if pity for her was all he had for her in the past, then he had nothing for her.

Her heart, on the other hand, burned as if it'd been stabbed with a hot knife.

Chapter Sixteen

Lydia put her finger to her lips to signal to Sheila to be silent. She watched as Lydia quietly inserted a key into the door to the armory. She winced as the latch clanged loudly in the silent building. They'd moved freely, even at this hour, as none of the guards would question the presence of their Captain. Once armed, things would be different. Only active guards were permitted to carry dart pistols regularly.

Lydia handed her a holstered pistol and pack of darts. She strapped on the holster, wincing as the strap struck a metal pipe fixed to the wall. She mouthed a silent 'sorry' at Lydia.

Locking up the armory, they darted back down the hall toward the medical wing. Knowing the guard rotations, Lydia planned the exact path they should take. With some effort, they managed to sneak to the end of the wing. Lydia peered around the corner and held up one finger, indicating a single guard was posted at Jez's door.

The finger opened to a hand, and Sheila got the message. *Wait here.* Lydia stood and walked down the hallway confidently.

"Evening, Captain. Didn't expect to see you this late. Why are you wearing a—"

Phoot!

Sheila could hear the body of the unconscious guard crumple to the floor, and she emerged from her hiding place. Lydia was whispering curses to herself when she approached.

"Didn't mean for him to hit his head," she whispered. "Appears he'll be okay, but the headache he'll have will be awful."

Sheila grabbed the keys off the guard's belt and fit them into the door handle. She held the door open as Lydia dragged the guard inside. She gently placed him in the corner, while Sheila shut and locked the door.

"What the heck are you two doing?" came a tired voice behind them. They whirled around to see Jez's eyes watching them in the dark.

"Jez, we need your help," Sheila said, not wanting to waste time.

"Ha! Right." Jez laughed through a yawn. "Do me a favor and keep the jokes to the daytime. I was finally getting some rest.

"We're serious, Jez," Lydia said forcefully. "We need you for a mission."

"A mission? In the middle of the night? And one that requires knocking out the guard outside my door?"

"We need someone who can handle Coalition systems. You up to it?" Sheila bit her lip, waiting for an answer.

"Easy. They put more than the ability to knock a few heads into my brain in that chop shop. And what is in it for me? I'm sure you've people here who are far less hated who can help." Jez raised an eyebrow.

"We do," Lydia growled. "I don't like this, but I have to. Suffice it to say what we're doing isn't exactly authorized, and we need help from someone equally unauthorized."

Jez smiled in amusement. "Aww, it's nice to feel needed. So, I'm supposed to go with you out of the kindness of my heart?"

Lydia turned to Sheila. "This is a bad idea."

"Definitely," Jez added.

Sheila placed a hand on Lydia's shoulder to calm her. She addressed both of them. "Okay, you two aren't each other's favorite people. No one disputes that. But—Lydia and I need your help, and I'm guessing being cuffed to a bed isn't your favorite way to spend your time." Jez raised an eyebrow. "That's right. You help us, and we set you free when we're done. Deal?"

Lydia turned away shaking her head. Jez scowled and glanced down.

"And what do I have to do?"

"You have to agree to go first," Sheila said.

Lydia raised a brow, indicating she was impressed with her command of the conversation.

"No hints?"

"We're searching for someone. That's all you get to know."

Jez pursed her lips to one side. She studied Lydia's face and then Sheila's. "Okay," she said, "I'll do it. You're right. These cuffs are getting old. Besides, I'm not sure what they'll ultimately do with me here."

"We're not the Coalition," Lydia clarified. "You would have had a fair trial."

"Fair, but hopeless. No thanks." Jez scowled again.

"So, do we have a deal?" Sheila stepped forward.

"Deal," Jez agreed.

Lydia let out a sigh. "Deal."

Sheila found the handcuff keys on the guard's ring and worked on the first lock. She stopped and stared Jez in the eye. "Can we trust you?"

Jez met her gaze. "Not sure you can, but you'll have to. But despite what you think, I'm not an evil person when the Coalition isn't controlling my head. I know how to survive. All I want is to get out on my own and control my own head. You give me that, and I'll help you."

Sheila nodded and unlocked Jez's arm. Jez flexed her arm a few times to work out the stiffness. She then poked at the bandage on her side to ensure it was still secure. Sheila unlocked her feet next as she rounded the bed. Finally, she freed Jez's other arm. Jez shot out of the bed in one motion, finding herself at the business end of Lydia's pistol.

"Jumpy, aren't we?" Jez joked. She stretched her arms in the air. "I couldn't last another moment in that bed. So many hours in one position, and the muscles get sore." She leaned to one side and then the other. "Oh, and one more thing."

"What's that?" Lydia still aimed the pistol.

"You might confine yourself to non-lethal methods like this

pistol." Jez wiggled the end of the barrel with two fingers. "Don't expect me to be Ms. Nicety-nice. I go with you, and I do this however the heck I want." She walked over to the guard, and Lydia lowered the pistol.

"What are you doing?" Sheila questioned.

"You were going to lock up the guard, weren't you? You don't want him pounding on the door or yelling when he wakes up, do you?"

Sheila could see that Lydia didn't like the idea, but it made sense. The more time they had, the better. They helped Jez lift the guard onto the bed, and Jez smiled as she locked the cuffs on his four limbs.

"Okay, I think we're ready," Sheila said.

"What, no pistol for me?" Jez cocked her head.

Lydia rolled her eyes. "Nice try."

Jez smirked, and Sheila saw the corner of Lydia's mouth turn upward slightly. *Maybe this isn't crazy after all.* Lydia led the way out the door. Jez followed. Sheila was right behind.

Minutes later, they found themselves at the back of the school building. The gym was dark, and the door made a large clicking sound as they opened it, which echoed in the empty space. The three tiptoed across the floor and around the obstacle course, when suddenly Lydia held up her hands to halt them.

She turned, her eyes wide with fear and pointed to her ear. *Do you hear that?* Sheila interpreted. She slowed her breathing and listened. Somewhere, they heard a soft sniffing sound. *Someone's in here!*

They scanned around the dark gym, but the shadows concealed anything that might be there. Sheila signed that perhaps they should make a break for the door, when a shuffling sound caught her ear. She signaled for Lydia and Jez to wait and walked in the direction of the noise.

In the corner, sitting behind a pile of safety mats, a form could barely be seen. As she approached, the dim shape became unmistakable.

"Perryn?" Sheila crouched, speaking loud enough that Lydia and Jez could hear.

The shape jumped at Sheila's voice. "Sheila?" she whispered back.

"What's wrong?"

Perryn shook her head silently as if to say it was too hard.

Sheila put it together. "You visit Willis?"

Perryn nodded.

"Perryn, he needs time. Whatever he went through, it was bad."

"It's not that."

Sheila turned back to Lydia, who gave her an impatient shake of the head. She subtly raised a finger to communicate they should give her a minute. She slid down next to Perryn.

"What is it, then?"

"I despised him. After my recoding, I couldn't stand to be in the room with him. So, he left. He left because of me." She paused to wipe her nose. "He's gone. There's nothing left. All because I couldn't get past this stupid idea in my head."

"It's not your fault, Perryn." Sheila meant it.

"It's not his, either," she countered.

Sheila sat lost for words. That's when she noticed the feet next to her. She glanced up to see Jez standing there. Turning back to Perryn, she saw her frozen, also staring at Jez.

"Jez, what are you—" came Lydia's voice, who emerged from the shadows. She grabbed at Jez's arm, who twisted out of it.

"Let me do this one thing," Jez demanded. She crouched in front of Perryn. "Remember what Will said to me in the tunnel?"

Perryn punched her in the mouth.

"You ruined him," she spat.

Jez fell backward, her lip bleeding. Sheila worried she might counter, but she chuckled instead. "Yeah, that's been coming a long time. Not the passive princess you were on the station anymore, are you?" Jez laughed, wiping at the blood on her chin.

Perryn said nothing.

"Anyway, Will told me to reinterpret the coding they put in my head."

Perryn was still silent.

"You're going to make this hard, aren't you? You need to rethink the words I said to you."

"And exactly how am I supposed to do that?" Perryn said through gritted teeth.

"I told you he pitied you because you were helpless and broken on the station. I can tell you all day that was a lie, but that won't help your brain. You have to make the decision yourself."

Perryn waited for her to go on.

Jez spat blood on the floor. "You've seen him, seen the brokenness from what the Coalition did to him. Do you pity him?"

"No. He's still strong. He doubts himself. Whatever I feel, it's not pity."

"Then maybe you need to figure out what that is and tell your brain that's what he felt for you. Redefine what pity means, and you may have found the way around your recoding."

Perryn's eyes widened at the realization. Jez stood.

"Come on," Jez said, "we need to get out of here."

Perryn appeared confused as if registering for the first time that they were leaving.

"Perryn," Sheila said, "I need to ask you to give us time. You need to trust me that what we're doing is the right thing. There'll be a lot of confusion about it, but the three of us are leaving for a while."

Perryn stared at all three of them questioningly. Then, she nodded.

"That's it. Let's go," Lydia ordered.

Sheila squeezed Perryn's hand and stood. A minute later, Lydia entered the code on the exit door, unlocking it, and stepped outside. The night was thick with moisture in the air. Outside a few vehicles were parked under the cover of trees. Lydia scanned around and waved them out.

Sheila stepped out into the fog as the door clicked behind her.

Chapter Seventeen

The morning sun cast long rays of light across the tiny apartment.
"Perryn! Please get in here. We're going to be late!" the woman
shouted.

"Coming, Auntie." Perryn shouted back. Her tiny hands
fumbled with the laces on her shoes.

"Perryn Davis, the Chairman of the Coalition and keeper of
our wonderful Law is speaking in our city today, and you're
making us late."

Perryn's aunt barged into the room. Her long hair was
graying, but Perryn could tell she tried to hide the gray inside her
braids. She wore a threadbare, floral dress that she'd spent the
last two days meticulously scrubbing and ironing. *She crossed her*
arms and stared down at Perryn with a frown of exasperation.

"Honestly, child. If you were any more uncoordinated—" She
cut off her words and pursed her lips in an effort not to say
something cruel. "Let me do it."

Walking forward, she knelt and grabbed Perryn's foot without
any pretense of gentleness. Snatching the laces, she furiously tied
them. The yanking on the laces produced a yelp from Perryn.

"Auntie, that's too tight!" Perryn tried to pull her foot away.

"Well, then, you won't lose them like last year's pair, will
you? Of course, my sister would have to have a daughter whose
feet grow three sizes every year. She never was practical." Perryn
glanced down at the mention of her mother. Her aunt sighed.
"That'll have to do. Let's get going."

A minute later they were walking on the street, the clip clop of
her aunt's shoes loud on the sidewalk. Crossing the street, she
hurried them around the corner into an alley.

"Auntie, you said never walk in the alleys." Perryn tugged at her hand.

"I did, but you made us late didn't you. We need a shortcut." Her aunt yanked on her arm as they walked into the damp alleyway.

Perryn could hear the coughing getting louder as they approached. About halfway through the alley, she noticed the pair of feet sticking out from the recessed doorway. The woman appeared like a heap of rags piled in the corner with arms and legs sticking out at sharp angles. Her faced was smeared with dirt and sores covered her skin. Her wiry hair stuck out in all directions. In her mouth, a cigarette clung to her lower lip, from which each inhale brought another fit of coughing. Perryn stopped and gazed at the woman.

"Perryn, we don't stop here," her aunt commanded.

"But she needs help, Auntie." Perryn pled.

"She needs nothing more than our pity. It's people like her that should make us sad for those who don't serve the Law and glad for us who do. Be glad you're not her."

"But Auntie!"

"No more, child! Not another word. Honestly, I hope for the day the Chairman finally rounds up all these lawless unfortunates. We'll all be better off, then. Now wouldn't we?" With that, she gave Perryn's arm another tug, forcing her to walk to the corner.

The dream had come when sleep finally overtook Perryn after sitting in the darkness of the gym for hours. She watched much of the night pass by unable to think of anything other than the image of Willis laying broken in the medical wing. Her thoughts spun in circles in her mind like the hands on a clock. She sat up, bleary-eyed, and rehearsed the thoughts she'd concluded the night before.

Willis and I became friends on the station after I was made team leader.

Friendship became something more as we prepared for the

elimination rounds, ran in the Chase, and hid out at the Thomson cabin.

That something never got discussed.

After many opportunities to do so, Willis was ready to say something when the raid on the Underground occurred.

Jez had done her dirty work then. Willis had said he loved her.

Perryn awoke from her recoding with the knowledge that Willis had confused his pity for love.

She despised his presence, and he'd left for her sake.

After months, he'd reappeared, broken and convinced he was dangerous to everyone around him.

She didn't pity Willis. Not the way her aunt had talked about it as a child.

What she did feel, she wasn't sure.

She listed these thoughts over and over in her head, trying to make sense of where that left her. She needed to process with someone. As good a friend as Maria was, she wasn't ready to give Willis a chance. *I know who I need to talk to.*

She got up and left the gym, hoping Jaden was up this early.

Jaden walked out of the cafeteria, still stuffing a piece of toast into his mouth when Perryn found him. Most were still barely up, but Jaden had always been an early riser. She hurried to him, and she could see he'd read her eyes.

"What is it?" Jaden's brow wrinkled with concern. "You look like you've been up all night."

"Pretty close," she said. "You got a minute?"

"For you, I've got hours. Do me a favor and let Chris know that I missed our decoding session because of you, okay? Those files Jez brought us from Solution Systems are locked down pretty hard."

A couple minutes later, they found themselves on their familiar steps. Jaden waited patiently while she gathered her thoughts. She wasn't sure how to share what she learned without giving away that she'd visited Jez or that the three women had left the night before. Honesty was best.

"I visited Jez in her room," she started.

"You what?" Jaden exclaimed. "Perryn, I don't think you—"

"Please, let me finish."

He closed his mouth and nodded.

"Thank you. She told me that what she told me in the tunnel wasn't true."

"That's great! That should fix it, then, right?"

"It's not so simple. You can't undo recoding. You *can* reinterpret it. So, then, I went to see Willis."

Jaden threw his arms out to the side. "You're killing me with the play-by-play, Perr!"

"Sorry, the short version is that I saw him broken and hopeless much like he saw me when we first met on the station." She leaned in to emphasize her next words. "Jaden, I didn't pity him." She paused. "I mean, I felt something. I was sad, but not in a way that looks down on him. I wanted to help. I wished him to find the strength I know he has. But what am I supposed to do with that?"

Jaden folded his hands and pressed them to his lips in thought. He stared off into the distance for several seconds, letting out a sigh and turning to her.

"Perryn, the difference between pity and what you feel is that pity is selfishness. Pity comes when I see something awful, and all I can think about is how badly it makes me feel. Pity doesn't want to help; it wants to feel better."

"That sounds a lot like how my aunt used to be. She couldn't wait for the Chairman to get rid of all those who made her feel bad."

"Exactly!" Jaden exclaimed, trying to contain his excitement. "What you felt made you want to help. You wanted *him* to be better, not because you would fix him but because you longed for him to be who he is. What you sensed makes you want to enter into his pain and walk with him. Am I right?"

She nodded nervously.

"Perryn, that's not pity. That's friendship and compassion. You might even call it empathy. You could even call it—love. It's at least rooted there."

Jaden stopped talking and watched her. A thousand thoughts exploded in her mind all at once like fireworks. Memories of her and Willis flooded her brain, and she could feel each one transform like images finally coming into focus. Moments she despised because of Willis's unwelcome pity became moments where he took care of her. Memories that made her want to shrink away changed into ones that made her want to run to him.

"Jaden, I don't pity Willis. I—care about him."

"Yes, you do."

"And he cares about me. He always has."

"Perryn, Willis—loves you."

Her heart burst inside of her. She could almost feel Jez's words morph in her mind as she redefined what they meant. She trembled with excitement. Everything in her desired to run to Willis and confess everything. She itched to declare her love for him to anyone she met.

"I—I need to go see him!" she said.

"I think you do." Jaden smiled.

That's when the lights flashed. Alarms blared. Someone had discovered Jez's absence.

Chapter Eighteen

"No!" Kane shouted. "I won't believe it!"

Perryn jumped as he swiped half the contents of his desk against the wall with one motion of his huge arm. Pens and clips clattered to the floors. Papers swayed and drifted in several directions. Glass shattered as a cup rolled to the edge of the desk and finally plunged to the floor. Everyone in the room stood silent, afraid to question Kane amid his rage.

Guards had gathered everyone in the gym for a head count, discovering Sheila was missing in addition to the Lydia and Jez. Outraged families voiced their distaste at the rude awakening, and Kane was forced to talk them down. A search was ordered for the entire building. No sign could be found of the three missing women, though the two missing dart guns were noted. Once it was clear they were no longer in the building, Kane had dismissed the crowd and ordered senior staff to his office. Chris suggested that Lydia had helped Jez in some way, and Kane wasn't having it.

"She didn't betray us. She wouldn't!" he continued.

"Chief?" Chris finally asked after a minute. Kane turned to him, his eyes wild like an injured animal. "I know it's hard to imagine, but there are two possibilities here. Either Jez escaped her bonds, overpowered the guard, and took two capable women as hostages—"

"Or?" Kane growled, daring him to say it.

"Or—" Chris hesitated. He appeared as though unsure he should finish. "Or Sheila and Lydia freed her."

"No!" Kane shouted again, clearing the other half of the table. Perryn saw it coming this time, but she still couldn't help jumping at the outburst.

"She could have manipulated them. You know? Like talked them into it or something?" Maria offered.

"Not likely," Chris said, shaking his head.

"I don't think so either," Brenda added. She wasn't technically senior staff, but her knowledge of Kane and Lydia's relationship made her valuable to the conversation. Kane had insisted. "Both Lydia and Sheila are highly intelligent. I don't think Jez could have said anything to sway them to do something so rash."

"And even with her new abilities, it seems far-fetched to believe she could break out of all four chains," Chris said, appearing a little sheepish in front of Kane. "Besides, Lydia or Sheila would have sounded an alarm the second something was up."

"Which means—" Maria started.

"Which means there must be another explanation!" Kane blurted.

"I'm not sure there is—" Chris said.

"There must be!" Kane interrupted.

"Kane?" Brenda said softly. "I think you need to tell them." She gave a knowing glance at Perryn.

"Now isn't the time for—"

"Yes, Kane. It is. If you want the others to know why it's so important that they come up with another reason, you'd better fess up."

Perryn smiled enough to communicate her thanks to Brenda for not revealing her knowledge of the relationship between Kane and Lydia. Maria would have been furious at her for not sharing.

Kane took a deep breath and sat down. He buried his face in hands, inhaling and exhaling slowly. After a moment, he waved a hand at Brenda as if to say, "go ahead." She turned to the others.

"So, you should know that Kane and Lydia are—" She paused to choose the word. "Close."

Chris and Maria stared as the thoughts apparently came together in their mind. Chris's eyebrows rose, and he turned to Perryn to see her reaction. Perryn couldn't help but smile, not because the news was any revelation to her, but because Maria's mouth was gaping open, her piece of gum hanging in the corner of her mouth.

"Is that true?" Chris broke the stunned silence.

Kane sighed. "Yes—it is."

"How long?" Maria whispered as if the idea were taboo.

"A couple months." Kane glanced down, uncomfortable with this kind of vulnerability. A long pause was shared as the group blinked and stared at each other.

Finally, it was Brenda who broke the silence. "So—I think we all need to cut Kane a little slack and try to come up with an alternate explanation that doesn't require he assume she betrayed him." Another long silence filled the room.

"I—I suppose they might have a good reason for freeing Jez," Chris suggested. Kane glared up at Chris, annoyed. "No. No. Hear me out. What if they learned something—something important— that would make them feel they had to get her out?"

"Like what?" The doubt was clear in Maria's voice.

"I don't know, but we all know they wouldn't just do this."

"I agree," Brenda said.

"I guess so," Maria added reluctantly.

Kane stared at his desk. Perryn sensed the eyes of the room slowly move in her direction. She didn't know what to say that would keep what she saw the night before secret, so she'd simply said nothing. And it was becoming obvious to everyone else.

"Perryn, do you know something?" Brenda softened her voice.

"Yeah, girl. Not like you to stay quiet," Maria said.

She breathed deeply, aware what she was about to unleash. "I saw them leave," she said. Kane's head shot up from the desk and gave her a stare that asked both "what did you see" and "why have you not said anything" all at the same time.

"Explain," Kane said, punctuating his expression.

"I—I," she stammered, "I was up late last night. They exited through the gym. No one was forcing anyone to leave."

"Did they tell you why?" Chris waved a hand, urging her to get to the point.

"No. Sheila simply said I needed to trust her. She said people would be confused by what they are doing, but that I could trust her," Perryn responded.

"And do you?" The question came from Maria, but Perryn sensed the whole room was asking.

"Yes. They seemed okay. Just in a hurry to leave."

"Seemed okay?"

"You know. They didn't act like they believed they were doing something wrong."

"So, all three of them left together and all were going willingly?" Brenda clarified.

"Yes."

The group collectively dropped their gaze, all of them pondering what was going on. Kane folded his hands in front of him and looked up. "We need to trace what Lydia and Sheila were doing yesterday. Where did they spend their time?"

"Sheila was with Jaden and me for most of the day," Chris said. "We were working on those files from Solution Systems. Nothing appeared funny or unusual. After that, she said she was off to find Lydia. Didn't see her again for the rest of the day."

"Lydia was with Willie-boy in the medical wing," Maria added. "The reason I know that is I was there after cutting my hand repairing one of the door locks in the women's barracks." She held up her bandaged hand. "Medic was almost done bandaging my hand when Lydia stepped out of Willis's room and ran down the hall. She didn't look good."

Brenda held up a hand, stopping the train of thought. "What do you mean?"

"Upset. She had her hand over her mouth like she was trying not to cry." Maria mimicked the gesture.

Kane waited for more details. "Anyone see her after that?"

Everyone shook their heads silently.

"Okay. Sheila's whereabouts are accounted for until she met

with Lydia. Lydia disappeared from her shift in the medical wing after leaving Willis's room. Do I have this right?"

Everyone nodded.

"Sounds to me like Willis has rested long enough. It's time we talked with him."

Chapter Nineteen

Sheila sat next to Jez in the van they'd taken from the Underground. They stared out the windshield watching the occasional car pass on the road at the end of the alley. Neither said a word, but she guessed they were thinking the same thing.

"Think she's coming back?" Jez finally broke the silence.

Sheila still couldn't believe that Lydia had even considered this plan. The chances of getting caught were extremely high, and it made her nervous that Lydia insisted on checking out the area by herself before they made their move.

"This whole adventure is going to be over very quickly if she doesn't." Sheila sighed.

A few more minutes of silence passed. Sheila had so many questions for Jez, but she didn't know how to ask them. *What did they do to you? To Willis? How did you get him out? And more importantly—why?* The thoughts swirled in her head. Normally, she had no trouble talking to people, but there was something about Jez that made her uneasy. Taking a deep breath, she tried anyway.

"Jez, I—uh—I was wondering what made you—" she began.

"Why did I save Willis? Like I explained to your people back at the school, he was my ticket out of there." The answer was so abrupt it was as if Jez had been waiting for the question, and Sheila lost her focus for a moment. She collected herself and continued.

"From what I hear, you did all the work to get him out. I'm guessing it would have been easier to get out without him. So why?"

Jez sat back and folded her arms. She stared out the window, and Sheila could tell she didn't want to meet her gaze. "I don't know," she said finally.

Sheila folded her hands and waited her out. For a full minute, Sheila sat quietly as she had in so many conversations with reluctant interviewees.

Jez finally rolled her eyes and turned to her. "For real? You're going to sit there until I answer?"

"Something like that," Sheila said unable to contain a grin.

"What if I don't want to talk about it?"

"Then you would probably have told me that. In my experience, people want to talk about what's going on inside them, but they are afraid."

Jez huffed at the word 'afraid.' "He didn't deserve to be there any more than I did. That place is a nightmare, and no one should be left there."

"So, you care about him?"

"Hardly." Sheila noticed the pained expression on Jez's face that betrayed her real feelings. Jez stared out the window blinking hard to keep the tears contained.

"Jez, do you remember when we met on the station—I was interviewing you about your experience as a Chase trainee."

"Yeah. So?" She still wouldn't look at her.

"You acted like you hated everyone, but it was simply that—an act. I'm pretty good at reading people, and I could tell you didn't feel that way. Now, you act as if everyone hates you."

"They should," Jez interrupted.

"I'm not so sure. You forget that recoding is a way of life in the Western Alliance. People understand and are more forgiving than you think."

"Whatever." Jez shifted in her seat, and Sheila could tell she was making Jez uncomfortable. "I don't need anyone's forgiveness. I—" She paused to take a deep breath. "I need to start over. I need to get away from this place and go where no one knows me—or what I've done."

Sheila took a chance. She reached over and gently placed her hand on Jez's arm. Jez straightened at the contact, but she didn't pull away. "Jez, you may not think you need anyone's forgiveness, but I know one person you need to let forgive you."

"Oh yeah? Who would that be?" she said, not trying to hide the sarcasm.

"You. You need to forgive yourself."

Jez wouldn't meet her gaze, but she could see the tremble of Jez's lower lip. Her face scrunched like she was trying not to sneeze, and her skin flushed. A tear escaped and rolled down her cheek, which she quickly wiped away. Sheila squeezed her arm to reassure her.

Suddenly, Jez threw the door open. Stepping out, she hurried behind the van. Peering in the mirror, Sheila saw her place a hand on the wall of the alley behind the vehicle to steady herself. Twisting, she threw her back against the brick and slid to the ground. Her face in her hands, Sheila watched her shoulders heave as she could no longer hold in the sobs. She expected she would hear about it from Lydia for letting Jez leave the van without her, but Jez deserved a moment to herself.

The armor had cracked, and Sheila believed it was enough for now.

Lydia returned a half an hour later. Sheila had almost been dozing when the driver's door suddenly flew open, and Lydia jumped in. She was out of breath as if she'd been running.

"Had to get out of there," she panted.

"What took so long?" Sheila glanced out the window.

"The officers were changing shifts, and the path to the local transport was right by my vantage point. Couldn't come out of hiding until I was sure that no more would be arriving."

"Are you sure this isn't a dumb idea? Storming inside a Law-keeper outpost is a little rash, don't you think?"

"Well, I agree that—" Lydia's voice cut off as she turned to Sheila. Her eyes turned to the back seat. Sheila watched as she scanned the inside of the van. Her head shot back to glare at Sheila. "Where is Jez?"

"She's fine, Lydia. She's—"

"Right here," Jez interrupted. Jez stood in the open doorway of the van. Climbing inside, she rolled her eyes at Lydia, who in turn gave Sheila an 'I told you not to take your eyes off her' frown.

"What were you doing?" Lydia demanded to know.

"None of your business," Jez spat.

"What was she doing?" Lydia was still staring at Sheila.

"Like she said." Sheila nodded toward Jez. "None of your business."

Lydia threw her hands up in exasperation and slumped into her seat. She shook her head as if talking to herself. Sheila watched in amazement as Lydia appeared to have an argument with herself. "Some team we are," she said at last.

"A regular group of misfits," Sheila added grinning, "including whomever it is you're talking to over there." She choked on a laugh that she could no longer contain. Examining Lydia, she saw her lips tighten as she tried to contain her own chuckle. In the mirror, even Jez was pursing her lips to one side, the humor not lost on her. Suddenly, Sheila burst out in a fit of laughter.

Lydia's hand went to her mouth as she laughed softly. Jez peered out the window. She was biting her lip in a losing battle to prevent losing her composure. For a moment, the three of them laughed, and Sheila noted how normal it felt to be sitting and laughing with these two women. *In another lifetime we might have all been good friends that went to dinner or on road trips together instead of fighting the World Coalition.* Finally, their laughter ended in a long sigh.

"So, what the heck were we talking about?"

"You wanted to know if this was a bad idea." Lydia pointed to Sheila.

"Actually, her exact word was 'dumb' idea," Jez corrected, "and it is. But—it's the only option we have."

Sheila turned to her. "How so?"

"All Coalition systems operate using a heavily encrypted

database of information. Everything from troop movements to prisoners to orders of paper towels for the Chairman's personal restroom are all in there." She paused, waiting for them to understand. "This is a Law-keeper outpost. It uses that same computer system, but as an outpost, it's a relatively small facility. If we're going to have any chance of finding this woman, we need to know what the Coalition knows. If they know the wife of the leader of the Underground still exists, they've no doubt been tracking her as best they can. Our chances are better here to get in and get access than anywhere else."

"But—those are still pretty low chances," Lydia added.

Jez nodded.

"Sounds like our choice is to take our chances here or return to base with a lot of explaining to do," Sheila summed.

"I can't do that," Lydia said.

"I won't do that," Jez said.

Sheila nodded. "Okay. Infiltrate the guarded Law-keeper outpost without getting caught is the plan. So, how?"

Jez leaned forward, placing her hands on both of their car seats. She whispered, "That's why you brought me."

Chapter Twenty

Sheila sat on the bench outside the Law-keeper outpost, her back turned to the entrance. She did her best to appear interested in the article on her digital publication. She had to remind herself to occasionally turn a page to play her part in the ruse. In reality, the dim reflection on the tablet was her way of tracking what was happening behind her.

"All is quiet," she said softly to no one, her radio earpiece picking up her voice for Jez and Lydia to hear. "One officer in the window. At least two more moving around behind him."

To her left, a figure emerged down the street and started walking toward her. Jez was wearing a white hooded sweatshirt with the hood up. She stared down at the street to hide her face and moved at a natural pace so as not to draw attention.

Sheila glanced across the street where Lydia stood silhouetted in the alley. Lydia had drawn the short straw as Sheila was too well known to get close, and Jez would be a known dangerous capture for Law-keepers. She wouldn't get within ten yards without raising an alarm. They needed the Law-keepers to allow one of them to get right up to the window before recognizing them.

"If you're going to do it, I would say now is the time," Sheila reminded Lydia, who nodded from her position. Lydia emerged from the alleyway and strode in her direction. She walked directly to the window of the Law-keeper outpost and pounded on the window.

"Hello? I need some help," Lydia shouted at the officer.

The man glanced up at her, and annoyance washed over his face. He rolled his eyes and grabbed the microphone to his left. Bending forward, he spoke in a mechanical, bored tone. "Do you have an immediate emergency that threatens the well-being of yourself or another close by?"

"Yes, I need assistance."

"State the nature of your emergency."

Sheila could see Lydia make a show of glancing to both sides as if fearful. She noted that Jez was almost in position and pounded on the window. "Please, I need help!"

"Ma'am, you must have a genuine emergency to seek the assistance of—"

Lydia clenched her fists in exasperation. Sheila's breath caught, fearful their plan might not work. Lydia had seconds to convince the Law-keeper to open the door, or their entire plan was a waste. She could see Lydia's jaw tense. She shot the Law-keeper an angry stare and pointed to the wall behind him.

"Hey, loser. Check out the screen on the wall behind you."

The officer sighed and turned to his right. Behind him on the wall, a rotating series of pictures displayed high-profile targets. The screen currently showed an artist's drawing and several security photos of Lydia. The man studied the picture and slowly turned back to Lydia uninterested. Even in the reflection, Sheila could see the moment he made the connection. His eyes shot wide open, and he shouted something inaudible through the glass.

"That's right, you half-wit," Lydia goaded.

The two other officers scurried to the doorway, throwing it open hard enough for it to slam into the wall next to them. They pounced upon Lydia, shoving her face first into the window. The Law-keeper in the window had moved to the doorway and was yelling for the officers to get her in cuffs. Sheila stood and turned. That was the moment Jez threw her hood back and sprang forward.

Jez's hand shot out, the edge of her palm connecting with the throat of the officer in the doorway. He fell to his knees, gasping for air that wouldn't come. Their backs turned, the other two were too late to notice Jez, and she leapt at them. She wrapped her arm around the neck of the closest officer. At the same time, she swung her left leg. Her heel connected with the jaw of the other, who fell backward.

The officer she held in a chokehold released Lydia and reached for Jez's arm. He stumbled backward, unable to breathe, and Jez kicked the back of his knee, which gave way. She shoved him forward, and his head struck the concrete wall. His unconscious body fell to the ground in a heap.

In a flash, Jez attacked the guard she'd kicked. A kick to the gut doubled him over, and a knee to the side of his head knocked him out. She bent over and grabbed the officer's sidearm. Walking swiftly over to the man still gasping in the doorway, she pointed the gun at his head. Lydia yanked her arm as she fired. Sheila's hand involuntarily covered her mouth.

"What are you doing?" Lydia shouted. Jez ripped her arm from Lydia's grasp. She struck the Law-keeper with the barrel, and he collapsed.

"I told you to let me do this my way," Jez snapped. "That was the agreement."

"He was already immobilized. Shooting him wasn't necessary."

Jez rolled her eyes and tucked the pistol into her waistband. She glanced from Lydia to Sheila, who still stood frozen. *Say something,* Sheila shouted to herself.

"I suppose you've an opinion on the matter," Jez scowled.

Her annoyance is a mask. See through it.

"You said you wished to leave your old life behind—to go where your past can't find you," Sheila said.

"And what of it?"

"Maybe today's the day to start being who you want to become."

Jez's expression softened. It was a brief moment, but Sheila saw it. Before it lasted, Jez shook her head as if to clear her thoughts. "Whatever." Jez pointed inside. "It won't take long for someone to see our mess out here. We've taken too long already."

"You stay with her," Lydia said to Sheila. "I'll pull these guys inside."

The outpost was a single room with a storage closet at the back. Two desks sat in an open space covered in papers with Coalition information. Beside the stool near the window ledge was a locked cabinet, presumably for firearms. Jez sat at one of the desks and worked on a computer. Sheila watched in amazement as Jez's recoding kicked in and her fingers flew over the keys.

"Breaking someone's neck isn't the only trick they taught me," Jez said with a smirk. "Besides, the clearance codes are changed once a week."

Sheila let out an impressed whistle. "You don't think they would have changed them after your escape?"

"Nope."

"What makes you so confident?"

"You don't catch a mouse by cleaning up all the crumbs."

Sheila smirked, impressed by the metaphor. A grunt from the door let her know that Lydia had pulled the last officer inside. "You mean bait."

"Yep."

Sheila sat silently, annoyed at the one-word answers. Jez rolled her eyes.

"They would create new access codes, for sure," she started, pointing at the screen. "But they would leave the old ones active so they could flag their use."

"Meaning?" Lydia joined them.

Jez sighed. "Meaning, the instant I enter the codes, we've a minute or two before they know I'm here and show up with an army."

"Oh," Sheila said, the shake in her voice betraying her anxiety. It made her uneasy that Jez was calling most of the shots on the mission, but she couldn't think of another way.

"I mean—" Jez said smartly, holding her hands out, "I'm good. You saw what I did to those Law-keepers. But—I'm not enough to take on the number of people they'll send after me."

"Just work fast," Lydia said, glancing back at the door.

"Entering the codes. Here goes nothing."

A few taps on the keys, and Sheila couldn't help but hold her breath. The computer processed for a long moment. A flash of the screen later, and the screen read 'Coalition Intelligence Database.'

"We're in!" Jez exclaimed. A radio in the corner chirped as a general alarm when out to Law-keeper stations.

"Attention all nearby units!" the radio squawked. "Converge on West End Outpost Two. Priority One target inside. Do not engage without authorization. Containment only. Suspect is considered armed and dangerous. All Law-keepers, converge on West End Outpost Two. Priority One target—" The radio continued to repeat the message. Once over, the airwaves lit up with the calls from Law-keepers reporting that they were on their way.

"Company is on its way," Lydia said.

"One second. Found the records of Kane's arrest." She read for a moment. "There it is!"

Sheila leaned in to get a closer look. Sandra's picture was in the corner of the screen. She appeared sad, likely having been told Kane was dead. She read the reports of her tracker being placed in her unknowingly during the birth of her son. Various locations were listed as the Coalition had kept record of her movement.

"Scroll down," Sheila said. "What was her last known location?"

Jez obliged, and the list ended with two entries, made about four months earlier. The first was a note about her presence near the capture of Willis by the Coalition. The second was a warrant for her arrest.

"They're searching for her." Jez pointed at the screen. "Says she illegally had her tracker removed by a man named Ben Brennan. Says they knew each other from living on the streets in Central City."

Lydia pointed to the screen. "So, this Ben Brennan was the last to see her, and that was months ago?"

Jez let out a humph. "Yeah, and it gets better."

Sheila sighed. "What?"

"They didn't catch Sandra, but they know she removed her tracker because Ben fessed up to in in custody. He's being held at the rehabilitation camp here in Central City."

A chill traveled Sheila's spine. It was the same camp where her father had been sent so many years ago. The one lead they had was a man behind the fences of a slave work camp that still haunted her dreams. She cursed.

"What is it?" Lydia appeared worried as she read Sheila's expression.

"Some old demons to exorcise," she said cryptically. "Looks like we get to go undercover."

"You're suggesting we break *into* a slave camp?" Jez's eyes betrayed her disbelief. She stood, and they all moved toward the door.

"Getting in will be the easy part," Lydia said as they exited. "It's getting out that's going to be the challenge."

Chapter Twenty-One

Willis breathed deeply as Kane, Perryn, and his mother entered the room. His heart raced, knowing they'd come for information. He'd heard the alarms go off and recognized it meant that Lydia had followed through on her plan. He had, in fact, heard the scuffle across the hallway when they broke Jez out of her room. He could imagine what everyone was feeling, and they were wanting answers from him.

More people who are hurting, and I'm the cause. Brenda sat at the end of his bed and placed her hand on his knee.

"Son, have you gathered what is going on?"

"Lydia is gone," he said.

"And so are Jez and Sheila."

Willis stared. *Jez I expected, but Sheila?* He glanced at his mother and the others, but he stayed silent. The notion of Sheila getting involved, and likely hurt, brought the tremor back to his hands. Kane stepped forward, a grim expression on his face, but he was stopped by Brenda's raised hand. Without a word, she communicated she would do the questioning.

"Son, do you know anything about why they would leave?" she continued.

He blinked slowly. He'd promised to keep his word, but he didn't want to lie. "Yes. I do."

They waited for him to continue.

"But I can't tell you," he finished. Kane let out a frustrated sigh. Perryn's eyebrows rose in concern. "I promised I wouldn't tell anyone, including Kane."

Brenda appeared puzzled and glanced at the others. Kane shook his head, and Perryn shrugged.

"Do you know about Lydia and Kane?"

"I figured it out."

"How?"

"Because what she's doing, she's doing for him." He pointed at Kane whose eyes grew wide. "You don't do what she's doing—sacrifice what she's sacrificing—unless you care about someone."

"What do you mean, 'sacrifice'?" His face tensed with worry.

"I—I can't say. I did promise. But—I can tell you it's good, and it's for you."

Kane shook his head again, obviously agitated by Willis's secrecy.

"Okay," Brenda said quietly. "You made a promise, and you intend to keep it. We'll take your word that what has happened was meant for good." Her tone communicated to the others that it was the end of the matter, though she still appeared confused by the little he'd said. "What *can* you tell us?"

For the next half hour, he recounted the details of his imprisonment. He left out many of the details of the things Dr. Campbell had made him admit, but he said enough for tears to begin falling from his mother's eyes. Kane's expression darkened as he explained the new neuro-booster and the Coalition's ability to change the way people think.

"If they can find a way to release the neuro-booster over large populations, they can reprogram entire cities—maybe even entire alliances—through suggestion," he said.

Brenda covered her mouth in horror. Kane's fists clenched in anger. Perryn leaned against the wall and stared at the floor. She hadn't met his eyes the entire time, and he couldn't read her.

"They could release it as a gas," Kane muttered. They turned to him.

"What?" Brenda suddenly snapped out of her shock over Willis's experience.

"Intelligence has been monitoring the production of pressurized containers. They've been unable to confirm what, exactly, is going inside, but it's not hard to put together. For all we know, they've been releasing it over populations for weeks. There's no way to know with the information we have."

"But they couldn't sit down and manipulate everyone one at a time," Brenda countered.

They sat in silence until Perryn gasped. The realization came to all of them.

"The Chase," Kane said solemnly, nodding as if to confirm their fears.

"Everyone watches it," Brenda added.

"And with enough of the neuro-booster in their system—" Willis continued.

"The Chairman can speak and control the entire world," Kane finished.

A chill ran down Willis's spine, and his lungs turned to stone. He couldn't breathe. He glanced at his mother, his mind firing over and over. *It's my fault. It's my fault. It's my fault.*

"It's my fault," he croaked. The corners of his mouth trembled downward. The tremor in his hands turned into a full body shiver.

"What? Willis, you can't believe—" Brenda said.

"No!" he interrupted. "It's all my fault! They tested it on me! I was their successful trial. I left the Underground, and they were able to perfect their—their—" His words faded as he clutched his stomach and rolled to his side. His body trembled violently, and he believed he might wretch. His chest pounded hard enough he thought his ribs might crack. He would have welcomed tears, but the guilt kept them at bay.

"Willis, that's not true," Brenda pleaded. She reached for him, but he turned away.

"Stay away," he said, his voice partially muffled by the pillow. "You'll only get hurt, too."

"Son—"

"No! I don't want you getting hurt any more. Everyone who comes near me gets hurt—like Dad."

The room went silent. He could feel his mother rise from the bed and hear her feet shuffle to the door. That was followed by some whispering between her and Kane.

"Son, we'll return in a little while. I love you. You have to believe this isn't your fault," Brenda whispered, patting his foot.

He heard the door open and click closed. Several minutes went by before the trembling subsided. He opened an eye and peered around the room.

Perryn still stood by the door.

Chapter Twenty-Two

Perryn saw Willis's eye open and stare at her. She inhaled long and slowly to calm her nerves. Inside, her gut split in two to see Willis reduced to the skeletal form quivering in front of her. She missed the Willis she remembered from the station, powerful in both his ability to conquer an obstacle and to lead those around him. The Coalition had shattered him, and she hated them for it.

An ember inside of her, something just and righteous, ignited, and she could feel the anger growing. The internal flame burned hot until it roared within her. *The Coalition robbed his childhood. It took his father. It abused his mother. It stole—him.* She realized in that moment, that she would do whatever it took to help Willis become the man he was meant to be. In this battle, the Coalition couldn't be allowed to win. Yet, as hot as the anger flamed, her compassion for Willis was warmer. Her heart both burned and melted at the same time.

His eye stared at her unmoving as if he was waiting for her to speak or leave. For a long moment, they watched each other in silence. Neither moved nor spoke. She couldn't imagine where to begin—where to start rebuilding what the Coalition had torn down.

"I don't hate you." The words popped out of her mouth before she could think about them. She froze, fearful she'd started in the wrong place. It was when Willis slowly turned his head to see her with both eyes that she considered she might be on to something. She continued in an indifferent tone to raise his interest, as though she was simply informing him. "Thought you ought to know. After much agonizing and discussion, Perryn Davis does *not* hate Willis Thomson."

His eyebrows scrunched together in puzzlement. *Good. At*

*least if I've thrown him off, he might listen before assuming he'll
hurt me.*

"Yeah," she said, placing her hands in her pockets, "there was
a rumor going around that I was recoded and woke believing you'd
felt nothing more than pity for me. But…that's the thing about
rumors. They're just rumors." She smirked.

Willis still lay silent, but his eyes widened as she spoke. His
lips parted as if he intended to talk, but nothing came out. She had
his attention.

"And do you want to know how I know that rumor is a dirty,
rotten lie?" She paused. After a moment she stepped forward and
placed her hands on the footboard of the bed. "You see, when you
met me, my life was at an all-time low. Diego had died. Blue Team
was doomed. I accepted I'd be recoded into my own death. It was
inevitable. Then, in walks this cocky guy who thinks he can
brighten my day by congratulating me on becoming team leader.
Annoying, am I right? I mean, how insensitive."

She held out her hands and shook her head as if indignant.
Inside, she urged herself to keep going to prevent losing her train
of thought. He was listening, really listening. If she had a chance
to reach him, it was now.

"So, anyway, I blew him off so he wouldn't get any funny
ideas, and do you know what he did?" She paused again. She
leaned forward and lowered her voice to a whisper. "He helped
me." She let the words hang in the room.

"He didn't look down on me. He didn't say 'too bad' as he
blew right by me in training leaving me to be recoded into oblivion.
He took the time to get to know me. He gave me pointers. He
picked me up when Jaden was suspended from the team. He made
sure I believed I could make it to the final selections. He saw I was
strong, even before I realized it.

"And why did he do all that?" she continued, her voice rising.
"It's not like he benefited. In fact, he suffered under our mutual
friend Jez for coming anywhere near me. So why did he do it?"
She lowered her voice again. "Not because of pity."

She shook her head. Willis sat up in the bed, an expression of doubtful amazement washing over his face.

"Jez was right that he felt something all that time, but she picked the wrong word. It wasn't pity. What I believe she meant to say is that he cared." She smiled and sat down next to him on the bed. "And even after he won the Chase, escaped to the woods, joined the Underground, and rescued his mother, he still didn't pity her. He needed a strong friend by his side, and that's what she was. She was strong. Strong enough to pick him up after his father died. Strong enough to see through Jez's lies. Strong enough to wait for him to get his act together and say what he felt. Strong enough to stand next to him as Jez held them both at gunpoint."

Reaching out she placed her hand gently on his, small and weak in her grasp. His body would take weeks to get back to full strength, but she could still feel its warmth that betrayed a strong will and selflessness beneath his skin. She gazed into his eyes, and she could feel hers begin to water.

"He's the one who has forgotten how strong he is. The world has taken one too many bites out of his soul, and he's struggling to remember how amazing he can be. But—*she* remembers. She wants to help. It's her turn to pick him up and help him see how tough he can be. Not because of pity, no. But—because she cares." She paused again as a tear escaped her eye.

"Because she loves him," she finished.

His lips trembled, and his eyes watered with tears. The air between them filled with electricity, and his slight fingers slowly closed around hers.

"But—" he whispered, "you can't— You'll get hurt. You shouldn't—" He was crying and couldn't complete his sentences.

She didn't let him say any more. She leaned forward and touched her lips to his. The saltiness of their tears mixed as they lingered in a soft kiss. She pulled away slightly and opened her eyes to gaze into his. Then, she kissed him again, a tender, long-overdue kiss.

They both sniffed as she leaned her forehead against his. Her insides burst with joy, and she couldn't help but smile. She placed both of her hands on the sides of his face and wiped his tearful cheeks with her thumbs.

"Willis Thomson, you're stuck with me. I love you, and I don't care if I get hurt. It hurts far more to be without you."

Chapter Twenty-Three

"How do I look?" Sheila gestured to herself.

"Far too clean." Lydia picked up a handful of dirt from the ground and spit into it. She rubbed her hands together and then wiped them on the sides of Sheila's face faster than she could pull away. "Now you match that prison jumpsuit." She pointed to the filthy uniform they'd rescued from the garbage.

"Thanks?" she said, not hiding the question in her voice. "You could have let me do that myself."

"Yeah, but that was more fun."

Sheila glanced at Jez who wore a smirk. Once again, Jez's newfound spark of humor had lit up her eyes, and she couldn't help but wonder if she was ready to call Jez a friend. *Danger has a way of doing that,* she said to herself. *People who would not otherwise come together become friends.*

The three of them peered over the edge of the open sewer access. A tower was visible down the street. The windows near the top faced in all directions, giving a clear view of anything the blinding spotlight atop the tower illuminated. About halfway up the tower, walls extended covered in razor wire. The entire place appeared trapped in a gray haze as if a storm cloud had settled right on top of it.

To the left of the tower, a small opening in the wall arched high enough to allow a transport truck to pass through. Currently, guards were sweeping the bottom of a truck ready to depart with mirrors. A call went out, and large steel pylons lowered into the road to allow the truck to exit. The engine roared to life, and the truck lurched forward. They ducked behind the dumpster, feeling the ground tremble as the truck lumbered down the street right over their heads.

"You think we can get in there?" Sheila bit her lip. "They're scanning the trucks."

"Only on the way out," Lydia corrected. "It was an early mission Kane considered. Breaking prisoners out of the rehabilitation camp might have given the Underground the boost in numbers it needed to begin standing up to the Coalition."

Jez tisked. "So why didn't they?"

"There's an easy way to get operatives in, but we never came up with a plan we liked to get people out." Lydia pursed her lips.

"Great." Jez rolled her eyes. "We can become prisoners, but we can't get out."

"Yeah, and your idea to get in seems anything but 'easy,'" Sheila added.

"Be glad you've been doing all those pull ups in the gym in the mornings," Lydia said.

"How did you—?"

"Head of security, remember?" Lydia smiled, pointing to herself. "Once inside, you need to allow the truck to move past the guard station and into the garage before getting down. It means holding yourself in place for more than two minutes, but anything less will leave you in full view of the tower." She gestured to the sweeping spotlight.

"Hold myself up underneath a moving truck for more than two minutes?" Sheila said, her voice full of doubt. "You give my workouts more credit than I think they deserve."

"Adrenaline will do what your muscles can't," Jez reminded her.

"Any of us falls and you're by yourself as far as they know. Don't call out or look at either of the other two trucks," Lydia added. "Here they come."

Sheila grasped the handles of the ladder, her heart pounding. She'd never done anything like this in her life, and the fear made her muscles cramp. She saw herself slipping as she climbed the ladder and missing her chance to grab the underside of the truck as it stopped at the intersection. Lydia's plan felt crazy, but she'd assured them it would work.

The rumble of the trucks caused bits of sand to fall through the manhole. The dim light of the setting sun disappeared as the first truck stopped over their access point. Lydia scrambled out of the hole. Rolling to her back, she jammed her feet over parts of the undercarriage. Grasping with her hands, she lifted herself as the truck rolled away.

The second truck arrived, and Jez repeated the maneuver with surprising ease. Sheila shook her head at the recoding effects of the Coalition's work. Jez appeared super-human to Sheila.

Sheila's hands trembled as Jez's truck rolled away. She slowly made her way to the top of the ladder. The third truck stopped overhead, and a blast of hot air entered the hole.

She couldn't move.

Now, Sheila, now! She was yelling at herself, but fear had taken hold of her. *This is your chance!*

She reached a trembling hand upward, finding the edge of the access hole. Seconds ticked away, and she recognized she was moving too slow. To her horror, the engine above roared, and she watched the undercarriage begin moving overhead.

No! she screamed silently.

She huddled near the top of the hole. Her face pressed against the ladder. She panted while cursing herself for her fear. Lydia and Jez would wonder where she was. She was left on the outside with no way to communicate to them. She lowered herself down the ladder.

How could I let this happen?

To her surprise, more rumbling came, and a fourth truck stopped over her position. She shot up the ladder and dragged herself out of the manhole. She rolled over and nearly cried out at how close the bottom of the truck was to her face. The engine roared, and she grabbed the first part she could reach. The truck lurched, and she couldn't help the cry that left her mouth as the lower half of her body dragged on the pavement.

Every pebble and imperfection in the pavement ripped into her skin through the thin fibers of the prison uniform. The truck gained speed, and she had to act before the pain became too great. Pulling upward with her arms, she raised as much of her body as she could and lifted her right leg. She thrust it outward, her right foot finding a gap in which to wedge itself.

Another cry escaped her lips as a bump in the road skipped her bouncing left foot into the bottom of the truck. She pulled with her three secured limbs and lifted her leg. No longer dragging, she searched frantically for a place to secure her left foot, but nothing could be found. Time and again, she thrust her left foot outward blindly, but no gap or support could be found. At one point, her ankle struck a particularly hot exhaust pipe, and she yelped at the pain.

The truck slowed to a stop as it approached the guarded entrance. Her muscles screamed as she did her best to hug the bottom side of the truck. Sweat beaded on her forehead and ran into her eyes. Her arms shook violently from the exertion, and she silently pled for the truck to begin moving again.

To her relief, she heard the guard pound the side of the truck and yell to the gate operator to let them enter. The truck rocked, and she nearly lost her grip. Gritting her teeth, she fought the urge to let go and allow her muscles to relax. Suddenly, the sound of the engine's echo changed as the ground shifted from pavement to concrete. The darkness around her told her they'd entered the garage. Moments later, the truck turned and parked near the wall on her left side. The engine cut off.

She planned to lower herself slowly to the ground, but her arms gave up as if they realized she'd arrived. She slammed to the ground, her head striking the concrete. She bit her lip to keep from crying out, and she silently rocked while holding her head.

The sound of the truck door opening froze her in place. Two sets of feet flopped to the ground on either side of her and made their way to the back of the truck. She could hear the guards grumbling about what they would be served for lunch.

It was then that she dared a glance to her right and left. A small gasp escaped her lips. *Where are Lydia and Jez?* There were no trucks on either side of hers, and she realized her truck hadn't been part of the same convoy. It was parked in a different section of the garage. She scanned the garage, but she couldn't see them anywhere. Sliding on her stomach, she made her way to the front of the truck and crawled out, thankful to leave the hot underbelly of the truck behind. She crouched between the truck and the wall considering her options.

I'm separated. I could search for Jez and Lydia, or I could search for Ben. She debated the options silently for a moment, deciding that searching for Ben was more important and might yet reunite her with the others. *Lydia will put mission first.*

A door opened to her right, and two armed guards entered.

"Get in here!" one shouted. "This truck needs to be unloaded immediately."

A single-file line of prisoners walked through the door. Sheila grit her teeth at their appearance. The Western Alliance had long bragged about its program for 'rehabilitation candidates,' calling it a 'chance for wayward citizens to prove their loyalty.' Propaganda had always portrayed the working conditions as ideal, but what Sheila saw was anything but that.

The prisoners appeared haggard, several wearing uniforms that barely held together at the seams. To a person, their faces bore the sunken features of neglect. Most were middle aged, but there were several that appeared younger. She bit back a shout as the second guard used the end of a rifle to prod an older man moving slowly inside, his thin arms and hands shaking with age and overuse. His back was hunched, and she guessed he'd spent many years here. She couldn't help but think of her father, who had lived out his days at this camp.

The final prisoner walked through the door, and the guard turned his back to guide them to her truck. She slid silently along the wall and jumped behind the final prisoner, who gave her a questioning glance. She held a finger to her lips, and he nodded.

Look tired and beaten, Sheila. She let her arms hang loosely and made her eyelids droop. She prayed her face didn't betray the adrenaline coursing through her veins. She silently thanked Lydia for the mud on her face as one of the guards studied her. His gaze lingered for a moment before moving on, accepting that she was part of the group.

"Get these boxes off the truck, now!" the first guard shouted again.

Two of the prisoners climbed into the back of the truck and handed boxes to the rest. Sheila accepted one and followed the prisoners as they marched across the garage. Her eyes darted left and right, searching for any sign of Lydia or Jez, but she saw nothing. She heard a grunt to her left and saw the elderly man straining under the weight of his box.

"Here, trade for mine," she said. She hefted his box out of his arms with one of hers, replacing it with her much lighter parcel.

"Bless you, young lady," the man said, a thick southern drawl to his voice.

"No stalling!" a guard shouted as he approached, startling Sheila. He placed the barrel of his rifle into the small of her back and shoved. She stumbled forward and nearly lost control of the heavy box in her hands.

"Sorry, child. That's my fault. I'm not as strong as I used to be," the elderly man whispered.

"Don't you dare apologize." She shook her head as they continued to walk. They exited the garage and entered an attached warehouse. On all sides, she saw food stores and other supplies on shelves. Based on the appearance of the prisoners, she assumed that little of it was being used to care for them. "Their cruelty isn't your fault."

They stacked their boxes on the shelves, and the man grabbed the shelf to catch his breath. He gazed at her with exhausted eyes. His face appeared like wrinkled leather, and the gray whiskers on his face gathered in patches as if some had been torn out. His forehead wore a scabby wound, the obvious abuse of a guard. She wasn't a medic, but even she could see the infection forming there.

"Young lady, you're not from here, are you?" He paused before heading back to the truck.

"What makes you say that?" She turned to him.

"You have too much fight in you. You're not broken like the rest of—" He coughed and sucked in a wheezing breath. "Sorry for that."

"You're not well, are you?"

"No, and I don't care to be. My day will be soon, and it will be a welcome relief when it comes."

Sheila's eyes teared up as she stared at the man. She desired to reach out and touch his face, to show him compassion that'd been missing from his life for years, but she didn't dare. "I'm so sorry," was all she could manage.

"Don't you worry about me, child. But tell me, why would you want to be in here?"

She studied his eyes, wondering if she could trust this man with her mission. His eyes creased in the corners, and he gazed at her with concern. "I—I'm looking for someone," she blurted.

"You two," a guard shouted rounding the corner, "get moving! No breaks. If the old man can't handle his own, then he can report for processing." Sheila guessed what 'processing' meant, and the two of them slowly marched back to the truck.

"Looking for someone?" the man whispered as they walked. "Someone special to you?"

"Not exactly." She didn't glance in his direction. "Someone with information I need. Ben. Ben Brennan. You know him?"

The man chuckled softly. "A trouble-maker, that one. Finds himself in the box more often than not. You don't spend as long as I have in here without knowing who the guards like to mind more than others."

"The box? Where's that?"

"About fifty yards east of this warehouse if you follow the wall. You can't miss it."

Approaching the truck, they grabbed more boxes and retraced their steps. Back at the shelves, Sheila glanced around to confirm if the guards were out of sight. She placed a hand on the old man's face and gazed into his eyes. Her heart split open as she imagined this was her father, old and worn down as a slave.

"I'm so sorry for what's been done to you here. I wish I could take you with me."

"Young lady, as tempting as that sounds, I would get you caught." He took her hand from his face and held it gently in both of his. He smiled, doubling the lines in his face. "You find your information and get yourself out of here. The last thing I want to see at the end of my days is a young lady so full of life get trapped in this place."

"Thank you," she said, her eyes watering again. She turned to walk away, and then glanced back at him. "What's your name?"

"Jack."

"Just Jack?"

"Only name I've needed in here."

"Thank you, Jack."

"Thank you, young lady, for showing an old man a little kindness." He patted her hand and turned to walk back to the truck. She stared after him until he rounded the corner.

"I'm sorry, Dad, that you had to live like him," she whispered aloud to the air. She crawled into the shelving unit and burrowed to the next aisle. Crouching she watched for her moment. The attention of the two guards within eyesight was elsewhere, and she scrambled for an exit door. She slid out and disappeared into the shadows outside.

Chapter Twenty-Four

Jack had been right. The box was unmistakable. A small row of metal boxes, about the size of small dumpsters sat in a row. Each had a side panel, through which a person could barely crawl, bolted with a large padlock. On the front, a small hole was cut, she supposed, to allow rations to be given to prisoners.

She studied the area from her hiding place, waiting close to an hour for the sunlight to disappear. The boxes sat within a few yards of the main wall, at too sharp an angle for the sweeping spotlight to illuminate. This left the boxes enveloped in shadow. A guard walked the perimeter of the wall, and she timed his route. She would have a few minutes between each pass to find Ben and get what she needed. Footsteps to her left told her the guard was passing again. As soon as he was out of sight, she padded quickly to the first box. Peering inside, she was met with inky blackness. Heat still radiated off the metal from the sun earlier that day.

"Hello?" she whispered.

Nothing.

She moved to the next one. Peering in the hole, she nearly wretched. The sickly-sweet smell of rot filled her lungs, and she shrank in horror. Whoever the occupant was, they were no longer alive. She prayed it wasn't Ben. Moving to the next, she again whispered. This time, a shallow moan greeted her.

"Ben? Ben Brennan?" she whispered, hopeful she'd found him.

"Who is it?" came a croaking voice.

She paused. She would get one chance to answer him correctly. "A friend of Sandra." A long moment passed, and she began to be afraid he wouldn't talk to her. That's when a hand curled around the rim of the hole and two eyes met hers. The left eye was swollen shut, a reddish-black bruise visible even in the near darkness. He'd been beaten, that much was clear. His swollen and cracked lips parted to reveal missing and cracked teeth.

"How do *you* know Sandra?"

"To be honest, I'm a friend of hers because I know her husband."

His good eye grew wide. "She's been searching for him."

"Yes. We were told. And we're looking for her."

"We?" His eyes scanned to see who was with her.

"We got separated from each other," she said, remembering she'd hoped to run into Lydia and Jez here. "Has anyone else come by to talk to you?"

"No one has come here in two days. I think I've caused enough trouble for them to let me rot in here permanently. They—they—" His voice faltered. "They took them. My wife and children. The Coalition took them. They promised help. They promised—" His voice broke, and a tear leaked from his eye. She waited for him to recover. He sucked in a deep breath and continued. "I turned in that famous Thomson kid at our camp by the bridge. They said they would take care of whoever helped find him. Instead, we were hauled in for questioning. Interrogated. Then, finally, they threw me out on the street alone. No wife. No children."

"You were the one who turned in Willis?" She sucked in, not hiding her shock.

"Yeah. Didn't want to hurt the kid, but I had a family to look after. He was going to be trouble, and I believed it would help me help my family. Guess the Coalition wasn't interested in helping a former slave."

"So why did they let you go?"

"I didn't put it together at the time, but I guess they thought I'd lead them to others. There was a small group of us under that bridge, including Sandra, and they managed to run off as the Coalition darted the Thomson kid. I don't know how they got away, but Scott—he was one of our group—had a few places we could meet in an emergency. I found them at one of those places."

"And that's when you removed Sandra's tracker?"

"They'd never been after us before, so we hadn't worried about it. Tracker removal is risky, but she insisted. It's located near the spine, so it's easy to cause permanent damage. I got lucky with her removal."

"Ben, do you know where she is?"

He hesitated. His eye scanned as if trying to come up with an answer. He glanced back at her. "You promise you're her friend?"

"All I want is to reunite her with her husband."

He breathed a long, raspy breath. "We had to move on as the tracker would send out an emergency signal. Scott took his family and Sandra with him. I was on the Coalition's watch list, so I said I'd meet them later. I never made it. Got thrown in here."

"Where are they? Ben, please."

"Twelfth Street off Plaza. Third row house on the right. The basement."

"Thank you," she said. She touched his gnarled hand, which chafed like sandpaper. "If you weren't in here, I'd bring you with us. I'm sorry."

"My family is dead. I've caused trouble in here, so they would threaten me with my family's harm if I didn't behave. They never have, which tells me all I need to know." He stopped and pulled his hand back in the box. "There's nothing for me out there anymore."

She shuddered. Two men she'd met in here, and both were resigned to death. "I'm sorry." It was all she could think to say.

"Besides, I can't imagine how you plan to get out of here. But if you do, tell the Thomson kid it wasn't personal."

"I will," she promised.

She retreated to her hiding spot and glanced back at the metal boxes. She cursed the Coalition for what they were doing and prayed her father had never spent time in 'The Box.'

How am I going to find Lydia and Jez? The guard circled

around again. As he neared the boxes, a faint voice could be heard from the box she hadn't visited.

"Please, I need water," the voice pled.

"Shut up, prisoner!" the guard shouted.

"Please, I have information to trade."

The guard stopped and stared at the box. "Oh yeah, what information could you possibly have?"

"Someone was here. Someone from the outside talking to Ben."

"Shut up, you imbecile," Ben shouted. "He's making it up! No one was here."

The guard reached for his radio, and Sheila realized her situation was about to get a lot worse.

"She's over there! Please, I need water. I'm helping, see?" the prisoner shouted.

"Shut up!" Ben shouted again.

The guard followed where the hand from the box was pointing. He scanned left and right until his eyes rested on Sheila. She was cloaked in shadow, but his gaze told her he could make out her shape. He raised his rifle and pointed it at her.

"You there, come out!" he shouted at her.

Her hands shook as she raised them slowly and stepped into the light. He stormed over to her and struck her in the stomach with the butt of his firearm. She doubled over, the pain turning her insides out. He pointed the rifle at her again.

"Who are you? What is your prisoner number?"

He reached for his radio. If he reported her, all was lost. The whole prison would know of her. That's when the alarms blared. His radio lit up with reports of a prison riot in the barracks. Shouts were heard and spotlights adjusted in one direction. Guards rushed toward the other end of the compound.

Jez! Lydia!

Chapter Twenty-Five

The moment of distraction was all that Sheila needed. She lunged at the guard, hurling her shoulder upward into his midsection. He grunted as the wind was expelled from his lungs. Falling backward, he grabbed her shoulder for support, pulling her with him. She landed on top of him, her instincts reminding her to drive her elbow into him as she did. She felt one of his ribs crack as she landed.

In a panic, she reached for the rifle, still grasped in his left hand which was outstretched next to him. His right hand flew upward and met the side of her face. Light exploded in her vision, and she fell to the side. Still, she flailed for the rifle. Her fingers met the stock of the gun, and she grasped it.

Realizing what she was doing, he yanked at the rifle, twisting her fingers. She yelped in pain but managed to hang on. He reached for the gun with the other hand, and she had one chance. She kicked wildly, bringing her knee upward. It connected with the same ribs she'd landed on, and he screamed in pain. His fingers loosened their grip on the gun while his free hand reached for his side.

Getting her legs under her, she grabbed the rifle with both hands and pulled. The firearm came free in her hands suddenly, and she fell backward. The guard rolled over to get up, and she scrambled to her feet. She raised the gun with both hands above her head and brought the flat of the stock down on the side of his head. He fell limp to the ground, no longer conscious.

She grasped the side of her face and fell to her knees. She cried, both in pain and desperation. Fear gripped her stomach like a vice, and she vomited.

The alarms and lights created a violent chaos around her. Her mind spun as she tried to clear her vision. Adrenaline surged inside her to the point of trembling. She tried to compose herself and figure out where the commotion was coming from.

Across the compound, she heard gunfire. Searchlights swept back and forth, illuminating the grounds. From her angle, she could see several of the buildings on the other side of the courtyard. Most of the activity was centered on the barracks, which glowed with flames. Guards surrounded the building and apprehended rioting prisoners who fled the building. That's when another sound caught her attention.

Amid the blaring sirens and shouts, Sheila heard the almost imperceptible sound of breaking glass. She turned her attention to the far end of the building next to the barracks in time to see two shapes climb out of a window and flee in the other direction.

"Lydia. Jez," she whispered.

Dragging the guard into her former hiding spot, she ripped his jacket off and put it on over her jumpsuit. There was no time for a complete costume change, and she prayed that appearing halfway like a guard would be enough while all attention was turned to the riot. Grabbing his hat, she put it on and forced her tired legs to begin running through the open courtyard.

Spotlights still swept the compound, and once or twice, they illuminated her. From a distance, she hoped all they would see was a guard jacket, hat, and rifle and assume she was running to help the chaos. None froze on her, and she ran toward the shadows in which she'd seen Jez and Lydia disappear.

Reaching the building with the broken window, she rounded the corner between the buildings. She stopped and peered into the darkness but saw no one. That's when she realized her profile might appear like an armed guard to the two of them. She lowered the rifle.

"Lydia? Jez?" she whispered.

"Sheila?" Lydia's voice came from the darkness. She stood and walked toward Sheila. Her head was bleeding, and she cradled her left arm in her right hand. "Where have you been?"

"Never mind. I found Ben. We need to get out of here," she said.

"Not likely. We never should have come here," Jez rolled her eyes as she stood. Her voice was harsh, but Sheila could see her fear.

"What happened?" Sheila glanced to her left and right.

"No time to explain." Lydia winced as she adjusted her arm. "We were discovered and pinned down. We started the riot as a distraction. Let's say Jez is good at picking a fight and leave it at that."

"Guilty," Jez agreed, "but I still see no way to get out of here. This was suicide."

Sheila stared down at her newly acquired rifle wondering if she would be required to use it. Glancing back up at Jez, she raised an eyebrow at Sheila as if asking if she needed a hand. The idea of giving the rifle to Jez unnerved her, and she turned away.

"So, what's the plan? Shooting our way out of here doesn't seem like an effective strategy." She glanced again at Jez who smirked.

"No, it's not," Lydia agreed. She partially unzipped her jumpsuit and reached into the back collar. The sound of a Velcro strap tearing could be heard, and she removed her hand, a long, almost-flat bundle in her grip.

Jez sucked in upon seeing it. "Subtle," she said, obviously recognizing it.

"What is it?" Sheila inquired, not sure she would like the answer.

"C4 explosive," Lydia said flatly. "Underground secured some after the raid. Grabbed this from the armory before we left. Kane and I had access, no one else."

Sheila's eyes widened as she realized the plan. They wouldn't be sneaking out of the prison. "You sure there isn't a quieter way for us to get out of here?"

"No, there isn't. It's the one plan Kane and I were ever able to invent that might have a chance. And—we might release a few prisoners in the process." Lydia's face hardened as she spoke, and Sheila could see she'd thought this through.

"Where's our blast point?" Jez's voice sounded frighteningly calm about the plan.

"The wall about a hundred yards from here is close to the street. Alliance couldn't build it very thick without rerouting the entire block. This facility is old, so I'm hopeful this is enough to open the way. I think it's our best option." Lydia held up a small, black switch in her hand. "Remote detonator will let us hide from the blast."

"And if it doesn't bring the wall down?" Sheila held her breath for the answer.

"Then, we're announcing to the entire place where to find us." Jez spoke in a sing-song sarcasm. "Sounds like fun."

Lydia waved her hand, signaling for them to follow. The riot had called any perimeter guards away, so the gap between the buildings and the wall appeared deserted. They ran at a crouch along the length of the building, ducking into the next alley. Lydia grimaced as she again shifted her arm.

"Are you sure you've got this?" Jez glanced at the wound. "I can—"

"I'm okay," Lydia interrupted. Her eyes steeled and communicated that she wasn't going to let anyone else handle the explosives. "You two stay here. I'll plant the explosives and return." Lydia slid out from the alley and ran to a spot on the wall in the distance. She crouched and slid the explosive into a crack with her good arm.

"Not good," Jez whispered.

"What?" Sheila glanced at Jez.

"Company." She pointed in the distance. The outlines of four guards could be seen running silently toward Lydia's position. "She doesn't see them. Stay here." Sheila watched as Jez stood and hugged the wall as she made her way toward Lydia.

A cry came from one of the guards, startling Lydia who stood to run. With a swift kick, one of the guards knocked her down from behind. She rolled over to find four rifles pointed at her. The men shouted at her, and Lydia did her best to raise her hands despite her injured arm. They never saw Jez coming.

"Run!" Jez screamed as she sprang at the guards. She kicked at the rifle of the first guard, knocking it to his left. The gunshot ricocheted off the wall nearly hitting Lydia, who scrambled backward. Jez followed her kick by striking the guard in the head with a stone she'd picked up. The guards turned their attention to their new attacker, and Lydia rose to her feet and ran unable to fight with her injury. Jez's body twisted in a fury as she struck the next guard, always keeping the guard between her and the firearms of the others.

A second later, Lydia returned to Sheila's side. "I dropped it," she whimpered, clutching her arm in pain. "The detonator—I dropped it!"

Sheila stood to her feet, willing herself to go help Jez, when the shot echoed off the walls followed by Jez's cry of pain. Sheila gasped as she saw Jez fall to the ground, her hand reaching for her stomach. Two new guards had arrived, one firing on Jez. The still conscious guards recovered and retrieved their weapons. Jez rolled over groaning and clutched her middle as she slid backward and rested her back against the wall.

"Hands in the air!" the guards were screaming. They inched forward, surrounding Jez, whose jumpsuit was turning red under her fingers.

Jez was paying them no attention. Instead, she stared at her hand on the ground, the fingers of which curled around an object. She gazed over in Sheila's direction, her face cold and determined despite how much her body was trembling.

Oh please, Jez, no!

Their eyes lingered for a long moment, a silent conversation happening in the couple seconds they had. Jez lifted her hand, and Sheila could see her eyes grow sad.

She ducked back behind the wall as Jez pushed the detonator.

Chapter Twenty-Six

The concussive blast shook the buildings, knocking Sheila to the ground. Her ears rang from the noise, and she crawled on all fours coughing on the increasingly thick cloud of dust. Making her way to Lydia, she examined her.

"You okay?"

Lydia coughed twice and squinted at Sheila. Her face was caked with stone powder where tears and sweat had been. She clutched her arm, and her eyes searched Sheila's face for answers, the fear and dread spreading over her countenance like a wave. "J—Jez?" was all she could say.

Sheila shook her head, letting out a long breath so as not to lose composure. Lydia closed her eyes, her lips trembling. Moments were precious, and they needed to move. She grabbed Lydia by her armpits and hauled her upward. Lydia let out a cry as her arm moved, but there was no preventing it.

"Come on. We've got to go," she commanded. Lydia nodded and pushed upward with her feet.

Wrapping her arm around Lydia, the two rounded the corner. The dust swirled in the eerily quiet compound, but her ringing ears might have been the reason she was unable to hear anything. The blast would have everyone's attention by this point, and they needed to escape immediately. They trudged forward.

As they neared, the newly formed hole in the wall gaped at them through the haze. Rubble spilled out on both sides. Overstretched razor wire protruded outward like wiry hairs. A late brick fell, bouncing to the ground in front of them. Somewhere, under all the stone, Jez lay. She shook her head, willing herself not to imagine the state of her body.

"I'm sorry, Jez," Sheila whispered, unable to contain her tears. "Be free—finally."

Muffled shouts came over the ringing in her ears, and spotlights swept the dust cloud refracting off the particles in the air and creating a blinding glow. The dust was their cover for now. Sheila shoved Lydia up onto the rubble pile, and they climbed. She slipped on a loose stone and gouged her knee, the blood beginning to soak into her jumpsuit. She cursed at the pain but kept her limbs moving.

When they reached the top of the pile, she could barely see the street beyond. In the night's blackness, the street had a welcoming darkness that would hide them away. Suddenly, a stone gave way in front of her, and Lydia disappeared into the dust cloud. The sharp sound of stone on stone sounded, and a thud was followed by Lydia's cry of pain. Sheila scrambled down, nearly losing her footing more than once. She found Lydia at the bottom, laying on top of her damaged arm. She was gritting her teeth, a guttural scream expelling between them.

"Come on, soldier," Sheila said in a hushed tone, aware of the growing number of voices on the other side of the rubble. "All this was for nothing if we get caught." Hoisting Lydia to her feet, she threw her shoulder under Lydia's good arm and supported her weight. "Okay, one foot in front of the other. We can do this."

"I can't believe she—" Lydia wept as they limped across the street.

"I know. Don't stop moving," Sheila said, urging her forward. She couldn't believe it either. Jez, the girl who simply intended to escape and live life on her terms, had made their escape possible.

They disappeared into the darkness of the alley. Guards yelled and sirens blared, a gradually fading noise as they made their getaway. The price for Ben's information had been heavy.

It had better have been worth it, Sheila said to herself.

Chapter Twenty-Seven

Willis could hear the shouting outside when the door burst open. Kane nearly ripped the door off the hinges as he stormed into the room. His eyes burned with a mix of rage and fear. Before Willis could even sit up, he bounded to the bedside.

"Kane, stop!" Brenda cried, appearing in the doorway. Her hand was extended, reaching for Kane's shirt. She grabbed nothing except air.

Kane swept Perryn behind him as she stood, ignoring her protest. Grabbing Willis by his robes, he lifted his still thin frame completely out of the bed. He hurled Willis against the wall. Willis's head smacked the surface, and a sick dizziness overtook him.

"Where is she?" Kane roared. He pushed Willis harder into the wall to make his point.

"Kane, no!" Brenda shouted.

"What's going on?" Perryn said in alarm.

"Where is she?" Kane's voice growled even lower.

"What—? I—?" Willis stammered.

Brenda pulled hopelessly at Kane's arms. Maria and Chris materialized in the door, a shared expression of panic on their faces. Instantly, they joined Brenda in trying to pull Kane off Willis, but his behemoth size was more than enough to keep them at bay.

"Tell me where she went! I won't lose her!" Kane shook Willis, who scanned the room, silently pleading for help. He stared in a breathless panic into Kane's face, meeting the huge man's wild eyes.

Kane searched Willis's face before staring down at his own

hands. The rage melted from his face, leaving distress behind. Tears welled up in Kane's eyes, and his grip on Willis's robes loosened. Willis's body slid down the wall until his feet met the floor. Kane stepped backward, staring at his hands, which shook slightly. He glanced back up at Willis, and his lip trembled.

"I—I—can't lose her. I—I can't lose—again—. I—can't—" Kane's words were disconnected as he backed away from Willis. The others let go of him, and he stepped all the way to the opposite wall. Meeting the wall, he slid until seated. He placed his head in his hands. "I can't lose her. Not again."

Willis's legs shook, partially from being unaccustomed to standing and in part from fear. He scanned the room for answers. Perryn's hands covered her nose and mouth, holding back the tears. Brenda was crying silently.

"I—I don't understand," was all Willis could think to say.

Without a word, Chris grabbed a remote, turning on the monitor mounted to the wall. An image of destruction appeared, a stone structure reduced to rubble. Smoke belched from fires being snuffed out. Dust filled the air, and guards covered in grime stood by the mess, armed with rifles. A reporter, wearing a dust mask, was pointing behind her and in the middle of a sentence.

"...in a massive act of violence, the terrorists leveled the wall, taking the life of numerous loyal citizens working at the rehabilitation facility." Faces of the deceased guards, smiling in Alliance uniforms, scrolled the screen. "Several rehabilitation candidates escaped during the chaos, and officials warn citizens not to approach anyone unknown to them as the candidates' rehabilitation is not complete, which may make them dangerous. Again, authorities are asking for anyone with information on the perpetrators to come forward. One terrorist was found dead on the scene. Through DNA signature, authorities matched her identity and have released this picture and request anyone with information—"

Perryn gasped as the picture of Jez appeared on the screen, while the reporter continued. Willis stared at the image. It was a photo of her from her days as a Chase runner. Her black hair, still long, draped down her shoulders. Her mouth was closed, and she smiled with a fierce confidence.

"Jez—is dead?" Perryn searched the room with her eyes.

Heads nodded.

"They keep repeating the information, hoping someone will know something," Chris said. "Earlier, they showed a picture of Lydia and Sheila, saying they were caught on camera breaking into a Law-keeper outpost with Jez."

"Chief kind of freaked when he realized who the report was about," Maria added. Kane had yet to look up, his face still buried in his hands.

"Son," Brenda said, almost whispering, "I think it's time you tell us what you know."

"But—" Willis protested, "I gave my word."

Kane's head finally lifted, no longer angry. His face pled with Willis. "I lost my family once. I—I can't lose her, boss."

Kane had always called him 'boss,' a leftover title from their days as Red Team on the station. Even as Chief of the Underground, Kane had always deferred to Willis. His desperate eyes took Willis back to the day on the station when Law-keepers had nearly arrested Kane. It was the first time Willis had learned anything about Kane's past, his family that he lost. Willis's heart broke, and he accepted Kane needed the truth.

He needs it, or this will break him. It would break me.

"Kane, you—you haven't lost anyone," he said.

"Willis, how can you know—?" Brenda shook her head.

"No, I'm not talking about Lydia. I don't know what's happened to her. I think if she was caught or worse, her picture would be right next to Jez's."

"Then what do you mean?" Perryn searched his face for answers.

The group waited in breathless silence. No one dared move as they sensed the weight of what Willis was about to say. He took a deep breath. His voice shook, and he swallowed, trying to compose himself.

"I—I gave my word I wouldn't say, but Lydia is searching for Sandra," Willis said. He stopped, and the words hung in the air like a fog.

"Who is—" Maria started. She stopped when she saw Kane's face. His eyes were wide with shock and wouldn't leave Willis.

"Kane, your wife—your child—they're alive," Willis said. "Before the Coalition caught me, I met her. On the street. The Alliance told her you were dead, and that's what she believed until she saw you run the Chase. She's been searching for you ever since. Lydia made me promise not to tell you—not yet."

"Not yet?" Brenda said, speaking for Kane who still sat in stunned silence. "Until when?"

"Until she found her and brought her to you." Willis spoke directly to Kane.

Willis glanced around the room. Chris stared at the floor as if assembling the pieces in his head. Maria stood with her mouth gaping open. Brenda walked softly over to Kane and knelt next to him, her hand squeezing his shoulder. Perryn slowly sat on the bed, her hands still covering her mouth.

Kane grunted slightly as he pushed off the floor. Slowly, he rose to his full height, Brenda stepping away from him. He approached Willis, and the entire room sucked in a breath, expecting Kane to explode. Instead, he gently reached out and placed his hand on Willis's shoulder.

"Boss, you saying she's—my Sandra—she's alive?" Kane's voice was a barely audible whisper. "She's really alive?"

Willis nodded.

"And—my child? There's a child?"

"A boy," Willis confirmed. "You have a son."

Kane's face contorted as if fighting over whether to smile or cry or rage. He searched Willis's face with his eyes. "And Lydia went searching for them—for me?" His voice whispered.

Willis nodded.

Maria put a hand to her chest and glanced at Perryn appearing love struck. Soft smiles grew on the others' faces, but a pained expression appeared on Kane's. Willis didn't blame him. *His new love went to rescue the love of his life. That's got to be confusing, at least.*

"How do we—? Where are they? What can we—?" Kane stammered.

"We can't. That's all I know. I've no idea where they went or what they were planning." Willis swallowed hard. "I guess we have to wait."

"But why can't we start our own search?" Maria held out both hands.

"Yeah. Why not?" Chris agreed.

"Guys, I don't think—" Brenda began.

"No! For real, we should start looking," Maria interrupted.

"I don't believe we can do anything about it right now," Brenda countered.

The room exploded into argument. Willis nodded at Kane for leadership, but he stared at the floor like he hoped it would give him answers. Willis pled with him silently to take charge, but Kane wouldn't meet his eyes. He glanced in desperation at Perryn, who was getting frustrated by the room. Without warning, she stood, her face hardening.

"Stop it!" she shouted.

Chapter Twenty-Eight

"Just stop it!" Perryn shouted again, her throat rasping. The room went silent, shocked by her outburst. She swallowed hard and scanned around her. Willis's face begged her to do something. Kane's eyes wouldn't leave the floor. Brenda, Chris, and Maria slowly turned in her direction. She lowered her arms, not remembering when she raised them. "I don't think Kane needs any arguing."

"I simply think we should—" Maria's voice trailed off as she met Perryn's eyes.

"I know," Perryn said, softening her voice. "Everything in me wants to help my friend." She gestured toward Kane. "But the truth is we know nothing. We don't know where to even begin. We know that she's out there. Nothing more."

"But if we searched in the Coalition databases like Lydia did, then we could get the information we need to start," Chris suggested.

"Yes, we could, but think about it. The Law-keeping stations are on high alert after Lydia's break-in. Whatever they found in there led them to the prison, and whatever happened there led to them blowing up the place and Jez's death."

The room winced when she mentioned Jez's death. Jez had hurt most of them with her betrayal at the original Underground headquarters, but the knowledge that she'd died helping Lydia was sinking into each of them. Even Perryn was surprised at the amount of compassion for Jez rising within her, and she'd received some of the worst treatment.

"It's not a trail we can follow," Perryn summarized. Slowly those in the room nodded. Her logic was getting through to them, and she breathed a sigh of relief. She wasn't sure where all those thoughts had come from, but she noted how good it felt to be able to think so clearly. It was as if a cloud had lifted, a fog of emotion around Willis and her, and she was free to be herself again. She imagined if she glanced down, she would see herself wearing a blue training uniform to lead a team of trainees.

Kane turned and walked toward the doorway. He stopped in front of her and placed his hand on her shoulder. He nodded.

"You're right," he said quietly. "We can't follow. And if anyone can find my Sandra, it's Lydia. She's the best we have."

"Sheila's no slouch at following trails of information, either," Brenda added.

"True," Kane agreed. "What do you suggest as our course of action?" He gazed at Perryn with expectation in his eyes.

She let out a long breath. "I think—I believe it's time we stopped waiting. I know it's been hard since the raid. We lost so many of our own, but we've added quite a few more. The Chase is coming in a matter of weeks, and we have to prepare. If the neuro-booster has been or will be released over the population, we can't let the Chairman take control of the world again. If he does—the message of the Liberated will be drowned out."

Kane's eyes showed pain when she mentioned the raid. The reminder had hurt him, but he nodded in agreement. It was time the Underground took action again, and they all recognized it.

Kane turned to her again. "A moment ago, I was in need of a new Captain. I think I found her." He patted her shoulder and left the room.

Perryn stood frozen by the statement. She wished to protest and tell him she wasn't qualified, but he was gone. Scanning around the room, she saw nothing but smiles. Chris nodded and exited. Maria danced over to her, wagging her head with supposed attitude.

"Captain? For real? Don't expect me to call you that. Girl, you're still my best friend," Maria said with a smirk. They both laughed as Maria left.

She turned to Willis, who appeared uncertain he belonged in the room. *Now to him.*

"You, sir, don't get out of this one," she said. Out of the corner of her eye, she could see Brenda's smile widen.

"What—? I—I mean—" he stammered, sounding quite unsure of himself.

"You heard me," she interrupted. "If this place is going to raise up an army of Liberated, you don't get to stay behind. It's time you left this room, Willis."

She could see the confusion on his face. He appeared like he would rather run away, but she needed to press him. His confidence was broken, and she had to make him try. *He'll never heal if he won't take the risk.*

"Okay," he whispered, sitting slowly in the bed. He wrung his hands together.

"Listen, we have time to get you ready physically," she said, sitting next to him. "But only getting out there will get you ready here." She pointed to his chest. Brenda padded over to them and studied their posture. She smirked and tilted her head playfully.

"Is this what I think it is? Have you two finally figured out—you two?" She pointed fingers at the both of them. Perryn smiled and nodded. She glanced at Willis, who still appeared scared, but he nodded as well. Brenda took a deep breath and let it out with a satisfying sigh. "Good. And for the record—it's about time." She raised an eyebrow, causing Perryn to chuckle. Even Willis laughed gently. Brenda smiled and turned to leave.

"I'm not ready," Willis said almost inaudibly once Brenda was out of sight.

"I know." She took his hand. "But *we* are. We're going to do this together."

"Captain's orders?" He still wouldn't meet her gaze.

"If that's what it takes."

He nodded.

"And we start first thing in the morning."

Chapter Twenty-Nine

Twelfth Street off Plaza. Third house on the right. Basement. Sheila repeated Ben's words to herself silently, not wanting to forget. The cost of those ten words weighed on her like an anchor around her neck. *Twelfth Street off Plaza. Third house on the right. Basement.*

Jez's face still burned in her vision. The grief she'd seen in her eyes as Jez realized her hope of a free life was gone tore through Sheila's soul like a bullet, and she choked for a moment on a single sob. She raised the back of her hand to her mouth and breathed through it lest she lose her composure.

Three days had passed since the explosion. The basement of the abandoned home they'd holed up in was covered in dust and cobwebs. A scrawny rat scurried along the wall board. She'd ducked between the city blocks during her provision run mindful of the complete silence in this part of the city. Whole neighborhoods sat vacant, left to rot after the Great Collapse caused the population of the world to plummet.

She rounded the corner and rapped on the wall three times, then two times. A knock further in repeated the pattern signaling that Lydia understood it was Sheila that approached. She walked in to see Lydia laying where she'd left her. Her arm was bandaged around the cut on her forearm. During the prison riot, Lydia had been thrown against a metal bunk, the corner of which had torn through her skin. It hadn't been until they'd found the hiding place that Lydia had even allowed Sheila to examine the wound, and that'd been hours later.

"Hey," she said flatly, approaching Lydia.

"Hey." Lydia nodded toward the street. "What's it like out there?"

"Quieter. If they're still searching for us, they're doing it somewhere else."

"Good. We need to keep moving."

Sheila shook her head. "Moving? I don't think so."

"Don't even start with me, Sheila. We don't know how long your information is good for or if it's good at all."

Twelfth Street off Plaza. Third house on the right. Basement, she said again to herself.

"Besides," Lydia added, "I think it's getting better."

Sheila gently pulled the bandage back on the wound. The skin around the wound appeared raw and puffy. Instead of scabbing normally, the cut was bright red and oozed. Lydia winced as she pulled the bandage off fully.

"Yeah, I'm not sure 'better' is the word I would use," she said to Lydia, who gave a pained smile.

"Look at you telling the one medic here what is and what is not 'better.'" She laughed, as did Sheila.

"As far as you're concerned, I'm the medic right now. If you'd like to advise your medic based on your previous experience, then she'll listen. If not, be quiet so I can change this dressing."

"Did you find the medicine I described to you?"

"All I could scrounge up were some clean bandages, and I think we need to be grateful for those. Our faces are all over the news, and we can't go anywhere where we'll be seen."

Lydia let out a grunt of pain as Sheila placed the new bandages on the wound and wrapped her arm. *She's as tough as they come.*

"As much as I think you're crazy for wanting to move," Sheila began, "I'll admit we need to. Your arm isn't getting any better, and we're going to need help."

"You think this Scott guy is going to be interested in helping us?"

"Well, he's been taking care of Sandra and her child. And the way Ben told the story, I would guess he was the one who helped Willis that night. Sounds like someone who might take in two fugitives."

"So how far is *Twelfth* Street?" Lydia grimaced.

Twelfth Street off Plaza. Third house on the right. Basement, Sheila repeated to herself again.

"It's about a half mile, most of which are in the abandoned part of the city. It's the last several blocks that'll be difficult."

Lydia nodded. "Nighttime it is, then. Cover of darkness."

"Tonight?"

"Tonight."

Twelfth Street off Plaza. Third house on the right. Basement.

The night air blew cold on their skin as they huddled in the shadow of the alley. Lydia stood with her back to the wall, catching her breath. She cradled her arm across her stomach, and Sheila could see the fluids soaking through the bandage. They'd been slowly making their way through the city for a couple of hours. The abandoned neighborhoods had been relatively easy to move through, but those had changed to a populated center several blocks earlier.

She'd been grateful to toss the threadbare prison uniform away, but she wished they had warmer clothes. Unable to make it back to their supplies, she'd swiped the first set of clothing remotely her size that she could find. The denim shorts were a little large on her, and she'd tied two of the belt loops together to keep them up. The men's red flannel shirt was missing the sleeves, and it made her feel like she should be up to her elbows in grease and working on a motorcycle. Lydia was sporting a pink t-shirt with a cat printed on the front and a pair of gray sweatpants.

What is Scott going to think when we show up looking like this?

Peering around the corner, she glanced both ways to see if anyone was present. A Law-keeper vehicle sat on the street, its lights off. She studied the window, trying to make out the outline of a driver, but she saw nothing.

"How's it out there?" Lydia whispered to Sheila, still breathless.

"Law-keeper vehicle about 100 yards away, but I think it's empty. I don't see any movement."

"You *think* it's empty?" Lydia questioned.

"'Think' is the best we're going to get."

Lydia nodded and pushed away from the wall. She placed her hand on Sheila's shoulder for support and waited for Sheila's word. She peered one more time around the corner at the vehicle. No movement could be seen.

"Okay. We go now."

"Now?"

"Now!"

She ran forward, mindful not to outrun Lydia whose fingers squeezed her shoulder. The alley across the street shrank from them as they ran. She dared a glance at the car, but there were no signs of life. She let out a sigh of relief.

She never saw the hole.

A chunk of pavement was missing in the middle of the road, and Sheila's foot landed hard as it caught the edge, rolling to one side. With a cry, she tumbled to the ground, her knee scraping along the pavement. Lydia landed next to her but managed to catch herself on one knee. Sheila winced and grabbed for her ankle.

The car lights turned on.

Chapter Thirty

Sheila stared at the car like a deer caught in lights, and her body froze to the spot. Lydia grunted nearby as she stood her feet.

"We've got to run!" Lydia shouted as the Law-keeper's siren blared. Sheila felt Lydia's hand tugging her shoulder, but she couldn't take her eyes off the flashing lights atop the Law-keeper vehicle. "Run, Sheila!"

Sheila blinked hard, her thoughts finally agreeing that flight was necessary. She pushed up with both hands and yelped as her ankle protested against her weight. Using her good leg, she stood up and limped to the edge of the street.

"Stay where you are!" a booming voice projected over the bullhorn mounted on the vehicle. The engine of the car roared to life.

Ignoring the warning, Sheila hobbled, her sights on the alleyway in front of her. *If we can make it there, maybe we can lose them in the darkness.* She willed her ankle to stay strong as she pressed forward. Lydia was already in the shadows, waving for her to hurry. She could hear the car nearing.

The corner neared. *I'm not going to make it.*

"Sheila, duck!" Lydia yelled. In her hand, she held a broken brick from the alley. She drew her arm back as Sheila lowered her head. The brick sailed over Sheila, and she could hear the crunch of glass behind her as it found its mark in the center of the Law-keeper's windshield. The spider-webbing glass obscured the driver's vision, and he overshot the alley. Sheila heard the squeal of tires as she ducked into the darkness.

The sound of a crash thudded behind her. She wasn't certain what the Law-keeper hit, but she hoped it would be enough to disable the vehicle. Lydia grabbed Sheila under her arm and half-dragged her through the alley. Shouts of cursing echoed as the Law-keeper leapt from the car.

The streetlights nearly blinded them as they shot out the other end of the alley. Throwing caution to the wind, they flew across the road in full view of anyone watching. Sheila didn't dare to glance around to see if any other patrols were nearing them as the Law-keeper had certainly radioed. Whether he was chasing them or not, they refused to waste the time to notice.

The next alley included a branch to the left and right, creating a private service drive for the buildings on either side. Lydia pulled her into the left branch to get out of the line of sight of the Law-keeper. They raced as best as their beaten bodies would allow.

Sirens wailed in the distance.

"Twelfth Street, right?" Lydia nodded, looking for agreement.

"Yes," Sheila said through gritted teeth. The pain in her ankle stabbed with each step, and she considered giving in to it. Before she could, Lydia turned at the next alley and yanked her toward the next street.

They emerged on a road lined with townhomes, old residences that'd once been trendy homes for people wanting to live near the hustle and bustle of the city. The years had taken their toll on these homes, and she guessed several were abandoned. Few had lights glowing from the windows.

"Here we are. Which house?" Lydia scanned the street.

"Third off plaza, on the right." Sheila spouted the rehearsed words, thankful she'd made a point to know them well. If she'd needed to stop to think, she wasn't sure she could remember in her current state.

The townhouse's brown brick sank into dim light of the night. The shutters, once black, were a drab gray or missing all-together. Lydia rested Sheila on the railing and flew up the front steps. She pounded on the door of the darkened home.

"Hello? Hello? We need help!" Lydia shouted. Sheila shot glances in either direction expecting the flashing lights of Law-keeper vehicles to appear at any moment. The wail of the sirens got louder with each second. "Hello? Somebody?"

Twelfth Street off Plaza. Third house on the right. Basement. Sheila remembered. *Basement!*

"Basement," she croaked, the pain almost unbearable.

Lydia turned to her, and a second passed before the word registered in her mind. She raced down the stairs and leapt the railing to the stairwell leading to the door under the porch. She resumed her pounding.

"Please, someone! We need—" Lydia resumed.

Sheila could hear the door fly open causing Lydia to cut off her sentence in surprise.

"Shhhh!" came a voice a second later. "Anyone with you?"

"Up on the street," Lydia whispered.

A man bounded up the stairs wearing a white button shirt tucked into a pair of faded jeans. His eyes widened with recognition when he saw Sheila. She glanced down at her ankle as if to ask him to notice her injury. He nodded in understanding.

Without hesitation, he approached and picked her up onto his shoulder fireman-style. Taking the stairs two at a time, he flew to the door. Sheila's head struck the doorframe as they entered, but she didn't care. The sirens sounded within a block or two, and she was thankful to be out of sight. She fell to the floor as the man set her down. The door slammed shut, and several locks clicked into place.

"Thank—" Lydia began.

"Shhhh!" the man interrupted again, holding a hand up to silence her in the dim light coming from the street. No lights were on in the room, but Sheila could see his outline. The sirens grew loud as the Law-keepers turned onto the street. The man peered through the edge of the basement window and watched as two Law-keeper vehicles sped by, their engines in full throttle. The flashing lights momentarily filled the room and then flickered as the cars passed.

The man let out a sigh of relief. He walked across the room.

Lydia and Sheila stared, not daring to speak. He pulled some books off a shelf and knocked on the back of the bookshelf. The muffled sounds of locks being thrown issued through the wall. To Sheila's amazement, the bookshelf swung on hidden hinges and light poured into the room.

"Help me with them," the man said to the new figure standing in the secret doorway. Sheila could tell from her outline it was a woman, her hair pulled back in a short spiky tuft of hair. She strode toward Lydia and helped her up.

The man approached Sheila, this time helping her up gently. Wrapping an arm around her back, he supported her through the door. She hopped instead of limping, not willing to place any weight on her ankle. Her foot flopped in the air radiating bolts of pain up her calf.

The room beyond the bookshelf was small, lit by a single bulb hanging from the ceiling. A table sat in the middle of the room. In the corner, a small sink sat next to a counter barely big enough to hold an electric hotplate. A pot boiled with something that filled the room with the savory smell of meat. A curtain shrouded the corner out of which the end of a small bed frame poked. Two small feet tangled in a blanket moved slightly as the occupant stirred while asleep.

At the end of the table, a woman sat with a young girl encouraging her to sip at the bowl of soup in front of her. The child ignored her mother's pleas and stared at the two visitors. The steam rising from the bowl made Sheila's stomach growl.

The man helped Sheila into one of the chairs at the table, which she grasped for balance to keep her foot still. Lydia sat down next to her and glanced from the man to the woman and back again. The man closed and locked the door. He rounded the table to stand next to the woman who had assisted him. The light illuminated his kind face, which smiled at them. The woman was beautiful, even though unkept, and she studied them with dark-brown eyes filled with worry.

"You sure about bringing them in here?" She nodded at the man while keeping her eyes on the newcomers.

"Yes, I am. I leave them out there pounding on our door, and the Law-keepers catch them. The next thing they do is investigate why they chose our door to pound on. Besides, did you notice who this is? They might be able to help you!" he said, a tinge of excitement in his voice.

"Or lead Law-keepers straight to us," the seated woman added.

Lydia straightened, and Sheila could tell she was ready to spring into action at the first sign of trouble. Sheila examined the situation. *These are families. They are more concerned about hiding than harming us.* Tact might be the best course.

"Thank you," she said, her voice raspy and dry. She swallowed to wet her throat. "Thank you for letting us in."

"You're welcome," the man responded. "I'm surprised you learned we were here. We've spent weeks observing, and the few neighbors on this street haven't even noticed us."

"How *did* you find us?" Her voice was soothing and low, but Sheila could hear an edge of anxiety that wasn't fully hidden.

"Ben sent us," Sheila said. Lydia shot her a glance, warning not to give too much information, but Sheila shook her head. "If they are who we hope they are, that's the one name to connect us."

"So that explains the prison scene," the man said, nodding to himself.

"Are you—?" Sheila began.

"My name is Scott," the man interrupted. He extended his hand across the table and shook hers.

Chapter Thirty-One

Sheila almost cried in relief at finding Scott. In that moment, she realized how much she'd doubted Ben's information, and she was thankful he'd been right. The relief spread to the rest of her body, allowing the pain of her injury to fully exert itself with the fading adrenaline in her veins. She winced as she adjusted in her seat.

"You're both hurt," Scott said calmly. "We need to talk, but will you let my wife examine your injuries?" Lydia gave the seated woman a doubtful scan before glancing at Sheila.

"I'm mostly a mother these days," the woman said, finally smiling, "but I was once a nurse." Her voice was soft and feminine. The child next to her stared at Lydia and Sheila expectantly awaiting their answer.

Lydia nodded.

"Yes, but her first. My ankle is wrecked, but I'm not sure there's much we can do for it," Sheila agreed.

"Not true. One second," the woman said. "By the way, I'm Janet, and this is Sandra. This little one with me is Hannah. My husband meant to introduce us, I assure you." She gave a playful smirk to Scott, who chuckled in embarrassment. Janet rose from the table and opened a small refrigerator. Grabbing the soup spoon off the table, she pried a chunk of frosted ice off the wall of the freezer compartment. Wrapping it in a towel, she approached Sheila.

"I'm Sheila, and this is Lydia," Sheila said.

Pulling a chair over, Janet cushioned it with a pillow. She gingerly lifted Sheila's leg, and Sheila let out a small cry as her foot moved. Janet placed her leg on the pillow and placed the towel gently across the already swollen ankle.

"Sorry to move you, but you need to keep this elevated. Keep that ice on for the next twenty minutes and try not to move," Janet instructed.

"Not going anywhere," Sheila said grateful for the cool sensation on her skin.

"Now for that arm." Janet pointed to Lydia.

Lydia raised her arm and allowed Janet to slowly remove the wrapping. Lydia sucked in through her teeth as she pulled back the bandage. Janet frowned as she examined the wound.

"Infected, I know," Lydia said.

Janet tisked. "How many days?"

"Three. Cut it in the prison."

Janet nodded and returned to the refrigerator. Retrieving a small vial, she uncapped a syringe and filled it from the vial. She wiped an alcohol pad on Lydia's upper arm. Holding up the syringe, she expelled the air and raised a brow to Lydia. Lydia nodded her silent permission, and Janet inserted the needle into Lydia's skin.

"You're fortunate you came to us," Janet said, disposing of the needle. "The infection is bad, but not beyond the reach of medicine, and I don't imagine walking into a hospital is an option for either of you."

"Thank you," Lydia said, holding a bandage where the needle had been.

"Are we good?" Scott tapped a foot impatiently.

"I still need to clean that wound, but yes, we can talk," Janet replied.

"How long has it been since you've had anything to eat?" Sandra's voice sounded less anxious and more kind than it had been.

"Anything real?" Sheila questioned. "Ages."

"Then we eat while we talk. There's enough."

Within minutes, everyone sat at the table, a small bowl of soup in their hands. Sheila had almost cried at the first sip. It was a simple broth with a few pieces of meat and potatoes thrown in, but it was the best thing she'd eaten in days. The soup sent a warm sensation through her body, and she momentarily forgot about her pain and worry.

"Well, I guess we start with the biggest question," Scott dabbed the corner of his mouth with a cloth napkin. "If the news is to be believed, you're no friend of the Coalition. But—you've gone to a lot of trouble to find us. Blew up a prison even. Lost one of your own." Sheila glanced down at the mention of Jez. "You found Ben and came running to us. The biggest question is this— why would anyone besides Law-keepers want to find this little ragtag group so badly?"

Lydia waved a hand at Sheila as if to say, "You're the better one with words, so have at it." Sheila set her nearly drained bowl down and took in a deep breath. She scanned the table and saw nothing but kindness on their faces.

She started with Willis's departure from the recoding center. Heads nodded as she rehearsed his short time on the street and faces darkened as she mentioned Ben's betrayal. Sandra shook her head in disgust as she described Willis's treatment by the Coalition and escape with Jez's help, the first experiment with Project Rebirth. She then explained how Willis had shared his information with Lydia, the information heist at the Law-keeper outpost, and their daring infiltration into the prison. Scott lowered his head into his hands as she recounted Ben's condition and words.

After a moment he raised his head. "Ben never meant harm. He loved his family and wished to protect them. But—he's right. They are probably gone."

Sheila described the explosion and choked again on a sob as she talked about Jez. Their flight from the Law-keepers finished the story.

"And that's how we ended up on the receiving end of your kindness," Sheila finished.

The three glanced at each other. Janet leaned forward and raised a finger. "What I don't understand," she said, "is why the three, now two, of you would come searching for Sandra. Why is Kane not with you? Why would you leave without telling him?"

Sheila glanced over at Lydia whose face blanched with dread. Clearly, she hadn't been ready for this subject to come up with Sandra so soon. She glanced at Sheila who angled her head back at Lydia. *It's your news to share,* Sheila said silently. Lydia licked her lips and breathed in to speak.

"It's because," Sandra spoke first, gazing at Lydia, "you two are close."

The words filled the room with a palpable tension, and the lone noise was the creak of a chair as Scott leaned back from the table. Lydia's eyes filled with tears, and her lips trembled. She glanced again at Sheila who clenched her eyebrows to communicate her concern for her friend.

"I—" Lydia's voice shook. "I don't know what to say."

Sandra's mouth turned up at the corners slightly, and her head tilted in a compassionate gesture. "Honey, it's okay. Both you and Kane believed me dead. And when you realized I was not, you came for me."

Lydia sat in stunned silence.

"All that tells me is that the man I love has thankfully not been alone. He's found the ability to love again, and that makes me glad. And—he's found it with someone who loves him enough to risk even her life to restore his family. That tells me everything I need to know about who you are."

Tears escaped Lydia's eyes, which she quickly brushed away. She looked down in embarrassment and folded her arms across her middle, careful not to crush her wound. Her breaths came in shaky stutters. Sheila needed to speak for her friend.

"As you can imagine, the news about you was hard for my friend to take in," Sheila said, gesturing to Lydia.

"You mean the fact that my husband, who couldn't express his emotions to save his life, has found himself in love with and loved by two women? Do you mean that little nugget?" A smirk spread slowly on Sandra's face. "I can't wait to see the confused frown on his face when he sees the two of us side by side. We should charge admission because it's going to be entertaining."

Sheila studied Sandra for a few moments. When she noticed Scott biting his lip with a smile, it occurred to her that Sandra meant the whole thing as humorous. A single laugh burst involuntarily from Sheila's mouth, and she glanced at Lydia in surprise. Lydia stared in shock and glanced over to Sandra to see her reaction. Sandra sat with her hand over her lips unable to hide her silent laugh. Slowly, the quiet laughter spread through the room until Sheila could no longer help herself. A laugh, hearty and loud, burst from her lungs, and the room joined her. The tension drained from the room, and the long fit ended with a collective sigh, a couple people wiping tears from the bottom of their eyes.

"I—I thought you would hate me," Lydia said.

Sandra smiled softly. "How could I hate you for loving my husband so selflessly?"

"I don't know," Lydia admitted. "I thought—" Her voice faded.

"Well, I don't know what this means for any of us, but I do know we'll get nowhere if you and I spend our time threatened by each other."

"No, I don't suppose we would."

Sheila couldn't believe what she was seeing at the table. Two women, who could otherwise see each other as rivals, connected through their shared love of the same person. Both were showing their worth, and Sandra was right. *Kane is going to have a mess on his hands.* That didn't stop Sheila from guessing that both women were also hurting inside.

"Mommy?" a tiny voice peeped from the corner.

At the edge of the curtain, a small boy peered from the end of the bed, rubbing his eyes with the back of one hand. Sheila guessed he was around four years old. Their laughing had apparently woken him, and he squinted curiously at the strangers at the table.

"Come to mama, honey," Sandra said, extending her arms.

The boy slid nervously out of the bed and moved quickly to his mother. She picked him up and placed him in her lap. He buried his face into her chest, peering around the room with one eye while chewing on the tip of one out-stretched finger.

"This, here, is Nathaniel," Sandra said. "He's Kane's little boy." She smiled down at her son. "Nathaniel, meet Ms. Sheila and Ms. Lydia. Remember how we've been searching for your daddy?"

The boy nodded sheepishly.

"Well, these nice ladies know where he is. Isn't it nice they came to find us?"

The boy pulled away and gazed up at Sandra. "So, we'll get to meet Daddy soon?"

"Soon. Can you say 'hello' first?"

Nathaniel pulled the finger from his mouth and curled his hand open and closed in a childish wave. Sheila waved back at him as did Lydia, but Sheila could read the confusion raging inside her friend. The women might be getting along, but things were no less complicated.

Lydia reached out a hand across the table. She opened her fingers slowly and turned her hand. "Hi, Nathaniel. It's nice to meet you," she said in a soft, shaky voice. Nathaniel reached out and grasped Lydia's finger in his fist, and the two shared a mismatched handshake.

Yes, this is definitely still very complicated.

Chapter Thirty-Two

Willis's arms shook, unused to the strain of holding his bodyweight off the ground. It'd been a week since he'd started training again, and his muscles ached from the prior day's work out. Rung by rung, he hoisted himself up the ladder. At the top, his teammates were waiting. They reached down and grabbed his arms to help him finish. Once on the platform, he turned his back to the wall and took a moment to breathe.

"So, what now?" The teenage girl in front of him sounded out of breath.

He studied the small group that Perryn had given him to lead. They were all young and inexperienced. All of them had been raised hearing stories about Willis Thomson, the next great Chase runner, and rumors of his experience with the Coalition had nearly made him a legend among the trainees. At least, that's what Perryn had assured him.

This is her way of showing me I can still lead. Perryn's intentions had been obvious, giving him this group, but he appreciated it. He didn't need to win their respect, something which his breathlessness after a ladder climb wouldn't have helped, he only needed to keep it. That meant winning the exercise.

"I'm confident Team A is hiding behind the wall over there," Willis said gesturing with one finger across the gym. "Team C is on the other side, either behind the pile of boxes or under the stairwell."

From their perch above the gym, they could see the entire room, including the flags in the middle atop a pyramid of boxes. One, labeled with a 'B,' was their objective. They had to retrieve their flag and return it to their corner to win the game.

Phoot!

A dart whizzed by Willis's head, striking harmlessly against the concrete wall. He crouched further from the edge of the platform to get out of view. It'd been Perryn's idea to use empty darts to simulate reality as close as possible.

"Someone on Team A thinks they have pretty good aim," a twenty-year-old male said.

"They do," Willis affirmed, choosing honesty over bravado. "That almost got me." He chided himself silently for making a dumb mistake. The tremble returned to his hands, and he clasped them together to hide it. "Okay, both of the other teams have taken up defensive positions. Exercises like this usually amount to all sides waiting the others out until everyone gets impatient and charges. That's why we're up here. We're going to do this differently."

"Taking it to them?" the first girl suggested.

"Exactly." Something inside Willis fluttered, and he started to feel some of what he used to on the station. He almost smiled.

Don't get cocky. You'll let them down in the end. His smile disappeared, and he shook his head to focus. *These are simply games. Relax.*

He scanned the group again. They all eagerly awaited his orders, staring through clear eye protection goggles. "Ryan and Michelle, you two use the rope to your right to get behind the barriers in the near corner. That'll let you begin making your way across the side of the room to flank Team A. Keep them occupied."

The two trainees who had spoken earlier both nodded.

Willis turned to three teenagers to his left. "You three. Steve, Nikki, and—" He snapped his fingers in frustration, unable to remember the third girl's name.

"Jolene," she reminded, smiling shyly.

"Yes, Jolene. Sorry. You guys use this platform to make your way over there." He pointed down the length of the wall. "Flank Team C, and like the others, keep them occupied."

They nodded.

"What about me?" came a quiet voice.

Willis examined the girl in front of him. She was sixteen, and barely old enough to go on missions for the Underground. She'd surprisingly volunteered for the training when Perryn had issued the announcement. Willis sized her up. She knelt with her shoulders slumped. She nervously fingered the dart gun in her hand, which appeared awkward and out of place in her grasp. For a moment, Willis was taken back to an image of Perryn sitting by herself in the recreation center of the space station, fingering her newly awarded leadership armband. The girl's eyes darted left and right as if measuring what the others were thinking. She radiated insecurity.

"Bekah," he started. Her eyes locked with his, full of worry. "You're with me."

"To do what?"

"We're going after our flag."

Her eyes grew wide, and she once again glanced at the others. "I—I'm not very fast. You sure I'm the right person? I don't want to lose this for everyone."

Another flash, and Willis was reminded of the Lake Placid Training Center years earlier. He'd talked with countless trainees for the Chase who were like Bekah. Young, inexperienced, and completely unsure of themselves, he'd delivered more than a few pep-talks to get them motivated.

"Bekah, you can do this," he said. He reached out and placed a hand on hers, lowering the dart gun. "Don't worry about that thing. You stay focused on getting that flag, and let these guys do the shooting. I—need—you to have my back out there. Can you do that?"

She studied his face, searching for confidence. Willis tried to conjure up some and found the well to be dry. He did his best to offer her his 'we've got this' expression. She smiled shyly and nodded.

"Okay. On three."

Willis slowly raised one finger. Then two. As he raised the

third, Ryan hooked his climbing belt to the rope and launched from the platform. The whirr of his carabiner on the rope as he zipped across the room was interrupted by the metallic tinging of darts missing him and striking the wall. Michelle leapt a moment later. They landed behind a stack of water barrels and yelled together.

Team A fired in their direction, drawing the eyes of Team C.

Willis waved his hand, and the three teenagers began their army crawl along the platform, staying out of sight. At the end of the ledge, they turned their bodies, barely exposing their heads and arms. They started firing, and soon shouts from Team C rose as darts found their marks eliminating trainees, who yelped from the pain and exited the floor with hands raised.

Willis smiled at Bekah, who shook with apprehension. "You ready?"

She stared at him, her forehead full of worry lines. She shook her head and then nodded a moment later. He grabbed her arm and gently pulled her to the ladder behind the pillar underneath them. Pressing the insides of his feet against the side of the ladder, he controlled his descent as he slid down to the floor. A moment later, Bekah hit the floor harder than she expected. She fell backward and scrambled forward to hide behind the pillar.

"Sorry," she whispered.

"It's okay." He tried to give her a reassuring smile.

He peered around the edge to see if anyone had noticed their maneuver. All signs pointed to everyone being preoccupied with their teammates. A shout from above signaled that Nikki had been hit and was exiting the game.

"We've got to go before they pick off our team. Stay low and try to make it to the base of the pyramid." The floor was littered with smaller objects, which could serve as obstacles or cover depending upon the situation. Once again, he counted off three fingers.

Darting around the right side of the pillar, he ran in a crouch. Silently stepping around the objects, he dove to the bottom of the pyramid. The sound of dart guns firing filled the room. He turned over and found himself alone.

Glancing back, he saw her. Bekah knelt huddled behind a large overturned chair halfway to his position. Her hands shook as she grasped her dart gun, and her face wore a wide-eyed expression. He waved at her to continue, but she shook her head. The chaos of the room clearly overwhelmed her, and she seemed paralyzed by fear. The darts weren't deadly, but even he didn't like the idea getting stuck with one, much less several. He waved again, and again she refused.

He grunted in frustration and turned to face the pyramid. Slowly, he climbed the boxes, willing his body to blend in with their surface. Reaching the third level, he extended his hand and slowly pulled upward with two fingers to lift his team's flag from its holder. He held his breath as the tiny motion of the flag was a dead giveaway to his presence. Seconds later, he breathed in relief as the base of the flag released from the base. He loosened his grip, letting the pole slide through his fingers so he could grab the middle of it.

Another shout, and he could tell that Ryan had been hit.

Extending his right leg, he slid backward. With luck, his escape would be unnoticed, and he would win before anyone realized the flag was gone. Reaching with his toes, he searched blindly for a foothold. He found the bare edge. A moment later, his body jolted as his weight pushed his toes off the edge. He caught himself with his hands, cringing as the flagpole struck the large metal crates, sending a hollow clang through the room.

"Hey, Thomson's on the pyramid!" someone shouted. The shouts spread, and he could feel the attention of the room turn in his direction.

Leaping from the pyramid, he hit the ground in a roll. His one hope was to dash to the corner which displayed a large 'B' painted on the wall. A dart flew by, and he could hear it hit the ground next to him. He sprang, ready to run. One step. Two steps.

He winced at the fire of a dart piercing his shoulder. A second later, another found his calf. He let out a shout and raised his hands.

"I got him!" a voice yelled.

"Me, too!" came another.

Chaos erupted in the room as the teams emerged from their hiding places. Desperation played into tactics as teams succumbed to the urgency of getting their flags. Willis dropped the flag where he stood and made his way toward the wall designated for those eliminated. Two more shouts, confirming that Jolene and Michelle were both out.

Of course. I messed it up for all of us. Let's see if they trust my leadership after this.

He reached the wall and turned to take in the scene. Team A and C were shooting frantically as they emerged from their corners. A couple made dashes toward the pyramid, only to pull up and raise their arms in surrender. Their faces winced at the pain of the darts. Few members of each team were left, and a final run for the flags would finish the exercise.

In unison, the three remaining members of Team C shouted and ran toward the pyramid, firing their dart pistols. Team A stood and returned fire, inching forward.

Here it comes, Willis said to himself. He crossed his arms, annoyed at his failure.

A member of Team C leapt up the pyramid, grabbed his flag, and jumped all the way to the floor. He ran for the corner. Eliminated Team A members shouted in desperation at their teammates. Miraculously, none of the darts found their mark.

Buzz!

The boy stopped where he stood, halfway to his corner. Players lowered their weapons and glanced around confused as to why the game had been ended. The boy raised his arms in exasperation and waited for an answer.

Doors opened on the side of a clear plastic observation box. Perryn emerged, with two other officers at her side. Willis couldn't help but smile as she strode confidently to the middle of the room, her captain's bars on her collar glinting in the fluorescent light.

"Captain, what's up?" The boy threw up his hands again, obviously annoyed.

"Yeah, we were about to win," a girl added.

"Captain, why did you end the game?" a third inquired.

"You didn't win," Perryn said flatly.

"What do you mean? Who did?" The first boy twirled, searching for a winner.

"She did." Perryn pointed to the far corner.

Willis followed her gesture to the corner. The rest of the room did the same. There, standing next to the large 'B' painted on the wall and appearing timid with all the new attention, stood Bekah. She stared downward, hiding her face behind her brown hair, not wanting to meet anyone's gaze. In her hand, she held the flag Willis had dropped.

Chapter Thirty-Three

Willis watched his teammates congratulate Bekah, something which had happened several times in the last few minutes. It wasn't until the other teams had left, cursing their loss under their breath, that Bekah had come out from behind her hair to reveal her smile that spread from one ear to the other. His team had been quick to surround her. Willis got the impression that they weren't used to winning the training games.

"Bekah takes the game for B Team!" Ryan laughed, clapping her on the shoulder.

"Stop it, Ryan," she retorted, her face blushing from his touch. "The whole team made this happen."

"Yeah, except you were the one out in the open with everyone going crazy at the end," Jolene added. "You're lucky you don't look like a pin cushion with all those darts flying around."

"B Team for the win, I guess!" Bekah said, laughing with her teammates.

Willis walked up to them, arms loosely crossed. They silenced at his approach, yet they were unable to hide their excitement. Nikki bounced in place. Steve wrung his hands as if he could barely contain himself and would take off running at any moment. Willis allowed himself a small chuckle, noticing the absence of the tremor in his own hands.

"B Team? Is that what we're going to call ourselves moving forward?" He raised an eyebrow.

"Yeah. You know, as in the team no one would pick." Ryan smirked.

"Or lose to," Jolene giggled. The group laughed together.

"Okay," Willis said. It was not a bad name for this group of misfits. "B Team it is. Workout will be later today. Take a couple hours off to enjoy yourselves, but then we get back to work. Chief wants us ready. Mission could begin at any moment."

The mention of the upcoming mission washed somber frowns across their faces. Willis hated to do it, but they needed to know this was more than a game. Even at that moment, plans were being drawn up to stop the Coalition before the upcoming Chase. Intelligence needed to figure out how and when the neuro-booster would be released on the population. Then, these young recruits would see real action. Enemy darts would be replaced with bullets. Games would become reality. Elimination would mean capture or worse.

"Yes, Willis," came the collective response of the group. They dispersed, still trying to maintain some of excitement as they whispered to each other. Bekah held back for a moment, waiting for Willis.

He smiled at her. "Something up, Bekah?"

"Why did you pick me?" She gave him a puzzled, yet hopeful gaze.

"What do you mean?"

"I'm not the fastest. Definitely not the most athletic. And—I wouldn't even say I'm the smartest on the team. So, why was I the one you picked to go after the flag?"

Willis carefully considered his answer. He remembered having these kinds of conversations with Chase trainees over the years, and he understood his next words could do a lot of good— or damage.

"Bekah," he started, pausing to look her in the eye, "you need to see yourself the way everyone else does." She retreated behind her hair again, unable to take the compliment. "I'm serious. When I picked you, you were the only one in the group that doubted you could do it."

"But—I hid, scared. I didn't follow you to the flag."

"No, you didn't, and good thing. You probably would have been shot right off as I was."

"It's embarrassing. Everyone saw me hide."

"But—you didn't give up. You remind me of our new Captain."

At this, Bekah's eyes widened, and she pulled one side of her hair backward. "The Captain?" She glanced toward the direction of the offices. "I could never be like her." Willis could tell that her awe of Chase runners extended to Perryn as well. He gave a sideways smile as he thought of Perryn.

"Yeah. She'd be the first to admit she wasn't the fastest or bravest on the station, and yet she's who she is today because she didn't give up—ever."

Willis couldn't be certain, but he swore he could see the corners of her mouth turn upward. She searched the floor with her eyes and nodded. He placed a hand on her shoulder, and she tensed under his touch. She blushed again.

"Thanks, Willis. I—I won't give up."

"See that you don't," he ordered, a large smile on his face. "You might want to join the others. I'm guessing they're getting some lunch, and the celebration isn't yet over. Don't want to miss that."

"No. Yeah. Okay." She turned to leave, trying not to appear like she was hurrying to catch up with others.

Willis scanned the room, strangely quiet. For a moment, he was transported to the station. He could hear the quiet sounds of the recreation room, which nearly always had a team scheming in at least one corner. He could smell the sterile, recycled air. He could feel the familiar snugness of a training uniform on his skin.

But how long until I fail them? What happens when this is real? Half the team was eliminated today. Tomorrow, that could mean more than a dart in their skin. That reality deflated him, and his shoulders slumped. He'd allowed himself to believe that he was the great Willis Thomson again, fearless and unquestioned leader, but he recognized the truth. *Everyone gets hurt in the end.*

He turned to leave when he noticed the figure standing against the wall by the doorway. Her brown hair was braided, and her eyes stared at him as if reading his thoughts. The gold Captain's bars stood stark against the black uniform she wore. Perryn had watched the entire encounter, waiting for Willis to notice she was there. The moment he did, she pushed away from the wall and walked toward him.

"Still got it, I see," she said.

"Guess I'm the leader of B Team, huh?" He laughed.

"I know they don't question it. I don't either." She searched his face, her eyes adding, *but I know you do.*

"Yeah. Well, I'm not so sure," he admitted. "They're a good group. They've got everything they need to become great."

"They need a leader who believes he can get it out of them," she interrupted. "Sounds a lot like a Blue Team I once knew on the station."

"That was different." He glanced away in frustration. She was trying to encourage him, but he wasn't sure he wanted to hear it.

"Willis," she said, taking his hand, "you're still the same man you've always been. The same leader who built the best Chase team in recent memory. The same one who stood up to Creed and his nearly-psycho control over his team. The same person who saw a broken Blue Team leader and made her believe she had what it took to lead."

"Until he got her hurt." The words were more honest than he intended, but he couldn't lie to her.

"Willis Thomson, you aren't solely responsible for the pain I've experienced. I won't let you take credit for choices that I made, either entirely or in part. I was there, too, if you remember. I didn't exactly try to stop you from bringing Jez out of Solution Systems."

"But—" Willis protested. She silenced him with a finger on his lips.

"No. Don't say it anymore. B Team? Sounds a lot like Blue Team. I think history is about to repeat itself."

Willis shook his head. His insides raged against the idea, but he couldn't be mad at her. She was saying what he would have said in her place. He changed the subject.

"Speaking of Blue Team, where is Jaden? I've barely seen him."

Her face darkened at the mention of Jaden's name. She glanced away as if searching for him. "Ever since word got out about the neuro-booster," she began, "Jaden's been obsessed with the idea. He's basically locked himself in one of the intelligence offices and hardly comes out to eat or sleep."

"What's he doing in there?"

"All he would say is that it's all connected."

"Connected?"

"Slaves. The Coalition. The Chase. The neuro-booster. All of it."

"Think he's on to something?"

"I don't know, but I do think he'd be more likely to talk to you than anyone. His mother put her hopes in you, remember? Jaden's never forgotten that."

"Then let's go. Kane's going to launch this mission any day. If Jaden thinks he's figured something out, we need to know what it is."

"Shower first. You smell. But yes, then we talk to him."

Chapter Thirty-Four

The knock on Jaden's door echoed in the hallway. Willis stood next to Perryn and searched her expression. A deep crease of worry was etched between her eyebrows. In many ways, Willis was aware that Jaden filled a hole in Perryn's life. He wasn't family, but they treated each other like a brother and sister. Their bond was never romantic, but the aversity on the station had welded them together permanently. Willis found himself amazed that she'd held herself together so well after the station was destroyed, and they believed Jaden had died.

He knocked again. Still, no answer came.

"Do you think he stepped out?" Willis gave her a doubtful glance.

She shook her head.

Willis tried the handle, and it turned with ease. Slowly, he cracked the door to peer inside. The stale air greeted him, causing him to wrinkle his nose. The dim light inside was nothing more than a thick blackness with their eyes accustomed to the florescent hallways.

"Jaden?" he whispered. He shook his head, wondering why he was whispering. "Jaden?" He raised his voice this time.

"Willis? That you?" Jaden's voice croaked from inside.

Willis pushed the door open further and stepped inside. Perryn joined him, and they took a moment to adjust to the darkness—and the smell. Willis had never seen Jaden like this. His hair stood out in several directions as if he'd run his hands through it in frustration more than a few times. His clothes were rumpled and unwashed, and he sat in a chair staring away from them. Plates and cups, used and unwashed, sat around the room. Each were covered in partial leftovers of unfinished meals, and Willis could identify a least one of them as the meal served a week ago.

The wall in front of them appeared like something out of a crime novel. Pieces of paper were pinned to the wall, covered in Jaden's notes. Here and there, papers were connected to each other with string. In some places, smaller notes with a question mark, covered documents. For a moment, Willis questioned Jaden's sanity.

"Jaden, what's all this?" Willis spoke after scanning the room for a long second.

"I'm close." He tapped his chin with a pen.

"To what?"

"The answer."

Willis glanced at Perryn for a clue as to how to proceed. She nodded in Jaden's direction, silently telling him to keep talking. She then pointed at herself and shook her head as if to say, *I've tried already.* In the center of the web of madness on the wall was a picture of Jaden's mother. Willis stepped over to the photo.

"This about your mom?"

"Yes. No. She's giving me the answers."

Willis raised his eyebrows. "Answers?"

Jaden took his eyes away from his notes and gazed at Willis. "Something about this neuro-booster you described has me thinking about my mom. When I went back to the station, she told me about how she was able to start sneaking out to find me."

"How?"

"She stopped eating."

"Eating?"

"She noticed that most problems between slaves and guards happened at night, hours after they'd last eaten. She never trusted the food they gave her and guessed that the Alliance was putting something in their food that was keeping them compliant. At night, the effects would begin to wear off, and some of the slaves would become difficult for the guards."

"So, she stopped eating to stop ingesting whatever this was?" This time, it was Perryn asking.

"Yes." Jaden addressed both of them. "It wasn't long after that you two met her. Her head was clear again, and she was able to think for herself."

"And you think the Alliance was using the same neuro-booster on the station slaves?" Willis pointed at the picture.

"Perhaps an earlier form of it. Injections would have been too obvious and might have generated resistance from the slaves."

"I guess that could be, but I don't see how it helps us."

"I feel like the answer is right there." Jaden pointed at the air as if the clue was hanging right in front of him. "Something that'll help us is right at the edge of my brain. I can't seem to grab it."

Willis chewed on his lip. "Wait. You said the effects wore off each day?"

Jaden nodded. "Every night."

"That's how it was for Jez. Without continual injections, she was able to rebel against her programming. In fact, they had to inject her with greater frequency to keep her under control. Eventually, it would have been every day."

Jaden nodded again.

"And yet," Willis continued, "I noticed at Solution Systems that some effects of the neuro-booster take more permanent hold on the person." He glanced at Perryn whose forehead wrinkled with understanding concern. He gave her a slight nod that communicated he wasn't ready for Jaden to know he was talking about himself. She grabbed his trembling hand, letting him know she understood. "What's the difference?"

Jaden ran his fingers across the stubble of his chin thoughtfully. He stared at the picture of his mother for several long breaths. Closing his eyes, he rubbed the bridge of his nose with two fingers. Suddenly, he shot up in his chair.

"That's it!" he exclaimed. Willis and Perryn started with surprise at his outburst.

"What's it?" Perryn's eyes darted from Jaden to Willis and back.

"It has to do with the suggestion."

173

"The suggestion?" Willis furrowed his brow.

"Yeah. Were those in this more permanent state told things that were true or that they believed to be true?" Jaden stared hopefully at Willis.

Willis glanced at Perryn. Something inside him sank. Deep down, the doubt he was experiencing had always been there. He'd been an expert at shoving it inside. The neuro-booster and Dr. Campbell's questioning had simply brought his fear to the surface.

"I—I think so." He couldn't make out where Jaden was going.

"That must be it, then!" Jaden was standing.

"Jaden, you're not making sense," Perryn said.

"Think about it. Slavery goes against who we are. We're not meant to live in oppression. Our minds crave independent thought." He paused to see if they were tracking with him. Their puzzled expressions must have frustrated him because he sat down right in front of them and leaned toward them. "Jez was no different. The last thing she ever desired was to be controlled by another person. She was a survivor who had always operated on what served *her* best, but the Coalition made her *their* pawn. It went against everything she was."

Willis noted that the word 'was' still chafed on all of them. He nodded, sensing that at any moment, the pieces would come together.

"Don't you see?" Jaden continued. "If the suggestion is counter to the natural instincts of the individual, the neuro-booster must be kept in their system to keep the person in line. If the suggestion rings true with what the person already believes, it doesn't require continual dosages to maintain potency."

Perryn stood abruptly. "That means—"

Jaden nodded and stood with her. "We're searching in the wrong place!"

Willis joined them, but he was still confused. "Explain."

"We've been watching the skies trying to figure out how the Coalition would release a gas over the entire population before the Chase. We believed if we could stop the release, we could prevent the Coalition's plans to control the world with a powerful suggestion. But—if the effects are so short lived, they'd have to release it daily to keep the suggestion in place."

"That would be impossible to hide if it was through gas," Perryn deduced.

"Exactly. So, where do you put a neuro-booster that's centrally located, easy to hide, and deliverable to most of the population daily?"

Willis scanned around the room. He couldn't believe the mess, but his attention focused on the glass near Jaden's chair. "Water," he said. "Everyone drinks water daily."

The three of them stopped and stared at each other.

"And who developed the treatment process used on most world's fresh water since the World Coalition declared most of the world's water unsafe decades ago?" Jaden bounced as he waited for them to answer.

"The Western Alliance did," Willis whispered. "We can't stop the release of the neuro-booster."

"Most of the world has already been drinking it every day," Perryn finished.

Chapter Thirty-Five

Kane's door was shut when Willis, Perryn, and Jaden arrived at his office. Sprinting through the hallways, Willis had knocked over at least two people in their hurry to share their discovery. He and Perryn both pounded on the door to get Kane's attention.

"Kane, open up!" Willis yelled. "We figured it out!"

A long moment passed, and they heard the lock on the door click. The handle turned slowly. Kane appeared, his expression switching from annoyed to surprised. Willis took a moment to realize how they must have appeared. The three of them were huddled by the door, out of breath. Jaden still smelled like a forgotten hermit, unshaven and dirty. Kane examined them once more before stepping backward to let them in.

"Captain. Boss. Jaden." Kane nodded to each of them as they gathered, and he closed the door cutting off the curious onlookers in the hallway. "What's this about?"

"Sorry," Willis said breathlessly. He leaned forward with his hands on his knees to catch his breath. "We know what the Coalition is doing. We think we've figured out their plan."

Kane's eyebrows rose, and he held up a finger to encourage Willis to wait. Picking up a radio he called for Chris and Maria. A minute later, both entered.

"Proceed," Kane commanded after explaining to Chris and Maria.

Their explanation was rushed, and Kane had to stop them more than once to ask questions. Maria smacked her gum in disbelief at their plan until Perryn assured her it made sense. Chris's eyes searched the ceiling as he mentally assembled the information.

"So, you're saying everyone's been drinking the stuff around the world, and they'll believe whatever they're told?" Maria couldn't hide the doubt in her voice.

"No." Willis shook his head. "It doesn't work that way. The suggestion needs to have a ring of truth to it. The wording is very important and needs to be paired with a heightened state of emotion, like when you feel threatened. Every day occurrences would be unlikely."

"And the Chairman is a master wordsmith," Perryn added. "He will be able to say the right thing. He'll be able to make people feel threatened without making it sound like he's the one threatening them."

Chris stood and paced. "I don't understand. Why wait for the Chase then? Why doesn't the Chairman get on television and issue his command to the world?"

"I've two thoughts about that," Jaden said. "First, I think it's possible the amount in everyone's system isn't high enough. Kind of like lead poisoning. It takes time for enough to get in your body for any real effects." He paused to make sure everyone was nodding and following him. "That's simply a hunch. The second I'm almost sure about, and that's the fact that the Chairman can't count on enough people to be watching by coming on at any other time. The Chase will be an event when almost the whole world will be watching. Emotions will already be heightened as people hope and pray their runners will perform well and make their lives easier. The Chairman will have the whole world as a captive audience."

"And then he'll have the whole world as captives," Willis agreed.

"Great," Maria said, crossing her arms. "So, we're doomed. It's not like we can stop drinking water. We're going to hear the Chairman, too, if we try to do anything."

"Not so," Kane interrupted. "Chris, how full are the rain barrels on the roof?"

Chris counted on his fingers. "They were nearly full

yesterday, and the weather is calling for more rain. Are you thinking—?"

"Yes," Kane responded before he could finish. "We'll begin immediately rationing water strictly from our rain collection. No one drinks another drop from the city supply until after the Chase."

"Will that be enough?" Willis noticed the room shifted. Apparently, everyone was thinking the same thing.

"Barely." Chris nodded. "Enough to get to the Chase anyway."

"So that means—?" Perryn started.

"We're going to finally see some action," Maria finished. "It's about time if you ask me."

"Captain," Kane pointed as he spoke, "are your teams ready?"

"They will be," Perryn said. "Another couple of weeks, and we'll have them ready to go. They'll still be rather green, though, having not been in the field. But—we've got some new squad leaders who show some promise." She winked at Willis.

"Good. Make it happen," Kane began. "Chris, I want all the surveillance we have on the Chase stadium. Captain, Willis, and Maria will join me after training to draw up plans. We can't allow the Coalition to gain control over the world. And Jaden?"

"Yeah, Chief?" Jaden raised his brow.

Kane wrinkled his nose and looked him up and down.

Jaden tilted his head to take a sniff near his armpit. "Right. I'll hit the shower."

Chapter Thirty-Six

Sheila hobbled over to the refrigerator. Three weeks had passed since finding the hideout, and she was beginning to feel like a drain on Scott, Janet, and Sandra. Lydia was at least able to be helpful with supply runs as her arm had been mostly healed after a few days of medicine. Sheila, however, felt like all she did was lay around with her foot up. It was only in the last few days that she had any confidence in her mobility to start moving around without fear. Tonight, she would make dinner. It was a small thing, but at least she would feel like she was contributing.

"When do you think they'll be back?" she whispered.

Sandra sat in the corner, rocking her son in her arms and singing softly as he slept. Hannah was asleep in the next room that Scott and Janet used. Sandra paused and tilted her head. "I think it'll be soon," she said. "Scott doesn't like to be out for more than an hour at a time, and he'll be extra careful to get back with Janet and Lydia with him. Supply runs are routine. Scott has a man he trusts to get them what they need."

Sheila was pulling out different vegetables and sniffing them for freshness. "I'm not much of a cook, to be honest, but my grandma did teach me a couple of her recipes before she passed."

"I'm sure Janet will appreciate the break, but you should be careful on that ankle, honey."

"I'll be fine. I can't feel useless anymore. It's not my style."

"Well, let me put Nathaniel down, and I'll lend you a hand."

"Seriously, I've got this. You quite literally have your hands full. I'd hate to wake him up."

"This young man? He'll sleep through anything. Been raised on the streets mostly."

Sheila stopped and turned to Sandra, giving her a concerned smile. Sandra met her with eyes that betrayed strength and courage. "I'm sorry things went the way they did for you. In another life, you and Kane would have been raising Nathaniel and living a normal life."

"Normal and ignorant. This life has let me see what the world is like, and I want to pass that on to my little one here. He has the chance to grow up truly free. If that happens, then all this will have been worth it."

She shouldn't pry, but the reporter in her had to ask. "I have to say, it has been pretty remarkable that you and Lydia have gotten along so well."

Sandra smiled. "So, it finally comes. I've been waiting for the 'best friend' talk from you."

"That's not what this is—I mean—I get why you might think that. Lydia is my friend, but so is Kane. I want what's best for both. And—for you."

"You're sweet for saying that. We've found ourselves in a rather awkward situation, but I can't hate Lydia. She's a woman who fell in love with an honorable man. I can't blame her for that."

"She's honorable, too. You need to know she's not going to stand in your way when you're reunited with Kane. She'll do it for him—and you—and especially for Nathaniel."

Sandra glanced down at the sleeping boy. "He's going to have a father again. I must admit, that makes me more than happy. But—" Her smiled disappeared. "I hate that a strong and giving woman is going to be left broken-hearted."

"Well, that's why she has me. She won't be alone." Sheila smiled and turned back to the food. She could feel Sandra studying her from behind.

"And where did you learn to become such a selfless person, Ms. Sheila Kemp? People like you are rare."

"My sister taught me."

"She sounds pretty special."

"She was." Sheila's voice caught on the word 'was,' and she took several deep breaths to calm herself.

"I'm sorry. How did she die?"

"She'd been sick all of her life. It's the Coalition that made sure it happened last year."

A long moment passed between them in silence. Sheila didn't want to talk about her sister to Sandra. Sandra had experienced loss, but her loss was going to be restored. *Mine never will.* That's when she felt the hand on her shoulder. She glanced up and saw Sandra's face. Tears fell from the corners of both eyes. She pulled Sheila into an embrace. Sheila resisted, her body stiffening. Then the tears came. Her body relaxed, and she let the months of grief that'd been stuffed away flow freely. Sandra said nothing but held her new friend for several minutes.

Knock. Knock. Knock, knock, knock.

They both started at the sound at the door until it registered that the frantic knock matched the code they'd arranged. Sandra wiped her eyes and walked toward the door. As she worked her way through the numerous locks, Sheila took several breaths to calm herself. She wasn't interested in questions.

The last lock clicked, and the door flew open. Lydia burst in, her arms around a hunched Janet. Janet's arms clutched her stomach, and Sheila could see the blood soaking between her fingers. Sheila grabbed the edge of the table and tilted it, causing the contents from the refrigerator to clatter to the floor. Setting it down, Lydia helped Janet to lay down on the table.

"What happened?" Sandra's face registered shock.

"Mama?" Nathaniel's voice came wearily from the corner. Sandra rushed to keep her son from seeing the scene in the kitchen.

"Ambush," Lydia said, the shock still in her eyes. "Scott's supply contact gave us up. They were waiting for us. Scott ran to lead them away so we could escape."

"P-please, I need to see," Janet stammered, her shaking hands reaching for her wound.

"No," Lydia ordered.

"You may be a g-good m-medic, but I-I n-need to l-look."

Sheila grabbed a pillow and propped Janet's head and

shoulders up so she could examine her midsection. Her clothes were soaked in perspiration, and Sheila could feel her body tremble.

"The bullet entered here," Lydia said, guiding Janet's hand the wound.

"D-did it exit?" Janet's voice shook, fear flooding her face.

Lydia nodded at Sheila, and together they rolled Janet to her side. Janet grunted in pain as they lifted her. The back of Janet's shirt was soaked red, and Lydia grabbed a cloth off the counter and placed it over the exit wound. Grabbing Sheila's hand, she placed it over the cloth and lowered Janet's body allowing Sheila to keep pressure on the spot.

"It went through," Lydia said, her voice grim. "You've lost a lot of blood."

Sandra emerged, having calmed Nathaniel. Janet's breaths came in shallow sips as she gently prodded the wound with her fingers. Her face contorted into anguish as the realization of the bullet's damage hit her. She searched the faces of the three women over her.

"B-bring me my baby," she whimpered.

Sandra, hand over her mouth, rushed to the next room. They could hear her whisper to Hannah to wake her. A minute later, she emerged with the bleary-eyed girl.

"Mommy? Why are you crying?" Hannah appeared confused by the scene. She walked over to the table and searched her mother's face.

Janet reached a shaky hand and brushed a lock of hair out of Hannah's face. "I-I'm crying b-because you're so b-b-beautiful," Janet said, her lips trembling. "I want you t-to know that M-M-Mommy loves you."

"I love you too, Mommy." Hannah stared at the three crying women standing around the table. "Ms. Sandra, is Mommy going to be okay?"

"M-Mommy loves you. Mommy loves you. Mommy l-l-loves—" Janet's voice trailed off, and her gaze faded. Her hand let go of Hannah's cheek and fell limply next to the table.

"Mommy? Mommy, wake up!" Hannah cried.

"Come here, baby," Sandra said, drawing Hannah to herself.

"Why doesn't Mommy wake up?"

"Your mama's gone, baby."

Sheila pulled her hand from underneath Janet. It was covered in blood, and she grabbed a towel to wipe it off before Hannah could see. Whimpering and sniffing could be heard around the room.

A sound at the door caught their attention. Scott stood there, taking in the scene of the room. Lydia turned to him and shook her head silently.

Scott fell to one knee and let out an anguished gasp. Hannah, hearing her father's voice, unburied her head from Sandra. She flew into her father's arms, and the two wept. Lydia rounded the table and quietly closed Janet's eyes.

The room stood quietly, allowing the family to mourn. Finally, Sheila made her way over to Scott and Hannah. She knelt and lay her hand on his shoulder.

"I-I'm so sorry, Scott," she said softly.

"She—she wanted some time together," he said through tears. "She never comes on supply runs, but she believed it would be a safe chance to get outside for bit."

Sheila nodded. She sniffed and rose to close the door to the secret space. Her eye caught the movement of a small red dot on the wall. It moved slowly until it came to a stop on her chest. She followed the laser's refraction off the dust in the air to the window. A sniper was perched in the window across the street, aiming right at her.

The door burst open.

Chapter Thirty-Seven

The scream caught in Sheila's throat as the Law-keepers stormed the basement residence. Before she could warn the others, the room was filled with armed men wearing body armor and masks. They shouted as they rushed into the kitchen.

Hannah squealed in fear as she was ripped from her father's arms. Scott protested, and then slumped to the floor as the barrel of a rifle was shoved in his gut.

"No. No," came Sandra's pleas as the Law-keepers charged her and her son's position.

Lydia grunted as she brought a chair down over the head of the nearest Law-keeper. She charged the next, but she was stopped when another officer swung the butt of this rifle. It struck her cheek, and she fell to the floor, barely conscious.

Sheila still stood frozen, staring at the sniper. His aim still held true, and a twitch of his finger would mean her death.

"Daddy! Daddy!" Hannah was screaming.

An officer appeared at the door, his rank pinned to his shoulders. The men parted ways as he entered, and he approached Sheila. Scanning the room to ensure his men had it under control, he shouted, "Shut that child up!"

The officer holding Hannah placed his hands over her mouth to muffle her screams. His pained cry let the room know that Hannah had traded her screaming for a powerful bite. He dropped the girl and staggered backward, holding his bleeding hand. Hannah scrambled for her father.

The officer pointed at Scott. "You get her quiet, or I'll shut her up!"

Scott quickly hushed his daughter, whose screams faded into

a whine. The officer turned his attention back to Sheila, and he scanned her up and down. He huffed as if unimpressed.

"So, you're the one that infiltrated the rehabilitation facility and blew it up?" he said incredulously.

Sheila stood silently.

"I mean, I get her," he said, pointing to Lydia who clutched the already swelling side of her face. "She's the soldier type. But you? Sheila Kemp, the infamous Watcher—I guess I expected more."

Sheila's teeth grit, but she refused to speak.

The officer laughed and turned away. "Cuff 'em! Looks like we might have all earned that extra time off before the Chase, men!" A grunt of agreement rippled through the group. A junior officer approached, his eyes filling with what appeared like remorse. He kept glancing at Janet on the table.

Sheila nodded in recognition. *He's the one who shot her, and he's realizing she was a mother and wife—not a hardened criminal.*

He held a pair of handcuffs. Cuffing one arm, he turned her around and cuffed the other behind her back. She noticed that he was gentle with her, so she avoided resisting. He led her out the front door and up the steps.

Along the street, people could be seen emerging from their homes, watching the scene. The officer guided her head into the backseat of the Law-keeper vehicle. Scott was next to emerge, still coughing from the blow to his stomach. Hannah, too, was handcuffed which made Sheila scowl.

Two officers carried a delirious Lydia. Sandra was led by an officer who carried Nathaniel, who reached with pleading arms for his mother. The last to appear were two officers carrying a black bag containing Janet's lifeless body.

Aside from the commanding officer, the others did their job with somber expressions. None relished the idea of arresting a mourning family and their unarmed friends. They obeyed quietly.

"Come on, men," the commanding officer shouted. "We've

brought in the catch of the day! Get this rebellious scum to headquarters." He climbed into the passenger seat in front of Sheila.

The car lurched, and Sheila watched the neighborhood pass by them. Men, women, and children watched, some with hardened expressions and others appearing close to tears. A few of the children pointed and were hurried inside by careful parents.

"Copy that. Suspects in transit," the commanding officer radioed from the front seat.

"It's about time, Captain," came the too-sweet voice over the radio. "His grace, the Chairman, is eager to see these rebels brought to justice. Please prepare Ms. Kemp for interview immediately upon arrival. I want to speak with her right away."

"Ten four," the Captain responded. He turned to Sheila. "Sounds like you've got a date with—"

"I know," she interrupted. "Penny and I go way back."

Chapter Thirty-Eight

Sheila could hear the clattering of bracelets long before the door opened. The muffled sound of Penny's voice, which dripped with sweetness, made her stomach turn. *How can she order people around and still sound like a weathergirl trying too hard?*

"Sweetheart!" Penny's voice exploded into the room as the door opened. Both clattering arms were extended as she walked toward Sheila. She wrapped her arms around Sheila from the side and rocked her back and forth like a baby. "Our little prodigal has come home!"

"I didn't realize home was being handcuffed to a table in a Law-keeper station," Sheila retorted, trying not to wretch on the stench of Penny's perfume.

"Oh, sweetie, there's no need to be that way. I have missed seeing you." She rounded the table and sat across from Sheila.

"Last time you saw me, you tried to have me shot."

"Yes, well, you *were* trying to escape the consequences of your actions. You can't blame me for that."

"I can, and I do."

Penny straightened and folded her hands in feigned offense. "Well then, that won't do. I *had* hoped for a happy reunion." Penny gazed anywhere but at Sheila as if the sight of her would make her lose her calm. Sheila grasped Penny's charade all too well.

She waited Penny out.

"Dearie," Penny leaned in as if to reveal a secret, "you are in a heap of trouble."

"Mmm-hmm."

"I mean, this business as the Watcher was bad enough, but you've found yourself the horrible pawn of that dreadful group of rebels."

"Dreadful." Sheila couldn't hide the sarcasm. She almost laughed as Penny's face contorted as she pretended not to notice.

"Truly it must have been. I'm so sorry you had to fall in with such an awful group. Oh, how I wish you had not left our care." Penny placed a hand over her heart and reached for Sheila's hand with the other. Sheila pulled away instinctively, stopped short by the metallic clank of the handcuffs catching. Penny grabbed her hand and squeezed it. "I can protect you." Penny nodded silently at Sheila.

"Protect?" Sheila played along.

"Yes, I am the Deputy Chairwoman of the Western Alliance after all, and I am in the good graces of his humbleness, the Chairman. Tell me you know the error of your ways and were forced to act as you did by the rebels, and I can get you leniency."

"And I suppose you'll want information."

"Well, of course!" Penny's voice rose as if surprised. "You tell us where to find this little rebellion, and I will see you restored to a place of influence. You can become *our* Watcher."

Sheila felt bile make its way into her mouth and swallowed hard, grimacing at the acid burn in her throat. She could believe that Penny would have rewritten history in her mind, but the idea that Sheila would outrightly betray the Underground was an idea beyond even Penny. Sheila wondered at her angle, but she could no longer hide her disdain.

"I don't think so," Sheila said flatly.

"Excuse me?" Penny straightened, legitimately shocked this time.

"You heard me."

"Dearie, I don't think you—"

"Oh, I do," Sheila interrupted. "I understand that you think I'm stupid enough to betray the people who can bring hope to this world. I understand you think I can't put together the fact that your need for information from me means that you haven't yet found the Underground. I understand that you think I haven't found freedom from the oppression of the not-so-glorious Law."

"Enough!" Penny screeched, slamming a hand on the table. "I might be able to take your unwarranted hostility, but I will not accept blasphemy against the one stalwart protecting us from total anarchy."

"Keeping us from freedom," Sheila corrected.

"Freedom to die in your case!" Penny growled. Her countenance had changed instantly. Sheila could see the red blotches growing from her neckline and into her cheeks. Her eyes were wild and filled with rage. Her lungs rapidly heaved in and out.

Sheila smiled. *Finally, I'm talking to the real Penny. Nothing I do here will change her plan. She's too calculated.* She leaned forward and lowered her voice to a controlled whisper. "You see, Penny, I've figured you out. You believe you've risen to a position of power and influence—a place that keeps you close to the Chairman you love so dearly. In truth, you're his pawn to move as he pleases. You have power as long as it suits him. Fail in stopping the Underground, and you'll see how quickly he takes it away."

She stopped and let the words sink in before continuing. "As for me, I might die. You *can* do that. But— I've found something for which I'm willing to die. And so—I die because I choose to— not because *you* choose. I'm free to make my choice, and I have. If you wished, you could be free, too."

Sheila imagined Penny's head might explode. Penny's nostrils flared with each heaving breath. Sheila leaned backward, a contented smile on her face. She cursed silently when her wrists caught on the handcuffs and kept her from crossing her arms to complete the moment.

Penny's lips trembled as she stood. For a moment, Sheila saw a crack in the plastic armor, but Penny reined it in quickly. She placed her hands on the table and leaned over Sheila. She snarled as she stared Sheila down.

"You think you've got me figured out?" Penny spat with each word. "You will see how much power I have, dear, as the Chairman sentences both you and your soldier friend to death for treason."

She stepped backward, unintentionally knocking her chair over. Penny hopped to prevent tripping, bracelets clattering in protest. Her face flushed as her façade of confidence was marred by the blunder. She smoothed her skirt and tugged on her jacket. She walked to the door without glancing at Sheila.

"Guard! Door," she commanded.

A moment later, the door opened, a Law-keeper stepping inside and holding it open for her. Penny stepped into the opening and stopped. Without turning to her, she spoke to Sheila in a low tone.

"And as for the two families you roped into this, we have special plans for them. You can count on it."

She left, the guard closing the door behind her. Sheila rested her head back. She could live with being doomed herself, and Lydia was ready to do what was necessary. The faces of Scott, Hannah, Sandra, and Nathaniel flashed through her mind.

They don't deserve this.

Chapter Thirty-Nine

Perryn scanned the room. She sat by herself at lunch, as Willis was stuck in an extra training exercise with his squad. They'd agreed to join up later, but she guessed their training had been halted by the same broadcast down at the gym. Everyone around her was staring at the monitors on the wall in the dining hall. The news had announced the capture of two high profile suspects, and the entire Underground understood what that meant. Currently, the screen was displaying the usual pro-Coalition propaganda with dreamy images of the Chairman overlooking canyons and grasslands, a voiceover describing his love for the Law and the citizens of the Coalition. Despite the gross display, everyone was riveted to the screen so as not to miss a second when the news returned.

The screen faded through black and into the image of an Alliance journalist in yellow sitting at a desk. She stared back at Perryn for those awkward seconds between when the cameras went live and when the journalist spoke. Wearing a well-polished expression of intensity, the reporter leaned forward and began.

"Officials today have confirmed the capture of two individuals sought for crimes against the Law," she began. The room gasped as pictures of Lydia and Sheila were displayed in boxes next to the reporter's face. Lydia's face sported a swollen eye and a large bruise across the side of her face. "Most recently, the suspects were believed to be involved in the heinous violence at the Central City Rehabilitation Facility, which caused the deaths of numerous loyal citizens employed there. Chairman DeGraaf weighed in on the capture earlier this morning."

The image switched to a prerecorded video of the Chairman.

"What has happened here goes beyond simple treason," the

Chairman said, his dark, wire-rimmed glasses appearing heavy on his large nose. "Treason is a crime of betraying one's governing authority. These two rebels have not only turned against their alliance, not to mention the greater World Coalition, but they have also encouraged others to do so. They have taken lives, innocent lives, in the name of a cause so perverse to the goodness of the Law, that treason cannot encapsulate its grievous nature. Truly, this is a crime against humanity. The world has been wounded by their actions, and the world will respond accordingly. There is but one measure for those who hold so low a view of the glory of the Law."

The reporter's voice could be heard again over images of the arrest. Perryn swiped with her hand at a tear on her cheek as the screen showed an unconscious Lydia being carried outside, while a dejected Sheila was loaded into a Law-keeper vehicle.

"Along with the two suspects," the reporter continued her voiceover, "two families were found harboring the fugitives. Officials have yet to release their names, but both are suspected of evading Law-keeping forces when sought for questioning."

Two faces appeared on the screen, a Caucasian male who appeared in his thirties and a young, beautiful black woman. An anguished yell came from the back of the room. Several heads turned, including Perryn, to see Kane collapse to his knees. His huge hands covered his face.

Perryn turned from Kane to the screen and back again trying to sort out his reaction. Slowly, the truth dawned on her, and her hand involuntarily covered her gasp.

"Sandra," Perryn whispered.

A couple sitting nearby heard her and turned to their tablemates. Gradually, the news spread through the room, the whispers growing to a dull roar as the room gave into the anxious tension. Shouts of "quiet!" and "hold on!" began as the Chairman again appeared on the screens.

The Chairman wore a grave expression as he spoke midsentence, "...which cannot be ignored. The world is in a place of questioning the Law, and I believe it is ready to once again have the protective veil pulled back to see the consequences of anarchy. It is for this reason that these criminals, both the two rebels and their accomplices, will be publicly reprimanded at the opening ceremonies of this year's Chase being held in the great Western Alliance. It is my firm belief that the world will once again find confident solace in the goodness of the Law when they see what happens to those who forget it. Obviously, the two rebels are guilty of a capital crime and will be punished in accordance with their guilt. As for their accomplices, I believe we have found a middle ground that will demonstrate both the grace and justice the Law has to offer."

The room erupted into shouting, no one paying any attention to the reporter's closing comments.

"They're going to execute the Captain?" a woman cried.

"Publicly?" another added.

"Don't forget Sheila!" a third sounded.

"Who were the others?" a man asked.

"Mommy? What's going on?" A child tugged at his sobbing mother.

The dining hall was a cacophony of voices, most of which were indistinct as people appeared to be shouting at no one. Perryn stood, knowing this could get out of control. The Underground felt safe, but seeing two of their own sentenced to death in front of them had shaken that security. Kane was in no place to restore that safety, and it was up to her. She steeled herself, setting her own emotions aside. Stepping up on her chair, she hoisted herself to the tabletop.

"Everyone! Please listen!" she shouted, louder than she believed capable. The room, seeing her, turned their attention, the noise slowly fading. Perryn held her arms out until everyone fell silent.

"Captain? What do we do?" A young man stepped forward.

She took a deep breath, realizing her next words would hold or lose the group. She resolved to speak calmly and without alarm.

"Most of you've been aware of Lydia and Sheila's departure weeks ago, and some have become aware that they were part of a rescue mission. Both women have fought bravely for the Underground and understood the risks, as do all of us who fight for freedom from the Law. That said, Chairman DeGraaf has, I believe, thrown down a gauntlet before us. He has told us both where and when our friends will be out in the open. What he's unaware of is that we've already been planning our next move for this exact same moment. Every, and I mean every, possible action will be considered to not only succeed in our mission but also to bring our friends—our family—home safely."

The room stared at her. Here and there, she could see heads nodding in agreement.

"This is what so many of you've been training for," she continued. "We are not unprepared. We are not caught unaware. We are ready to take the fight to the Coalition."

A few claps could be heard.

"Chief has led us into and out of danger on more than one occasion." Perryn motioned to Kane, who glanced up from his hands. "He has done so at great risk to himself. I'm one of the many whose lives he personally saved, and *all* of us owe him for providing a haven of safety from those who would seek to oppress us. However, you may have gathered that this mission has become quite personal for the Chief. The woman pictured—the accomplice to our Captain and Sheila—is the wife of our Chief, who we formerly presumed was dead. We believe there's a child with her as well. I say to you, my family, that we brace ourselves for what is coming. We should, not simply to save those that we know, but to save those loved by the one who has done so much for us. I ask you to join me three days from now, the day of the Chase, not for ourselves—not even for the world—but for our Chief."

Again, the room erupted, this time with overwhelming support.

"We got you, Chief!" someone cried out.

"You're not alone!" another shouted.

"For Chief!" one chanted.

The chant was taken up by the room, slowly at first, until the entire room shouted in unison, "Chief! Chief! Chief!" Fists thrust into the air with each shout, both in defiance to the Coalition and in support of Kane.

Perryn turned to her friend, who gazed in disbelief at the room in front of him. He'd never asked anything from the Underground for himself, and the whole room realized it. Kane's adopted family was rallying to his side. Kane stood up, supporting his massive body with one hand against the wall. He searched the chanting faces in front of him until his eyes met Perryn's.

She smiled at him, not out of cheerfulness, but out of loyal friendship. He breathed deeply and nodded at her.

Kane raised his hand to the room to quiet it down. With the other, he brushed away tears still clinging to his skin. The room quickly hushed, except for a small child who continued the chant despite his mother's protests.

"My friends," Kane began, his voice shaking slightly, "I can't tell you what this means to me. We fight for a cause greater than any of us, but that cause sometimes comes with a very real face. For me, it's the face of my wife and son—a son I've never met. I'm honored that you would join me in this. Report this afternoon to your squad leaders for instructions. We—will—win this fight. We have a chance to forever shape the world, and we're going to take it. And I must finish by saying—" He stopped and pointed at Perryn. "—I believe I've chosen my new Captain well."

This time, the room shouted so loudly Perryn felt the table under her feet shake. She stood wide-eyed, feeling exposed standing above everyone as the chant of "Captain! Captain!" began around her. All around her, members of the Underground gave her approving nods. Those closest helped her down from the table where she was greeted with high fives and confident pats on the shoulder.

Before the crowd could be calmed down again, Kane shouted with renewed strength, "Dismissed!" The crowd roared again and gathered to leave.

Chapter Forty

"You think I'm ready for this?" Willis stared down at Perryn's hand in his. The idea that they were back together and completely honest about how they felt was still unbelievable. He loved her and didn't want to disappoint her, but he didn't feel ready for this mission. Still, the Chase had arrived, and the time to act was now.

"Of course, you are. Don't doubt yourself," she whispered, squeezing his hand.

"But what if—"

"Stop it. The past is the past. I *know* you. I *know* you'll lead your squad with all the confidence and skill they need." He saw her glance over at his squad about ten yards away. He straightened up, trying to appear the part, but inside a knot was forming in his stomach.

"Perr, if something happens, I want you to know—"

"Shhh," she interrupted, placing a finger over his lips.

"No really. I love you. I won't let this mission start without making sure I've said it. I waited too long before, and I don't want to miss the chance again. I love you."

"I know." She smiled and rested her forehead on his. He kissed her, and they embraced for a long moment. For a few breaths, the world of chaos surrounding them faded into the distance, blurred by the tears in his eyes and drowned out by the pounding of his heart. Then, it all came crashing back as she turned to leave.

Turning to his team, he could see several of them poorly hiding their smiles. Jolene was biting her lips, trying not to giggle, while Bekah covered her mouth and glanced away shyly.

"What's with you guys?" He held his arms out to the side.

"Way to go, Thomson! You and the Captain, man!" Steve called out. The comment caused Nikki to snort, and she doubled over in laughter.

"Somehow I get the feeling Captain likes you, Thomson," Michelle commented. More laughter escaped from the mouths of the group.

"Real mature guys." Willis feigned annoyance. "If she liked me so much, how'd I get stuck with you guys?"

"Ohhhh!" the group called in amused unison, pretending they were offended.

For a moment, Willis again felt his old self rise to the surface. The confidence to lead showed up. The ability to connect with his team while still demanding their respect seeped from every pore. Then, it was gone.

Which is the real me? He shook his head and put a smile back on. He couldn't let them see his doubt.

Two hours later, he found himself in the sweaty bowels of the arena where the Chase would begin its opening ceremonies that afternoon. It'd been Chris that found that the service tunnels to the arena were separated from the old train tunnels they'd previously used as the Underground by a hasty wall of brick erected during construction. The arena sound check had provided the cover they needed to make quick work of the wall with a sledgehammer. They crouched by their new entrance and prepared to enter the empty tunnels.

Jaden sighed. "Anyone else wonder if it was too easy to get in here?"

"Remember, the Chairman practically dared us to try something, so security might be lax letting us in. It's getting out that'll be the greater challenge," Chris reminded. "Okay, all squads ready?"

"We blow the southwest tower to create a distraction." Willis repeated his team's instructions.

"And we get ready to blow the exit doors when all hell breaks loose," Maria added, pointing to Jaden and her team.

Chris nodded. "Right on both counts. My team will be disabling security communications, which should slow the response time of the Law-keepers. Kane is leading the infiltration team who will attempt to gain control of the stage during Willis's distraction. Perryn is leading two squads who are blending in among the crowd to assist with the extraction of the prisoners. Radio silence the entire time."

"If only it were as easy as it sounds," a man in his thirties on Chris's team offered.

"Hey, if we pull this off and get the right message out to the world," Jaden countered, "the tide could forever turn in our favor. The world is watching. We get that stage, and we win."

"Jaden's right," Chris agreed. "Everyone, stay focused. It's time the world heard the truth."

With that, Chris motioned to his team, and they quietly jogged down the tunnel. Maria gathered her team, pointing to their objective on a diagram of the arena. Jaden approached Willis.

"You got this, friend," he said.

"You, too. See you out there?"

"Race you home afterward!" Jaden smiled and slapped Willis on the shoulder, returning to his team.

Willis turned and met the nervous eyes of B-team. None of them had any field experience, and they'd been given the job that would start the entire process. Still, they would be able to get their job done before security was put on full alert, so he saw the wisdom in their placement.

Perryn knows what she's doing.

With two fingers, he pointed in the direction of a door about fifty yards up the tunnel. The team nodded and began their near-silent movement in that direction. Steve and Nikki tightened the straps on their backpacks containing explosive ordinance.

Stepping out into the tunnel, the air changed from the hot dampness of the train tunnel to the cool dryness of the new tunnel.

Pipes and electrical conduit lined the ceiling in all directions. They hugged the tiled wall as they moved, dart guns drawn. Willis prayed they wouldn't encounter anyone in this relatively open space.

He motioned for the group to stop, and Ryan stepped forward with a pair of bolt cutters. Making quick work of the chain on the door, he opened it to reveal a closet containing nothing but a ladder disappearing into the ceiling.

Without a word, he pointed for Ryan to lead the ascent. Michelle, Nikki, Jolene, and Steve followed. Willis turned to Bekah, whose head was on a swivel in nervous tension. He placed a hand on her shoulder and smiled. She tried to smile back.

"After you," he mouthed.

Holstering her dart gun, which still appeared awkward in her hand, she grabbed the rungs of the ladder and climbed. Willis glanced right and left before closing the closet door, shrouding the ladder in darkness.

The narrow tube around the ladder echoed with the sound of labored breathing as the team ascended upward from the foundations of the arena to the roof. Glow sticks cast a pale green light on the ladder in front of each of them, serving as dim relief to the suffocating darkness.

"We're here," a barely-audible whisper called out from above. Ryan had reached the hatch. Willis could hear him working on the lock, and he cringed at the loud creak the door made as it opened. Blinding sunlight poured in from above and filled the tube.

One-by-one, the team scrambled out onto the roof of the arena. In front of them stood a towering antenna, one of many around the arena. Willis steadied himself as the high perch made him momentarily dizzy. Far below, the arena appeared like a gaping mouth with thousands of Alliance-yellow seats appearing like teeth. The structure was six-sided and sank into the earth around a stage at the center. Each side featured two archways, out of which teams from all the alliances could, in theory, introduce their teams. Willis expected some of them would go unused.

"Subtle," Ryan remarked, taking in the sea of yellow. "You sure people will get which alliance is hosting this Chase?"

Willis smiled in amusement but held up a finger to remind Ryan to keep his voice down. Pointing, he directed the team to begin placing the ordinance around the feet of the antenna on the outside edge. The idea was to force the tower to crumble and fall outside the stadium and not endanger the spectators inside. With luck, the explosion and crashing antenna would give Kane the moment he needed to storm the stage and take control. While Perryn's team rushed the prisoners out, a prerecorded message would be installed in the tech booth beneath the stage to send a message to the watching world.

Save the prisoners.

Tell the world the truth.

The mission goals were simple, but they wouldn't be easy.

Willis continued giving silent directions. One by one, the outside foundations of the antenna were wired to explode.

A few more minutes. We'll be done and can hide for the remainder of our time. The team will be relatively safe compared to the others. A few more minutes.

Click.

The unmistakable sound of a firearm's safety switching off came from behind him. Slowly, he turned to stare into the eyes of a Law-keeper whose rifle barrel was pointed squarely at his chest. His hands felt like lead as they rose into a position of surrender. He needed to act—to do something. He stepped forward.

"Freeze, or I'll shoot!" the officer screamed.

"Listen, you don't want to do this," Willis said calmly. He stepped forward again.

"I said freeze!"

"It's a harmless protest. No one was going to get hurt." He stepped again.

Willis's muscles tensed in the standoff. He calculated his next move, envisioning the step he would take to the side to draw the aim of the rifle away from his team. If he was right, the nervous

Law-keeper would fire early, and the shot would miss. He would then have his opening to disarm the Law-keeper.

Click. Click. Click. Click. Click. Click.

Half a dozen more Law-keepers burst out of a doorway, rifles moving into position. The moment was gone. The first officer reached for a radio. Willis cursed.

"Sir, we have them," he said into the radio.

A minute later, the door opened again, and a man in a suit bearing an Alliance insignia stepped out. He wasn't a Law-keeper, but he was clearly the man in charge, as Willis could see the officers straighten at his appearance. He was short with greasy, black hair slicked straight backward. He straightened his jacket lapels and nodded to the officer. Willis supposed this was the man on the other end of the radio. He stepped over to Willis and examined him closely, walking a full circle around him.

"Good day to you, young man. I'm Charles, the head of security at this facility. I'm pleased to inform you that your little rebellion ends today. As always, the Chairman was correct in his interpretation of events. Willis Thomson has decided to attend another Chase." His voice betrayed a high society upbringing, and he curled his lips at Willis in obvious distaste. Willis wondered how a man so short could manage to look down at him. "My recommendation was to shoot on sight, but my instructions are to bring you in alive. Apparently, he wants to talk to you, Mr. Thomson. Lucky you."

He reached out and took Willis's dart pistol in his hands. Willis dared a glance back at his team, all of which were frozen in fear. Ryan appeared ready to grab his pistol, and Willis communicated with his eyes to hold. Nikki and Jolene hunched over one of the backpacks. Michelle and Steve were half-way through taping the final explosive. His eyes met Bekah, who was pale with fright. Her eyes blazed bright white as they were wide open, her pupils appearing like dark bouncing balls as she glanced from the officers to Willis and back. She was kneeling behind a metal support. It was her hand, however, that caught his attention. He caught her sliding a small black object into her boot. At their angle, the officers couldn't see that side of her, and there was a chance none had noticed.

Turning back to the man, he tried to hide that he'd noticed something. None of the officers moved to intercept Bekah, and Willis let out a long, shallow breath to stay calm. The man turned the pistol over in his hand several times.

"It's an honorable thing you do, carrying a non-lethal weapon, Willis Thomson. Not effective, but honorable. Nothing inspires so little fear in your enemy than the knowledge that you live by a code," the man continued. "In this case, however, you can be thankful for your weapon of choice. Today, it serves you well." The man turned Willis's own weapon on him and fired.

The world faded to black.

Chapter Forty-One

Bright light. It was all Willis could see for a moment when consciousness returned to him. For a second, he considered that he was still at Solution Systems, and the weeks with the Underground had been nothing more than his delirium. He blinked several times until the room started to come into focus. He wasn't strapped to a table. Instead, he was handcuffed to an office chair. *Definitely not Solution Systems.*

Two Law-keepers stood bracketing the doorway. He met one officer's eyes, who cleared his throat. Keeping his back to the door, the officer reached behind him and rapped twice on the large wooden entrance. A minute later two more officers entered. They parted upon entry leaving Willis a view of the man behind them.

Chairman DeGraaf.

He stood with his hands folded piously in front of him. The black robes with yellow trim ruffled as he entered. He never took his eyes off Willis. His gaze through the wire-rimmed glasses pierced him and made Willis feel like he was reading his soul.

"Leave us," Chairman DeGraaf said after several moments of silence. The officers glanced at each other as if this was an unexpected command. DeGraaf spoke again, increasing his seriousness without raising his voice. "I said, leave us. Mr. Thomson and I have a long history, and I do not believe he is any threat to me. There is much we need to discuss in private."

One of the officers nodded his head toward the door, prompting the others to begin moving out of the room. Taking one last glance, the lead officer shut the door. Willis could hear the click of the lock. He turned back to the Chairman, who hadn't stopped staring. Willis searched the room to avoid his eyes and noted that the few wispy hairs combed carefully across his head appeared fewer than their last meeting.

If the Underground has accomplished nothing else, we've not made it easy on the Chairman, he mused silently.

DeGraaf kept staring in thick silence.

"You want me to speak first?" Willis pointed to himself.

"Do you want to speak?" DeGraaf countered.

"Not really."

"Very well. I will ask you to listen carefully, young man."

Willis nodded.

"Good," DeGraaf began, sitting down in a chair facing Willis. "It is clear to me that I could speak to you regarding the glory and goodness of the Law all day, and it would be lost on you. You care nothing for the way the Law has prevented anarchy in our world and have openly sought to undo its protections."

Willis sat unmoving. The Chairman's candor unnerved him.

"That is why I will speak to you plainly. You were the best of us, Mr. Thomson. You had everything in you to become the greatest peacemaker in the history of the Law. Last year in the Chase, victory was in your hands, and you squandered the opportunity. As such, you became our greatest failure."

Where is he going with this? Willis wondered.

"While the Law is perfect, I am humble enough to know that I am not a perfect administrator of it. But—let it not be said that I do not learn from my mistakes. Last time, I tried to force you to do our bidding. This time, you will volunteer for the job."

Willis sat frozen.

"You doubt me? Dr. Campbell has assured me that you are more than ready for my proposal."

Willis winced at the mention of Dr. Campbell.

"Ah, I see you remember the dear doctor. You see, young man, you might be one of my greatest failures as steward of the Law, but I *know* you. I have raised you from afar to be the Coalition's greatest asset. But more than that, I *know* you inside. Your motivation is not secret to me. You are a failure, aren't you?"

He waited for Willis's response. When none came, he continued. "You have failed your teammates. You have failed your friends. You have failed your fellow rebels. You have even failed your family. Haven't you, Mr. Thomson?"

Willis tried to maintain his composure, but the Chairman's words cut to his heart. *I am a failure,* he told himself. He breathed in quickly, trying to dismiss the thought as nothing more than Dr. Campbell's manipulation, but it rang true all the way to his soul. His hands shook violently. *I have failed everyone I've ever met.*

Chairman DeGraaf closed his eyes and bowed his head slightly in a sympathetic gesture. It was clear he could read Willis's emotions without requiring a word. There was no doubt in Willis's mind that the Chairman understood him—really discerned who he was.

"Mr. Thomson, I have excused my loyal officers because I want to do something that some might question as weak. However, I believe it to be a mercy. I am willing to accept that you have been a formidable adversary and offer an opportunity for you to save all those you love—to undo the failure of the past and see to it that those you care most about are protected from what is to come."

Willis raised his eyebrows and spoke, "Which is what?"

"We know of your little infiltration of the arena today." He let the words hang in the air, and they filled the room with terror that choked Willis. The Chairman nodded. "Yes, more than your little band atop the arena, we know of the others. Your stunt with the explosives has been prevented as the detonator we found in one of the bags has been deactivated. The explosives will be removed the instant the crowds lining up outside are gone. We know of the team positioned by the exit. We know of those trying to disrupt our communications. We even know of those entering the arena as spectators as we speak."

Perryn! Willis shouted silently.

Reading his face, the Chairman smiled. "Yes, your beloved is among them."

"What are you going to do?" Willis surprised himself with the anger in his voice. Had his hands been free, he was certain he would be reaching for the Chairman's throat.

"Nothing, Mr. Thomson. We know that simply arresting your compatriots would provoke violence and stir the crowds to distraction. And—I think we both know that we need them focused today. Care for a drink of water?" The Chairman smiled coyly.

Willis's lip quivered with rage. *He's one step ahead of us, and he doesn't even care that we know all about the neuro-booster!*

"No, we will allow them to believe they are being successful until the critical moment."

"And when is that?" Willis growled.

"While there would be great power in my words should I choose to instruct the world with the help of Dr. Campbell's creation, there are those who are so confused in their relationship to me that they would resist the effects. You, however, are one of them. The critical moment will come when *you* tell the world they need to submit to the Law again."

Willis burst out laughing. He couldn't help it. The idea was so idiotic, and he couldn't believe the Chairman had suggested it. "You must be joking!" he cried out, still laughing. "I'd die before I did anything like that."

"Then, so will all your friends and family," DeGraaf said flatly.

Willis stopped laughing.

DeGraaf leaned in until his face was inches from Willis. His lips curled in disgust, and his acidic breath made Willis want to retch. "Young man, you will assist us, or your friends and family will die in front of your eyes. Your oaf of a leader—your friends—those young people you led to their doom up at the tower today—your mother Brenda—and your precious Perryn—" The Chairman paused to let the names hang in front of Willis's mind. "They will all die while you watch. And you—you will spend your life rotting in a forgotten cell, kept alive enough to remember every day that you could have saved them and chose to fail—again." DeGraaf sank slowly back into his chair.

Willis could feel the salty wetness that clung to the edge of his eyelid.

"You—you can't," Willis whimpered.

"I can." DeGraaf let the words hang in the room. "I can, and I will be praised for it by most of the world. Your rebellion will be reduced dramatically after the Chase. It may take longer without you, but we will crush them in time."

"Th-then why do you need me?"

"Because I would much rather end this peacefully and without bloodshed."

"B-but my family—my friends."

"Cooperate, and they will be spared."

Willis stared.

"Yes, as I said, you have been a worthy adversary, and I am ready to cut my losses. I cannot win you over to my side, but I can guarantee you a safe existence if you will deliver my words to the world. They will believe you of all people, and the rebellion will end without another shot being fired."

"And you'll leave us alone?"

"We have prepared an island off-shore. It is uninhabited, but there are dwellings there ready for all of you. The land has been cultivated and is growing crops already. Medical supplies and a few creature comforts have even been put in place. Help us, and I can give you my assurance that you and yours will be safely transported there and allowed to live out your days in peace."

"I don't believe you. You can't have arranged all that so quickly. There's no island like that—not this quickly."

The Chairman sighed and rubbed his face. Replacing his glasses, he stared at Willis in exasperation. "Oh, dear boy, you haven't put it together. The young lady who broke you out was not acting in rebellion. She was a failed experiment, but she proved useful in the end. One more unconscious idea placed into her mind was all it took." Pausing, he waited to deliver his next statement. "And what was that thought? 'Break you out and deliver you to the people you wished to help.' It was all she needed to believe to do our bidding. She didn't know, of course, but that was the beauty of it. She exercised what she believed was freedom so well that it got her killed in the end."

Willis's eyes grew wide. "So, you're saying—"

"I'm saying that you didn't escape Solution Systems."

Willis gaped in stunned silence.

"Mr. Thomson—we let you go."

Chapter Forty-Two

Perryn scanned around her, keeping the hat low over her eyes. The crowds pressed in all around her threatening to turn the orderly lines entering the arena into a mob. Shouts and cheers rose as various pockets of fans cheered for their alliance. Brightly colored clothing, alliance flags, and even face paint were normal at the Chase. She was grateful because she would otherwise feel exposed in her bright-yellow Western Alliance jersey that read "home team" on the back.

Outside the lines, a group of protestors had taken up a chant. She noted that several wore the colors of the United African Cooperative, one of the three alliances that chose to boycott this Chase. Law-keepers stood nearby waiting for the slightest hint of disorderly conduct to shut down the protest. Still the UAC protestors shouted in brave earnest.

To her left, she counted several of her squad members in other lines, all in various alliance gear picked up at street vendors nearby. Kane was in the line to her right, trying his best to hide his hulking form in the crowd. They communicated silently as they inched their way toward the front of the line.

Perryn wished she could be armed, but all attendees were being searched by the guards at the doors. Detectors scanned everyone. Dogs sniffed each passerby. Bags were turned out on tables. The process was slow and arduous, but the Alliance was clearly taking no risks. She would have to go without her dart pistol this round. Approaching the front, a guard waved her through a metal detector. She held her breath as she walked through, even though she believed nothing would set it off.

Calm down, Perryn.

"You, over there," a guard said pointing to a female Law-keeper to her left. Perryn walked over.

"Arms to your side," the new guard instructed.

She held her arms out and endured the rough pat-down. With a wave of her hand, the guard allowed her to proceed. The blazing sun disappeared as she entered the tunnel into the sea of people eager to find their seats. Above her on the next floor, she could see dignitaries and powerful guests of alliances walking behind a glass wall. Each was proceeding to special boxes where elaborate parties would be held in private suites. She walked toward the field entrance in front of her.

"Ticket please," a man in a blazer said, holding out his hand.

She held out the plastic card in front of her, which he took without raising his eyes to hers. Inserting it into his scanner, the screen chirped in approval at her valid ticket allowing her into the infield. Walking past the man, she felt the warmth of the sun return on her face as she stepped into the open air.

So far, so good.

The infield was a swarming sea of sweaty people all vying for the best spot in the standing-room-only section. Here and there, she could see people arguing over supposedly 'reserved' spaces that groups had tried to stake out. Another group shouted at two men who held up a huge banner in support of the Joint Mediterranean States that blocked their view.

Perryn kept her head down and silently shouldered her way between the people. She whirled around when a shove came from behind. She turned in time to see Kane's large mass press his way through the crowd to her left. She breathed a sigh of relief.

He's letting me know he made it.

After several minutes, she found a position she liked by the right corner of the stage. Chairs were set up to the left of the podium for the Deputy Chairmen and Chairwomen present, and that left this side of the stage for the prisoners to be standing. She scanned the faces and mentally checked in her squads.

"Hot day for a Chase, isn't it?" a voice came from her left. She turned to see the wrinkled face of an elderly woman. Perryn noted that she sported the same jersey as her.

"Oh yeah. Nice jersey by the way!" She tried to sound excited.

"Thank you, young lady. I never miss a Chase when it comes to the Western Alliance. Been at the last four, but never got this close!"

"Yeah, pretty good spot, huh?"

"I think so. I wish I could get closer where the Chairman will be, but at least I'll get a good view of those rebels getting theirs. Misguided young people they are. I tell you, in all my years, the Law has never done me wrong. My late husband, Gerald, did quite well for himself supporting the Alliance with his business."

Perryn nodded quietly, hoping her silence would encourage an end to the conversation.

"He had a bit of a gambling problem," she continued, ignoring Perryn's disinterest, "which is why I can barely afford an infield ticket. Lost all our money betting on the Chase one year, and that was that. Still, I'm no slouch when it comes to skills, and I've done okay for myself since he passed. These old knees would love a seat to sit in, but you can't beat how close you can get here." She patted her right knee and waited for Perryn to respond.

"Yeah, pretty close," she responded. She glanced around trying to end the discussion, but the woman stared, obviously eager for conversation.

"Say, you know, you look familiar. I bet we've met before today."

"I don't think so."

"No, I mean it. My mind is old, but faces always stick. I know I've seen you somewhere."

Perryn could feel the sweat beading on her forehead and said a prayer of thanks for the hot sun to hide her nervousness. Her face had been on world broadcast, and this woman clearly had seen it a year earlier. She needed to get away from the woman before she put it together. The opening ceremony would begin in minutes, and she needed to focus.

"I don't think we've met," she said, forcing a smile.

"You sure? Let me have a good look at you." To Perryn's surprise, the woman grabbed her arm and turned Perryn to face her. She held her breath as the woman studied her features. "Maybe you used to live in Centerville? Are you from there?"

Perryn forced the panic down into a ball in her stomach. "I—I have cousins there. I hardly know them, but I'm told the family resemblance is uncanny," she lied.

"Hmm. That must be it," the woman let go of Perryn.

Perryn darted glances left and right, searching for any reason she could excuse herself. The ceremony would begin soon, and she needed to stay close. Any minute, the fanfare of the World Coalition anthem would announce the beginning.

Oh God, please let the music start. She'd never longed to hear that terrible song so much.

"Let me go?" Willis stammered. "What do you mean? How—why—?"

The Chairman's expression turned from penetrating to cool. "Mr. Thomson, you can't be so naïve to think that you could simply leave our custody and go about your own business, could you?"

"I—I—" Willis stammered.

"You were a prize capture for us, no doubt, but I needed more. I recognized that if we released you, you would run to your companions and put together some kind of foolhardy mission to stop us. All you've done is round up all the troublemakers and made my job easy. Except for your mother and those staying at that little schoolhouse of yours, of course."

Willis's mind raced as he put all that the Chairman was saying together in his mind. It was unbelievable to him that he could have been manipulated so well, but it explained how they stayed ahead of everything in their plan.

Knock. Knock. A rap on the door startled Willis.

"Enter!" the Chairman barked, annoyed at the interruption.

An official in a yellow suit entered the room. He chanced a glance at Willis and approached the Chairman. Bending over, he whispered in DeGraaf's ear.

"Is that so?" DeGraaf said, winking at Willis. "Thank you. You have been most helpful. But please—no more interruptions."

The man in the suit nodded and hurried out of the room. Chairman DeGraaf leaned back in his chair and placed his hands across his stomach. He stared at Willis for a long moment, appearing to enjoy what he was about to say.

"I have received word that your little girlfriend has entered the arena. Taken a spot right near the steps of the stage. I wonder why she'd want to stand there."

Willis searched the floor for answers, but it provided none. His stomach tightened to a knot, and he was afraid he might vomit. *This is an impossible decision. Betray my friends to save them or stay loyal to them and watch them die.* Bile rose in his throat.

"Mr. Thomson, I need to take my place to start the ceremony. I will be needing your decision. Is *failure* an option for you today?"

Willis's whole body shook as he considered what he needed to do. He understood one thing, and that was he couldn't let his friends die. He couldn't let them capture his mother again. He couldn't let any more harm come to Perryn. They might hate him for it, but he could live with that—and so would they.

"W-what do I need to say?" he whispered, his voice catching on the words.

The Chairman leaned forward, a smug smile spreading across his face.

Chapter Forty-Three

"There's the Smith family with their kids and grandkids," the woman said to Perryn. For several minutes, she'd been recounting all the Centreville families she could remember. At some point, she would realize that she'd never met Perryn's fake cousins, and her cover would be blown. "Are you sure you can't remember your cousin's family name, dear?"

"Like I said, they changed it when they moved to Centreville after their dad was arrested. The shame was so great, they stopped communicating with our side of the family. It's why I haven't seen them in so long." Perryn wiped the nervous sweat off her brow. She was getting deeper into her lie, but she simply needed minutes. With luck, the ceremony would begin, and the woman would be too preoccupied to keep considering the matter.

"Loyal Citizens of the World Coalition, please rise as we welcome our world leaders to the stage to open this year's Chase." came the voice over the loudspeaker.

"Thank you, God," Perryn whispered.

"What did you say, dear?" The woman placed a hand on Perryn's arm.

"Thank God it's starting. I'm so excited."

"Me, too!" the woman exclaimed, clapping her hands. She craned her neck trying to catch a glimpse of movement behind the stage.

Perryn allowed herself a sigh of relief. The World Coalition anthem began in its overdone pomp, and the entire stadium began cheering at once. Deputy Chairmen and Chairwomen filed onto the stage, fully dressed in culturally appropriate attire for their region. Perryn noted the conspicuous absence of the deputies from the

United African Cooperative, the Union of Free Southeastern Territories, and the Southern Federation of Allied States. Each deputy waived to the section of the hexagonal arena where their dignitaries were seated together. Cheers rose each time a section was acknowledged. The deputies stood by their designated seats at the far end of the stage and continued waving, none more than Penny who waved two bracelet-jingling arms at the infield crowd. Sheila's gross description of Penny had been spot-on.

A line of Law-keepers filed on stage, standing shoulder to shoulder across the back of the stage. Each held a rifle at the ready. That's when she saw them.

Lydia appeared like she'd been through a battle. Her face was less swollen, but the bruise had set into a deep purple. She was shoved roughly by a guard who kept one hand on the handcuffs that held both of her arms behind her back. The crowd booed at the prisoners, and Perryn worried she might be sick.

Sheila was next, not appearing as bad as Lydia. Perryn could see her searching the crowd with fearful eyes. She glanced away, not wanting Sheila to see her. As much as she might want to offer hope to her friend, the last thing she needed was to be identified. A child fell on the last step and was picked up roughly by the guard. Her father, who Perryn recognized from the broadcast, pled with the guard to be gentle. The girl hugged her father's leg, unwilling to part from him. Finally, Perryn saw Sandra and her son. Sandra held her chin up, and Perryn marveled at her courage. She dared a glance in Kane's direction, but she couldn't find him in the crowd.

Perryn blinked hard, trying to contain her tears over the display. She couldn't believe the world viewed this as normal, and she prayed that today would change that. Suddenly, the boos transformed into questioning remarks, and Perryn's eyes shot open. She gasped at the sight.

Willis's squad was filed onto the stage, each handcuffed and escorted by their own guard. Perryn named them off in her head to see if they were all there.

Michelle, Ryan, Jolene, Nikki, Steve, she recalled. *Oh, and Bekah. Oh no!* Bekah stood at the end of the line, her tear-stained face searching the crowd in front of her. Perryn sucked in as the parade of prisoners ended. *Willis! Where is Willis?*

The fanfare ended, and the crowd settled.

"Loyal Citizens of the World Coalition," the voice on the speakers blared, "please welcome to the stage, the honorable keeper of the Law, Chairman DeGraaf."

The crowd roared to life in approval as the Chairman slowly marched on to the stage. He stopped once or twice to half-wave to the crowd. Stopping at the podium, he raised his hands to quiet the throng.

"Greetings and welcome to the Loyal Citizens of the World Coalition," he announced. The crowd boomed again, prompting him to raise his hands one more time. "My humble office as protector of our glorious Law gives me the privilege of opening this year's Chase to determine the law change that will shape the generations to come. It is the Law that protects us all."

"The Law is good!" the crowd shouted in almost unison.

"The Law that preserves us all," DeGraaf continued.

"The Law remains!"

"The Law that saves us all," finished the Chairman, clasping his hands together in his usual fashion.

"The Law is good!"

"I want to take a moment to thank our host alliance and its Deputy Chairwoman for their gracious hospitality. Without their loyal assistance, I am certain we could not accomplish all that we hope to at this year's event." DeGraaf left the podium and approached Penny, who stepped out from her chair to meet him. Taking her hand, DeGraaf bowed and kissed it. Penny smiled widely and fanned herself as if overcome. The Western Alliance section and much of the infield cheered in approval.

Retaking the podium, the Chairman again held his arms out to quiet the crowd. This time, he waited until the noise had settled beyond a dull murmur to near silence, broken by an occasional cough. He placed his arms on either side of the podium and stared down as if pained by what he was about to say. Perryn fumed inside, knowing what was coming.

"My dearest loyal citizens," the Chairman began, "it grieves me that a sacred day as this must be marred by the next events. Our near-perfect world has been protected by the glorious Law for generations, and we stand as the blessed inheritors of the Law-makers' dreams. That bliss, however, has been marred in recent memory. Rebels, who have the audacity to declare themselves above our Law, have caused strife around the world and sought to undo peace in our world. They are lovers of anarchy and seek to spread pain wherever they go.

"I cannot say enough how much it grieves me to spend part of this celebration with those who have joined me on stage here this morning. I lament that I must disrupt your happiness to undertake a necessary measure—and it is necessary. It is necessary because I ask you, the loyal and faithful, to join me in declaring once and for all that this is our world, and those who would do us evil cannot have it. It is because I love you, my friends, that I would ruin a moment of this day for our sake."

The crowd stood transfixed on the Chairman. Here and there, Perryn could see people whispering, but none took their eyes off DeGraaf. She glanced over at the woman next to her, who clasped her hands together in hopeful agreement with the Chairman. Suddenly, she leaned into Perryn.

"Isn't it wonderful? The Chairman loves us so much, he would ruin this day for our sake," she said, never moving her gaze from the stage. Perryn's eyes widened at the effect of the neuro-booster. The woman was ready to adopt anything she heard from the Chairman today. The gravity of their mission grew heavy, and Perryn's breathing quickened.

"Loyal friends, with me stand the rebels captured earlier this week. Two of them are guilty of the deaths of countless loyal Law-keepers and those on the path to rehabilitation. Here today, I declare them guilty of treason against the Law, a punishment of death to be carried out immediately after this morning's ceremony," the Chairman continued. Several solitary jeers at Lydia and Sheila could be heard from the crowd around the stadium. "But first, I begin with mercy. In a display of gross negligence for the well-being of the next generation, these two forced families to conspire with them. While conspirators are as guilty as those they assist, the Law teaches me that I am not above grace, which I extend today. In my first order of the morning, I hereby order a stay of execution for the conspirators in lieu of blessing them by taking their children into our care, that they may train for their alliance Chase team and ultimately have the chance to bless future generations with their lives."

Perryn gasped. *Oh God, no!* she screamed silently.

"He's so merciful," the woman next to her whispered.

Chapter Forty-Four

Sheila's wrists stung, raw under the handcuffs that rubbed relentlessly against her skin. She scanned the crowd endlessly, searching for a familiar face. Once or twice, she caught a glimpse of someone, but they would quickly turn from view or move behind another person. She comprehended enough not to linger on any one location. She'd tried to ignore the stares of the Underground team next to her, who pled with their eyes for a sign of support. She couldn't risk their safety by identifying herself with them.

"…that they may train for their alliance Chase team and ultimately have the chance to bless future generations with their lives," the Chairman finished.

While Sheila had been half-listening in an effort to prepare herself for action if necessary, these words snapped her to attention. To her horror, two Law-keepers moved toward Nathaniel and Hannah. Her eyes shot in the direction of Scott and Sandra.

Scott appeared bewildered, as if unable to process what was happening. The first guard reached for Hannah, grabbing her by the upper part of her arm. "Daddy!" she cried. That's when Scott's confusion dissipated.

"Wait. No!" he yelled, trying his best to break the grip of the Law-keeper. With his hands cuffed behind his back, he futilely lunged with his shoulder to no effect. "No! You can't have her!"

"Daddy!" Hannah screamed, as the guard pulled her away. She reached for Scott with both arms.

"You—" Scott began, preparing to curse the guard as he leapt violently. The club from the second guard stopped his words before he could speak them. Scott crumpled to the stage floor in a heap. Hannah shrieked as the guard continued to pull her across the stage toward a partially hidden stairwell that led below.

The second guard replaced the club in his belt and turned to Nathaniel. Sheila glanced at Sandra, whose jaw tightened. Sandra coolly stepped around Nathaniel, placing herself between the guard and her son.

"You can't have him," she declared holding her head up in defiance. "You took my husband already for your sick games. You can't have my son."

A grunt from her left drew Sheila's attention. Lydia, attempting to move to Sandra's assistance, was being restrained by two guards. "No. No. No!" Lydia growled.

No matter which way the Law-keeper moved, Sandra moved to match him. Slowly, the guard drew his club. He hesitated. Sheila realized that clubbing Scott had been one thing as he'd attacked the other guard. Sandra wasn't moving toward him. She stood with passive defiance.

"Get on with it!" a voice shouted from the crowd.

"Come on, lady. Don't you understand what an incredible gift he's being given?" came another voice.

Voices slowly rumbled through the crowd as impatience spread. Still, Sandra kept herself between the guard and her child. Uncertain, the guard turned to the Chairman, who bowed his head as if to say, "Get on with it."

Tightening his grip on the club, he raised his arm to strike. Sheila watched his eyes, which glistened with the beginning of tears. Sandra was unmoving, staring down the man in front of her. Sheila watched the guard's muscles flex, ready to swing.

A commotion in the crowd rose as people protested the movement of someone rushing the stage. Partially veiled by the podium, Sheila leaned to get a view of the disturbance. She breathed in quickly at the sight of Kane easily shoving members of the crowd to either side.

"No!" he shouted.

He leapt upon the stage, grabbing the first Law-keeper to intercept him. Heaving the guard off the ground, he hurled the man with inhuman strength into the next two guards. All three toppled off the back of the stage. Kane engaged a fourth guard, but the rifle of another caught his chin. Another blow to the stomach doubled Kane over. Seconds later, multiple guards had Kane restrained and at gunpoint. Handcuffs were placed on his wrists, but it still took several men to keep Kane under control.

The guard in front of Sandra had joined the fray, and for the moment she was safe. The stadium was deathly silent as Kane and Sandra gazed upon each other for the first time in years. Sandra's lip quivered with emotion.

"Kane?" she whispered. A tear escaped the corner of her eye and rolled halfway down her cheek.

"Sandra." Kane spoke in a deep voice, betraying his heartache.

Sandra stepped to the side, revealing Nathaniel. "See that man, Nathaniel? That's your daddy. That big, strong man is your daddy."

The world froze in the moment. Sheila glanced around, amazed that no one on stage or in the crowd moved. A moment of selfless love was on display, and the world was watching. A world, unknowingly controlled by the neuro-booster, was watching every moment.

The Chairman tisked in annoyance, breaking the silence. He waved to Penny to come to the microphone. Whispering in her ear, she took his place at the podium.

"Ladies and Gentlemen, we appreciate your patience during this disruption. We assure you that all will be back on schedule in a moment," Penny addressed the crowd.

DeGraaf waved as he walked toward Sandra. Obeying the command, the guards forced Kane closer. Separated by mere feet, Kane stared, his eyes moving from his wife to his son and back. An occasional twitch of resistance showed the never-ending fight between Kane and the guards who restrained him.

"My, my," the Chairman laughed away from the microphone. "Isn't this precious? Husband and wife reunited. My suspicions were correct. The hopeless leader of the Underground would not be able to resist this moment."

"You leave her alone!" Kane growled.

"As far as anyone here knows, I have," DeGraaf said confidently. "This crowd, as you know, is well under my control, and what they are about to see is going to be left to my interpretation."

Sheila watched as DeGraaf slipped his hands into his robe. He removed a small, black device that appeared like some sort of remote. He fingered it in front of him, out of view of the eyes of the crowd.

"This, my friend, is something I made sure to have with me the moment we made the connection between our prisoners and you. You see, your wife may have had her tracker removed on the street, but no street surgery would have been competent enough to recognize the second device placed inside her all those years ago. You, Mr. Leader-of-the-rebels, are about to appear to complete the narrative we want to world to believe."

Before anyone could protest, the Chairman pressed the remote. Sandra let out a gasp, and her face froze in fear. Tears streamed from her eyes.

Sheila realized that something horrible had happened inside of her body.

Sandra gazed down at her son. "Baby, I'm so sorry. I'm so sorry."

The Chairman nodded with his head, and the guards shoved Kane in Sandra's direction. To the crowd, Sheila grasped, it must have appeared that he lunged at her. The Chairman feigned being knocked backward, falling to the stage, eliciting a shocked gasp from the crowd. Kane, still restrained, was hauled away from the body of his dying wife.

He made it appear like Kane killed her! Please God, no.

"I'm sorry, baby." Sandra continued to whisper to Nathaniel. "Stay with your daddy. He'll take care of you. I love you, baby. I'm so sorr—" Sandra's words were cut off as her last breath escaped her lungs.

Chapter Forty-Five

Perryn's hand covered her mouth as Kane leapt upon the stage. Her mind raced as she realized the plan was blown, and she scanned around to see if she could non-verbally communicate with other members of her team. None were visible.

The next moments were filled with confusion as Penny attempted to calm the crowd. Perryn watched closely as the Chairman approached Sandra. Most were watching the podium, and she supposed that the Chairman's almost imperceptible reach into his robes had gone unnoticed by the crowd.

Next thing she saw, Kane was lunging at his wife, knocking over the Chairman. The guards got him under control and pulled him backward. Sandra lay on her back, in obvious pain. She touched the face of her son with one hand for a moment until it fell limp beside her. Kane let out an anguished shriek.

The Chairman stood and made a show of brushing off his robes. He walked slowly over to the podium, waving aside a shocked and worried Penny. He dropped his gaze and took a deep breath as if upset by the moment.

"My loyal citizens," he said, "what was meant as a moment of mercy has become tragedy. In front of you, the evil ideology of the rebels has taken another soul. In retribution for offering her son to her alliance in a show of loyalty, the rebels have taken her life in a senseless act. Such is the cost of anarchy. Such is the face of those who would tell you they are free. It is the Law that sets us free. Not this rebel who would take a life before your eyes. Not these next to me," DeGraaf gestured to Willis's squad, "who were captured infiltrating this arena to commit an act of terror."

The woman next to Perryn had tears streaking her face. "It is the Law that sets me free," she whispered to herself. Around her Perryn could see others doing the same. Sandra's death was deepening the story in their minds, and she stood helpless to stop it.

What do we do?

DeGraaf continued, raising his hands in the air. "My loyal friends, let us here today display our courage. Let us show these rebels, who, yes, stand among us." Murmurs spread among the crowd at the revelation that more of the Underground were present. The Chairman's voice rose in volume and urgency. "Let us show them that we cannot be moved. We cannot be swayed. We are the loyal, the faithful, the true followers of the one glorious Law. If you would today call yourself loyal and faithful, I invite you to bow with me. Kneel before the glory of the Law and show yourself devoted. The rebels are among us. Reveal them. Bow in trust of the Law and show the world how few the unfaithful are."

As if a wave had hit them, people around the stadium fell to their knees. Some were crying. Others were shouting their allegiance. Most were silent. The scraping of feet could be heard all around as people bowed.

Perryn's knees shook in fear, but she stood. To her left and right, she could see squad members also standing. They stared at her in fear, and she nodded to them. They nodded back in agreement. They would stand. In front of the world, the Underground would stand.

"You!" the woman next to Perryn exclaimed. "You ran in the Chase! I know you." She shook a defiant finger at Perryn. "You ungrateful little—" Perryn ignored the rest of the sentence.

"Loyal citizens around the world, left standing are the minority, the voice of anarchy. They are terrorists who would take your life for the slightest act of disloyalty to their cause. They are the cancer that threatens this world. They stand in defiance to goodness and justice and grace. But as you see—they stand alone."

Shouting began as people stared in hatred at Perryn and her friends. The Chairman's manipulation had them riled to the point of boiling, and Perryn was sure the crowd would see them dead if DeGraaf continued.

"My friends, before we deal with these terrorists and commence with this morning's celebration, I invite you to hear from one person who may shed light on true freedom." The Chairman softened his voice. "Once a member of the rebellion, he has seen the light of the Law and the error of his ways. His is a voice of reason. I ask all, loyal and disloyal, to hear his words and take them to heart. Perhaps, even those left standing among us may find the courage to bow their knees to reason." DeGraaf pointed to his left.

Perryn watched the stairs at the side of the stage. Willis appeared. He wasn't restrained. He wasn't guarded. He was free and walking toward the Chairman.

Sheila held her breath as the crowd fell to their knees. Within moments, she picked out the members of the Underground who stood. Part of her wished they would hide among the crowd and bow, but she realized what they were doing. When Kane stormed the stage, she guessed their plans had been ruined. Even more so, she glanced at the members on stage with her. Whatever the Underground had planned, it'd been discovered.

All they had left was to show the world they wouldn't bow to the Law.

The Chairman continued to talk about loyalty and invited another to the stage. Sheila turned to her left, and she sucked in a breath at the sight of Willis. He strode slowly up the steps. His gaze remained on the podium, and he didn't even throw a glance in Sheila's direction.

"Willis?" she said before she could restrain herself.

He stopped and turned to her. She noticed he appeared unable to face the members of the Underground next to her. His eyes met hers, but he said nothing.

"What are you doing?"

Still he stared.

"Willis?" came a voice next to her. Sheila thought a moment and remembered the girl's name was Bekah. "Why would you--?"

"I have to. I can't fail again. I may not be able to save the world, but if I can save you—all of you—I must."

"Willis," Sheila said, desperation lacing her tone, "do you think they'll live up to whatever bargain they've offered?"

Willis hung his head. He turned back to the podium and continued his walk of shame.

"How could he?" Bekah sniffed as her tears flowed.

"I don't know," Sheila offered. "But he must feel like he has no choice."

Chapter Forty-Six

Perryn's lip quivered as she watched Willis cross the stage. He appeared defeated and ashamed. For a moment, he exchanged words with Sheila, but her angry glare told Perryn that nothing had been accomplished.

Willis slowly sulked to the podium. Perryn cursed under her breath as the Chairman placed his arm around Willis's shoulders. It was an embrace meant to communicate, "He is mine."

"Loyal citizens, I give you the once hero of the Western Alliance. A young man born to a family of loyalty to represent his alliance at the highest level. In a tragic occurrence at the Chase, his moment of glory was stolen—a lifetime of loyal service lost. He has been a story of misguided searching since that day, which unfortunately led him to join the terrorist rebellion that stands among us."

Jeers rose from the crowd as people cursed Willis openly. The Chairman raised a hand to quiet the protests.

"Friends, in what has been a ceremony of tragedy, I ask you to turn your thoughts to happiness. Willis Thomson, Chase-runner and one who could represent the best in all of us, has seen the error of his ways. He has volunteered this glorious day to come among us and share his new-found loyalty to the Law—and to call all who have gone astray to join him."

The Chairman stepped backward to allow Willis to take the podium. This was greeted by a few solitary claps among the crowd, but mostly the stadium awaited what was to come next. Perryn examined Willis's face as he scanned the kneeling crowd. He glanced back at his squad behind him. Bekah's eyes pleaded with him, and he hung his head.

He's terrified. Not of what will happen to him, but to them—to all of us.

Willis took a deep breath and pulled out a written statement. He examined it for a moment and began to read.

"I, Willis Thomson, invite the world to know my story. The world I believed in was one of incredible peace and provision under the guidance of our Law. I was the fortunate recipient of grace when I was chosen to represent the Western Alliance as a Chase-runner trainee. I rose in the ranks to the point I was able to represent, not only my Alliance, but also the goodness of the Law in the Chase. An accident late in the race led to an unthinkable betrayal by my teammate, leading to a loss. My chance to help the world and future generations benefit from a Law-change was gone. This left me lost and uncertain. The world-wide rebellion that followed cost us all dearly, including the death of my father, Max Thomson."

Willis paused. Perryn could see the pain on his face as he mentioned his father. The words were tearing him apart inside, and she could almost hear his soul ripping as he spoke the words.

Don't be afraid, Willis. You don't have to do this.

"In my desperation, I searched for answers," he continued, "In my search, I was taken captive by the rebellion and indoctrinated in their cause. In my fragile state, I was unable to resist their zeal and joined them. I participated in many so-called missions that broke the Law and damaged world peace. I was a terrorist, but I believed my cause to be one of freedom."

"Willis, stop!" Sheila shouted.

"No, Willis!" Bekah cried.

Perryn watched Willis resist watching as guards trained their weapons on his friends. He wiped his chin with a trembling hand and turned the page of his notes.

Somehow, he must be thinking he's helping them. He would never believe these lies. He certainly would never speak them in front of us—unless he believed he was helping. Her mind zipped from one thought to the next.

"I can't undo the actions I've committed, but I can stand here today to try to right the wrongs," Willis said, his voice shaky. "As one who has participated and even urged others to join the rebellious cause, I stand before you to urge the whole world, loyal and disloyal alike, to—"

Willis's voice caught.

"I urge you to—"

The Chairman reached out and touched Willis's arm. Willis glanced at him, and DeGraaf inclined his head to whisper in his ear. Willis breathed in heavily.

Oh, no. He's going to tell the world to follow the Law. The Chairman has promised him our safety if he'll turn the world back to the Law! Please don't do it, Willis!

"I urge you to—" Willis started.

"Willis Thomson!" Perryn shouted.

All eyes around her shot in her direction, including Willis. Their eyes met, and her heart broke for him. He was trying to save them. He was afraid to fail all of them and see them come to whatever fate awaited. And she had to do something.

She opened her mouth to speak.

Chapter Forty-Seven

Willis stared at the paper in front of him. He read the final words the Chairman had provided. *I stand before you to urge the whole world, loyal and disloyal alike, to turn to the Law and its administrators, accepting its goodness and absolute authority in your lives.* He understood the words would change the world. He'd watched from backstage as the neuro-booster had swayed the crowd into almost robotic allegiance to the Chairman's words. He'd seen Kane get hauled below the stage. The body of Sandra lay on the stage as he walked up the stairs, and he was left to guess what had happened. He was supposed to chain the world to the Law—to the Chairman—with a few simple words.

The Chairman grabbed his arm and leaned toward him.

"Young man, your friends stand condemned in front of you," he whispered. "You have one chance to save them. Speak the words unless you intend to fail them one last time."

We will be safe. Perryn and I can live in peace. The whole Underground can. The war raged in his mind over the right thing to do. *I can't fail them. I can't condemn them to death.*

"I urge you to—" Willis started.

"Willis Thomson!" Perryn cried out.

He'd been afraid to meet her gaze since taking the stage, but he couldn't resist any longer. He stared at her, standing in the crowd by the stage. Everything in him wanted to leap from the platform and hold her. He longed to explain to her that he loved her and was trying to save her. He wanted to tell her the plan the Chairman had and how saving a few was better than condemning them to death. He was afraid of failing her, and he wished he could tell her.

He saw her take a deep breath.

"Willis Thomson, I love you!" she cried out, her eyes pleading with him. "Before the whole world, I want you to know that I love you, and you do not have to be afraid. You aren't a failure because you act out of love. And where there's love, there's no fear."

The words surged in his heart, flooding his body with warmth. He scanned the crowd, the sea of faces bowed in the presence of the Chairman and the Law. The world was ready to receive his next words and adopt them whole-heartedly.

And where there's love, there's no fear. He gazed at Perryn, his love for her filling him with courage. His back straightened, and his lungs breathed as if for the first time. The air smelled fresh and filled him with life, even in the hot sun.

I love you, Perryn. I won't fail you.

Perryn watched as Willis stared at the paper in front of him. Her words had stopped everything, and the entire crowd waited for what Willis would say next. Suddenly, he gazed at her for a long moment. His eyes had changed. The sadness was gone from them, and he beheld her as if he hadn't seen her in ages.

Willis took a deep breath and glanced backward. His eyes met his squad, who studied him. He stopped at Bekah, who stared at him imploringly. Then, to her surprise, Willis gave a slight nod. Perryn couldn't be sure, but she thought she saw him smile slightly.

The Chairman stepped forward, getting Willis's attention by placing his hand on Willis's. He communicated with a firm pat, and Willis nodded. He glanced one more time at Perryn and breathed in.

"I stand before you to urge the whole world, loyal and disloyal alike, to—" Willis paused and locked eyes with Perryn. "—to be free to love your neighbor—to give and to share—to forgive those, even those up here ruling over you, because that's grace—real grace. The Law was meant to show us the way, but it was never the way itself. Be free!"

Perryn's heart leapt inside her. She let out a yelp and ran for the stage. All around her, people stood, confusion on their faces. Some even shook their heads as if to clear their mind of cobwebs.

"Willis!" she shouted, climbing up on stage. He ran to her and threw his arms around her. They held each other tightly.

A murmur rose in the crowd and steadily grew into a roar. People pressed in on the stage.

"He's right!" someone shouted.

"The Law isn't freedom! It's slavery to you," another cried.

"No!" the Chairman shrieked into the microphone. The noise was so loud, many covered their ears as the speakers squawked with feedback. The shouts ceased. "Enough!" He turned to Willis, his eyes filled with fury. His face was red, and his cheeks puffed in rageful breaths. "You have crossed me too many times. You have condemned yourself and your friends to death, right here and now. Guards, take aim."

A long pause. The guards didn't move.

"Guards," DeGraaf shouted, "I command you. Take aim!"

Perryn could see the Law-keepers acting as confused as the crowd had a moment ago. A couple were rubbing their eyes as if something was in them.

"Now! Shoot them. Put an end to these lies."

"Mr. Chairman—" one of the Deputy Chairmen said, standing from his chair. Many of those around him appeared dazed. Penny stared into the distance, frozen like a statue.

"Oh, shut up!" the Chairman shouted. "Guards, now."

Still no one moved.

"Chairman DeGraaf," Perryn said, "I'm afraid the world has heard the truth. And if there's one thing we both know about the change of the neuro-booster, it's that it's permanent when it encounters the truth."

DeGraaf seethed, sucking in breaths through gritted teeth. He stormed to the nearest guard and wrenched the rifle from his hand.

He clicked the safety off and raised the barrel at Perryn. His finger found the trigger.

Life slowed to a crawl as Perryn watched the Chairman. She needed to move, but her feet were frozen. She felt pressure on her arm as Willis grabbed her. He pushed her sideways, replacing his own body in the gun's sight. She protested, but her arms moved heavily. She couldn't fight off his movement in time.

The rifle fired.

Chapter Forty-Eight

Perryn fell to the floor of the stage. Her head struck, and her vision clouded. The sound of the rifle's report still rang in her ear, and she could hear fearful shouts coming from the crowd. She turned over and pushed herself up on all fours. Rubbing her eyes to clear them, she scanned around.

Willis stood where she'd been. His eyes were wide, and he didn't move.

"Willis, no!" she cried. She scrambled up and over to him. He was shaking. "No. Tell me you didn't."

"Apparently, I didn't," he said.

"What?" She examined him up and down, but she saw no wound. "What do you mean?"

Willis pointed at the Chairman. She turned her attention.

The Chairman stood in shock. The end of the rifle was still in his hands, but the barrel was pointed skyward. A nearby Law-keeper's hand on the underside of the stock held it there. A moment later, the guard yanked the firearm from the Chairman's hand.

"What? What are you doing, you imbecile?" the Chairman snapped.

"They are unarmed," the guard said.

"So what?"

"They've done nothing to threaten you."

"You idiot! You report to me. I dictate the Law. How dare you stop me? Have you decided to become a Law-breaker?"

The guard stood stone-faced, staring at the Chairman. "There's no law against protecting the innocent. All they did here is tell the truth."

The Chairman spat and ran to the next guard, attempting to

pull his rifle from his hands. The guard held his grip, unwilling to give up his weapon. Frantically, he ran around the stage, pleading for support. He found none. Even Penny stood motionless except for her eyes which darted back and forth as if trying to sort out what had happened.

Turning back to Willis and Perryn, he spat again. "You think you've won. We have worn down the truth in the past. I still have a captive audience. A few more words, and I can sow the seeds of confusion. In time, I'll regain control."

Willis stepped forward, still holding Perryn's hand. He gazed at her and squeezed her hand. He had that 'trust me' smirk he used to give her on the station. The Willis she remembered was back.

"Mr. Chairman," Willis said, "you're right. The crowd—the cameras—they're all right there. You could try to confuse them. That is—if they pay attention to you. I think they are going to have something far more interesting to stare at."

"And what would that be?" DeGraaf glowered.

Willis turned to Bekah and gave her a nod. She smiled and pressed the detonator she'd pulled from her shoe.

The explosion on the southwest tower shook the stadium. People screamed and whirled, searching for the source. Fire and smoke rose from the tower. Moments later, the sound of twisting metal screeched as the tower bent harmlessly toward the outside of the arena. With a loud crash, it fell to the ground outside.

The crowds continued to scream and rushed for the exits. Cameras turned to capture the drama of smoke and fire atop the building. People poured out into the parking lot, knocking over security gates on their way.

"Now!" Perryn yelled. She rushed for the prisoners. Holding a hand out to a guard, he handed her the keys to the handcuffs without asking. She began to free everyone. Releasing Sheila, the former reporter turned to her.

"What can I do?" Sheila rubbed at her wrists.

"Know how to work those monitors in the control room downstairs?"

"Worked in broadcasting long enough to learn more than how to face the camera."

"Good. Upload this." She handed her a portable drive. "We're all carrying one. And free the Chief while you're at it."

"Got it." Sheila announced and ran for the stairs behind the stage.

Perryn unlocked Lydia who quickly grabbed Nathaniel in her arms. She glanced at Perryn and noticed the Captain's bars on her collar. She smiled in approval. "Seems I've been replaced," she said.

"Hardly. I need your help to get us out of here," Perryn said.

"How are we supposed to do that with this crowd?"

Willis ran over. "Appears the Chairman knew of the other teams, but never thought it necessary to arrest them. The others must be hiding out. The tower was the signal to set everything else off."

"What does that mean?" Lydia shook her head, not understanding the plan.

"That means that Chris should be knocking out security communications." As if on cue, the radios on all the guards screeched with feedback, forcing many of them to pull out their earpieces.

"Okay, not necessary at this point. Anything else?" Lydia continued.

"See that maintenance entrance over on the side there?" Perryn pointed. They all took note of the garage door that led to the infield yards away. Sparks flew around the edges. Seconds later, the door fell inward with a metallic clash. "That would be Maria."

"Kane picked his new Captain well." Lydia smiled.

"Speaking of Kane, who is going to—" Willis began.

The large screens around the arena showing the images

broadcast around the world turned to static for a moment, cutting Willis off. The image reappeared with text over top of it.

You are free from the Law.

You are free to make this world better.

"Sheila did it!" Perryn pumped a fist in the air. Seconds later, Kane bounded up the stairs, Sheila right on his heels carrying Hannah. Hannah leapt from her arms and ran to her awakening father. He stopped and gazed at Lydia, his eyes soft with compassion. Then, he turned to the body of Sandra. His lip quivered.

"I have your son," Lydia said, the words snapping Kane back to the present. "I'll get him out of here."

Kane nodded and walked over to Sandra. He brushed her hair with his hand and leaned over to touch his forehead to hers. Picking her up, he cradled her body in his massive arms. He took a step toward the exit, and an angry expression flashed across his face. Perryn saw the hatred in his eyes as he turned to glance back at the Chairman who ran around begging someone for assistance, to no avail. DeGraaf pulled on Penny's arm, demanding she help him escape. She slapped him, sending several bracelets flying and retreated from the stage. The Chairman held his face in shock staring after her.

"Kane?" Lydia said, placing a hand gently on his arm. "He's not worth it. He won't make it far on his own. This world has abandoned him."

Kane looked down at her, his glare melting into sadness. He nodded and turned to Willis. "Free to forgive, right boss?"

Willis nodded. "Right."

Perryn glanced around her at her friends reunited. Fire, smoke, and screaming people surrounded them, but she shut that all out for this moment. This was her family. These were the ones for whom she would gladly give her life. In her hand was the hand of the man she loved—in all his brokenness and flaws. She squeezed his hand and smiled at him.

He smiled back and kissed her.

Willis sighed. "Can we get out of here?"

"Yes, let's go." She squeezed his hand again.

"Captain's orders?" Willis smirked.

"Shut up and run."

Everyone laughed as they ran for the exit.

Chapter Forty-Nine

FINDING THE WAY
By Sheila Kemp

There are few things in the history of mankind that could measure up to the world-rocking events of this year's Chase opening ceremonies. Wars, famines, plagues, and even the Great Collapse—have all been devastating tragedies humanity has been asked to overcome. And we have, leaving us with a sense of our own fragility.

Our world is different, shaken to its core. The Law is gone. The slave caste has been freed. The Chairman has disappeared. The world is free. Unlike previous times in history, this time the change is one of incredible hope. This time, the change does not force-feed us the truth of our own mortality, but rather we get to indulge in the truth so that we leave a legacy far greater than the span of our lives. What we do with our days lives well beyond us.

This writer, for one, believes this was the intent all along for the Law-makers. They saw a world in chaos and confusion, and they happily gave us the Law to help us find our way. However, instead of embracing this hope, our fear of our mortality caused us to exchange the roadmap for the destination. As so eloquently put by Willis Thomson on the world stage, "The Law was meant to show us the way. It was never the way itself."

For generations, we have lost our way, believing adherence to an outward Law to be the end and not the means. Rather, the Law was meant to provide boundaries to help us learn again to love and care for each other, until we were ready to establish our legacy free from it.

Are we ready now that we have been freed?

I believe so.

And how do I know?

I know because I live in a world that has people, whom you may never meet, who love each other to the point of sacrifice. The Sanchez family, who gave of the little they had, to provide for those under their care up until the day of their arrest. There are people like Chris, Jaden, and Maria, my friends in the Underground, who lived and fought, not for a cause, but for friendship. Kane and Sandra, a family separated, who longed to be reunited as a family. Willis and Perryn, former Chase runners at the center of it all, who when it mattered most, put their love first. And most personal for me, Audrey, my sister in heaven who taught me years before that speaking the truth was an act of love. I will miss you forever, Audrey.

And so, my friends, we are left to find our way. It is time for us to leave the relative safe confines of the Law to search for the way to love each other and make this world the place it was meant to be. No, we have not collapsed into anarchy again. Order continues, but with a newfound purpose. In the words of our president elect, the former Deputy Chairman of the United African Cooperative, Charles Mwangi, "Our world identity was lost in a sea of hopelessness driven nearly to the point of drowning in endless slavery to mere survival. But we hope, and it is in that hope that we begin to really live. We have found ourselves again."

Yes, my friends. We are finding the way again.

Epilogue

Willis rushed through the hallways of the old schoolhouse. The acrid smell of paint burned his nose as he passed through the hallways under construction. Over the months, the building was slowly being converted. One of the leading initiatives of the new president had been to reestablish houses of education around the world, and the school that'd housed the Underground would be the flagship of the venture.

The families living inside had long since been relocated, and Willis had been a part of the crew that was getting the building back in shape for the first class of children to attend. Most days were spent overseeing crews who were rewiring the building for up-to-date electronics and lighting. Other than that, he spent his time making certain the paint crews left the "Go Fighting Bulldogs" mural alone at the front entrance.

"Where have you been?" Perryn waved as Willis raced around the corner.

"I couldn't find my good shoes. Someone got into my room while I was gone to paint it, and they moved everything around." Willis pointed to his feet.

"You doing okay since your trip? Glad you went?"

Willis recalled the trip they'd taken to clean up the cabin. Brenda had accompanied him, and the visit to the old cabin hadn't been easy. They set up a small memorial where his father had been killed and spent the better part of two weeks cleaning and fixing up the cabin.

"Yeah. I am. Mom wants to live there with Dad. She says she's not afraid of the quiet. In fact, she's looking forward to it." He fingered his pocket, flipping the ring box in it several times. He hadn't told her about his side trip on the way home. His mother had given him the key to a lockbox in a bank halfway between Central City and the cabin. Inside the box had been the ring, a family heirloom. He would propose tonight. Despite their still young ages, he couldn't bear to wait any longer. After the party, he would find a quiet place to slip away and ask her. There was no rush to get married, but he wasn't going to wait again to tell her how he felt.

"Well, we'll have to go up and visit her plenty. But we need to move, or we'll be late."

He smoothed his hair with his hands. Perryn made a face and fixed it for him. Her brown hair was curled and pulled back elegantly. Her brown eyes sparkled as she noticed him studying her.

"What is it?"

"You look beautiful today," he said.

"Are you saying I don't appear that way every day?" She feigned a frown. After a few seconds, she let it morph into a smile. She burst out laughing. "It's too easy with you sometimes." She placed her hand on his face and kissed him.

He rolled his eyes at her and smiled. Grasping her hand, he pushed open the door. Outside, the school grounds had been meticulously groomed. Gardens had been planted over the months, and the formerly overgrown scrub brush was replaced with blooming plants in all sorts of colors. Rows of chairs filled the garden as nearly all of the former Underground had come in for the celebration. Most of the seats they could see were full until they spied Maria's waving hand.

Tiptoeing to the front, they sat in the third row. Maria leaned over to them.

"Thought you'd make an entrance?" she joked.

"There was a shoe issue," Perryn said, pointing to Willis. He threw up his hands in resignation.

Music started, and Kane walked from the side. He was dressed in a white linen shirt, which ruffled in the slight breeze. A minister took his place nearby. As if on cue, the entire crowd turned to gaze behind them. There stood Lydia.

Willis had never seen Lydia outside the world of the Underground. She was usually all business and wore her Underground uniform as if she slept in it. Today, she wore a simple white dress and sandals. Her hair blew gently to one side.

"She's beautiful," Perryn whispered.

"Yeah, until she makes you do pushups." Willis joked, eliciting a poke in the ribs from Perryn and a snicker from Maria.

"You guys are so disruptive," Sheila turned from the row in front of them, smirking. She liked the joke, too.

"Seriously, you two are ridiculous." Jaden grinned next to Sheila. They both chuckled.

She stopped at the mouth of the aisle, where she was joined by Nathaniel. He reached up his hand to escort her, which she took smiling. In his other hand, Nathaniel held a picture of Sandra. The two walked the aisle, and Nathaniel smiled broadly. He wore a shirt to match his father, but at his request, was also sporting a bow tie.

People on both sides of the aisle smiled at the display. Several wiped tears from their eyes. Willis reached into his pocket and fingered the ring box once again. One day, this would be them, and he ached that Perryn's family was long gone.

Looking around him, he realized the truth. These faces, smiling and happy—these were their family. These were their people. They were all so different. Some had come from wealth, and others came from poverty. Some had been Alliance workers, loyal to the cause before their liberation, and others had grown up scarred by the Law. Some had happy homes with parents who loved them, and others like himself who had been taken for the Chase, had little to no memory of home.

He grasped he was one of the lucky ones. He still had his family. He had a woman who loved him. He had friends who had been willing to do anything for him. So many had lived and died for the freedom they were finally beginning to enjoy.

The minister was asking who was giving the bride away. The crowd answered with several sounds of 'aww' as Nathaniel had declared that he and his mother were giving the bride away. Lydia handed her flowers to Nathaniel who proceeded to sword fight an invisible opponent with them. Taking Kane's hands, she gazed in his eyes.

"We come together today to celebrate love," the minister began.

Willis sighed and settled into his seat.

"You sure you're okay?" Perryn whispered. "You don't seem yourself."

He turned the ring box over in his fingers one more time before pulling his hand from his pocket. With it, he took Perryn's hand and kissed it. He gazed at Kane and Lydia as they began their vows. He peered at Nathaniel who was showing the picture of his mother the flowers he was holding. He glanced at Jaden, Sheila, Maria, and Chris. Scanning, he found his mother in another row. He gazed at Perryn, whose brown eyes met his.

"I'm definitely okay. I'm right where I'm supposed to be."

Author's Note

This is it. The final chapter of *The Chase Runner Series* is in print. As fulfilling it is to put a bow on this story, I am sad to say goodbye to these characters. Each one of them reflects a part of my story as I've recovered from burnout and found a place of emotional health. As with the story, it has been the truth that has restored me to health.

Writing about Willis in the early chapters was difficult for me. I know well the sorrow of having what were once successes reinterpreted as massive failures. I had to dig back into the feelings of brokenness I experienced to get in Willis's head. Yet, I firmly believe that dystopian fiction needs to show that light can shine brightly in the darkness. Seeing Willis finally let go of fear because of the love of others reminded me of the love I have been shown by my heavenly Father and my family. From Perryn finding her voice to Sheila reinventing herself to Kane forgiving himself to even Bekah discovering she's not useless, my story is written all over these pages.

The title *The Change* comes from the curveballs that life inevitably throws at us. Even with the best of intentions and the purest motives, hardship will come. There is no promise of a life full of ease and happiness. Yet, it is in these moments when life is turned upside-down that we can find strength and assurance we otherwise would have lacked. God meets us in the painful corners of life. And when fear threatens to drown us in sorrow, his love reminds us that we are not alone—not forgotten. Friend, there is remarkable hope in the darkness when you know the last chapter of your story is already written.

I would love to connect with you to see what you thought of the final end to this story. What were your feelings when Willis and Perryn finally figured out their relationship? Thoughts on Jez's end? Which character had you cheering the loudest? If you haven't already, sign up for my newsletter to get all the latest news on book releases, book recommendations, and get your free copy of my prequel, *Kane: A Chase Runner Story* to learn how Kane made it to the station in the first place. I have other projects in the works, and you'll want to be the first to know.

Here's how to connect with me:
Website/Newsletter/Free book - *BradleyCaffee.com*
Facebook - *Facebook.com/bradleycaffeeauthor*
Instagram - *@bradleycaffeeauthor* (tag me in a picture of you with *The Change*!)

Most of all, PLEASE LEAVE ME A REVIEW AND TELL YOUR FRIENDS. Authors' success can live or die by reviews and referrals. If you loved *The Change*, please consider saying so on Amazon and Goodreads and telling another reader about the series.

Thanks for reading, fellow Chase Runner.

CPSIA information can be obtained
at www.ICGtesting.com
Printed in the USA
BVHW031015280822
645712BV00017B/210